BLOOD OATH

THE DARKEST DRAE: BOOK ONE

RAYE WAGNER & KELLY ST. CLARE

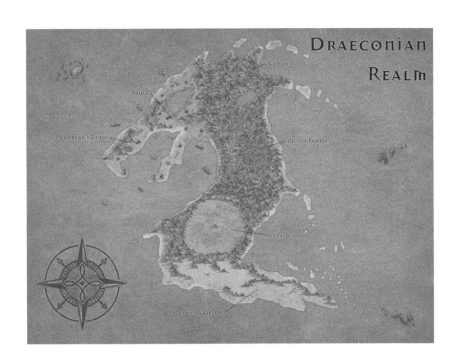

1

"What's on the menu tonight, Ryn?" a man heckled from the far end of the crowded bar.

I didn't acknowledge him straightaway, sliding two hazy tankards of Dyter's brew to a couple men still too young to be enlisted.

I glanced across the crowded room, wiping my hands on my apron. Recognizing the hunched man, a regular at Dyter's, I hollered back, "What do you think is on the menu, Seryt?"

He held up his stump of an arm and, with a drunken grin, replied, "Roasted chicken? Grilled mutton?"

A burst of uproarious laughter followed his quip. *Smart arse.* Chicken or mutton? After two generations of famine?

"Potato stew," I called over the ruckus, sighing inwardly as my belly rumbled. Talk of meat made me ravenous even though I ate better than most in Harvest Zone Seven, thanks to my mother's green thumb.

Ever since King Irdelron started hunting the land healers, the Phaetyn, ninety years ago, the land had been dying, slowly but surely.

He'd hunted them because he wanted to live forever and allegedly drank their blood to do so. The Phaetyn had been extinct for almost two decades, and the famine worsened every year without their magic. Now, the peasants of Verald worked relentlessly to fill the Draecon emperor's food quota. And when the emperor's quota was filled, the other kingdoms in the realm got their portions. After that, we, the peasants, got to keep or trade what was left—mainly potatoes. *Yay.*

Suffice it to say, no one really loved our king. Disliked might be a more accurate term—and loathed more accurate still.

"Potato and what soup?" the same man wheezed. He'd had enough of Dyter's brew to think he was funny—my favorite type of intoxicated male.

"Seryt, do us a favor and shut your gob," Dyter, my boss and friend of the family, boomed from the kitchen.

Those who heard the exchange grinned and continued their buzz of conversation. The crowd here was in an unnaturally excited mood tonight. I only recognized a third of the people in the tavern, which meant many had traveled from the other Harvest Zones and maybe even the other two kingdoms to be here for the meeting. To see so many different people here was a rarity. The kind of rarity that could draw attention from the king's soldiers. *Or worse.* I hoped Dyter knew what he was getting into by holding the meeting here.

I pulled my stiff cinnamon-brown hair up and fanned the back of my neck. The extra people crammed into the Crane's Nest tonight made it hotter than usual.

"Al'right, Ryn?" my friend, Arnik, asked from where he sat on the other side of the bar.

I smiled and dropped my hair. If I didn't watch myself, he'd be up trying to help, and he was too big to weave in and out of the patrons without causing a fight. "Just warm in here."

With plenty of rain, like today, the humidity and the stench of male sweat mixed with sweet fermenting ale beat down my patience almost as quickly as the senseless, roundabout arguments of the newcomers.

"Excuse me, is there any stew left?" a man asked. His voice was so quiet it didn't immediately register.

I shoved two more tankards down the line before turning his way. Wiping at the bar with my dishrag, I blinked as I took him in. I blinked again, but the apparition didn't change.

There before me was a man who was not young. The difference between him and the eighteen and nineteen-year-olds either side of him was plain. But neither was he old and wrinkled. I scanned him anew. He didn't seem to be maimed—though I couldn't see his legs. He'd asked me a question, so his brains weren't addled to the level of insensibility. He had sandy-blond hair and an open smile, yet something in the set of his shoulders and his blue-gray eyes spoke of secrets.

My mouth fell slightly ajar. I'd never seen a twenty-something man. He was *totally* illegal. He was meant to be away fighting in the emperor's war! A thrill ran through me.

"Is there any stew left?" the man repeated, his smile slipping.

It was possible I was gawking at him. I couldn't wait to tell Arnik I met an illegal person. "Let me check for you," I said, straightening.

"Thank you. I'd appreciate that," the man said, and he dropped his gaze back to his brew.

I hustled through the low door into the kitchen so I could go and stare some more at the twenty-something man. There was always more stew in the caldron over the fire in the kitchen, and I filled a wooden bowl and hastened to set it in front of him. That was how desperate I was for a bit of excitement; I was sprinting for stew now.

I stared as he held out his payment. There in his palm was a single coin. We mostly accepted carrots, apples, and potatoes as trade for the meager food and brew we offered. Not wanting to appear odd, I plucked the stamped piece of gold from his hand, holding it gingerly.

"My thanks to you," he said with a nod. He was being jostled on both sides by Arnik's exuberant pals, but the strange man didn't seem bothered in the slightest. That was how I knew he was older. In my experience, any male under twenty took it as a personal insult to be pushed around.

He dragged his spoon through the thick broth and overcooked vegetables. My staring was on the weird side, I knew. I could see his eyes shifting as he avoided my regard.

"You from around here?" I prodded, not put off by his discomfort. This was by far the most interesting thing to happen in a year. At least.

"Here and there." He grunted and put a heaping spoonful of stew in his mouth.

"Where?"

Dyter grabbed my arm. "Ryn, there's a load of dishes larger than the Gemond Mountains back in the tub. I need you to get started on them, or we'll be here all night."

"I'm not sure Mum meant for me to do dishes when she sent me to work for you." The old coot was the closest thing to a father I'd ever known so I didn't hesitate to try to get out of the work.

Dyter gave me a pointed look that made the scar on his cheek tighten. "I'm sure she meant for you to do anything other than kill her gardens."

"Hey! I'm good at weeding." I scowled, and it bounced straight off his stocky frame. He knew me too well.

He patted me on the shoulder, turning it into a push that propelled me toward the kitchen. "Sure, you are, Ryn. Sure you are."

I whipped my dishrag over my shoulder, *accidentally* smacking him, and headed to the kitchen. The mound of dishes that waited for me had spilled off the counter and onto the broth-sticky floor. With a sigh, I grabbed a pot off of the top of the pile and started on the enormous task.

I'd only worked at The Crane's Nest for a few months, though I'd known Dyter forever. After fifteen years of gardening, Mum announced I'd never be able to do more than weed and move dirt, so she sent me here.

I was a plant killer. A poisoner of growth. A farming fool. I liked to do it; I just sucked at it. Big time.

Most women in Verald learned the skills of their mothers to prepare them to run their household when their husbands left to join the war—and most likely die. Serving ale and stew was respectable enough, I thought, and it would be the only way for me to provide for a family, if my future husband and I had a child before he was sent to the lines. *Ugh,* that sounded so . . . planned and boring. But that future was drawing closer and closer. In three months, I'd be eighteen.

I held a huge pot over my head and let the pot drop into the sudsy water below, laughing and lunging away when water exploded everywhere. A cheap thrill, I had to admit, but a thrill nevertheless.

All I really wanted at seventeen years old was something different, something *more,* some interruption to the path of this mundane life.

My sleeves were soaked, my fingers pruny, and as I got down to the few remaining dishes, I rushed to finish so I could go back into the tavern room and eavesdrop on the meeting. The rebel gathering was Dyter's real reason for sending me back here. Miserable coot.

"Clear out!" Dyter boomed from the tavern room. His deep voice carried over the din of male voices, and I rushed out of the kitchen, tightening the ties of my apron over my green aketon and brown ankle-length skirt.

Dyter bellowed, "Curfew is in ten minutes and the king's Drae has been spotted in the skies the last few nights, so don't any of ya get caught. And if you do, don't squeal."

I shivered and saw several men exchange nervous looks. Everyone had to work to conceal their fear at the mention of Lord Irrik, the sole Drae in the kingdom of Verald. He was the horror story mothers told their children. A dragon shifter, sworn to be the king's muscle—brutal, terrifying, and invincible.

And he was hunting in Zone Seven.

*T*he men spilled out of the doorway, disappearing into the inky darkness of night. The muggy air rushed in, and I closed my eyes and took a deep breath, relishing the smell of heat and night—much better than sweaty man bodies.

"Want me to walk you home?" Arnik asked, joining me at the end of the bar.

His familiar voice brushed over me, making me smile, as he drew closer. Arnik and I had been friends forever. Best friends. Our histories were so enmeshed I couldn't imagine life without him. We'd grown up next door to each other, played together, and confided in each other. Everyone in Harvest Zone Seven knew everyone, but I didn't have any close friends other than Arnik. Most people found me a bit useless, I think. Or maybe I'd killed their potato plants at some point. People were fiercely protective of their potato crops in Verald.

"Sorry, Son. Ryn is staying on. I need her help," Dyter said, sliding a long bench on top of a table using his sole arm and a bump of his hip. "This place is a mess thanks to your revolutionary puppies."

I did my best not to smirk at the owner's jab at Arnik's new friends. I tended to keep to myself, but this was no reflection on Arnik's abundant social life. Of late, he'd gravitated toward young males full of indignant rage at the king and those who declared a burning need for glory.

Lips twitching, I turned to Arnik. "You're on your own for the walk. I'll see you tomorrow, though. Mum said there are deliveries to make, and I know your ma's been asking for soap."

I could make soap, a skill I was quite proud of, actually. Unfortunately, nearly everyone could make it, so I probably wouldn't be the soap queen of Harvest Zone Seven when I married.

"I'm pruning the pinot gris vines in the southern fields tomorrow," Arnik reminded me. "For all the good it'll do. Half of them are withered and black. The roses at the end of the rows haven't bloomed in years."

Arnik's gentle reminder made me sigh. At eighteen, he had adult responsibilities. Two weeks had passed, but I still tended to forget our schedules didn't match anymore. I'd been hoping he'd help me let the Tals' donkey out of its stall.

"Maybe you could come by for my supper break?" he asked in a rush.

He accompanied the question with an intense look, and I gave him a blank one in return. Why would I come to see him in the southern fields? We'd never . . . That would mean . . . I flushed.

"Aye, now, lad. I told you to clear out." Dyter bustled over, his presence pushing Arnik out the back door. "And no more telling those upstart laddies 'bout the meetings here. If you think the houses of Ers, Ets, and Als are interested in joining, you let me know and *I'll* decide if they can come, but you had the third son of Tal here." Dyter's voice showed exactly what he thought of the third son of Tal. The serious undercurrents to his words were unmistakable. The tavern owner rarely laid down the law, but when he did, he expected us to fall in line. I supposed that was why Dyter was so high up in the rebellion. He had a natural air of command.

"I thought you were recruiting," Arnik said, turning his frown on Dyter. "If Cal is really, truly coming, everyone will want to meet him. We could recruit a heap more to the cause if we told people. My friends want to help."

Dyter wiped the sheen from his shaved head. "Aye. We're recruiting, but only those willing to fight with their hands and weapons, not their ruddy mouths. The Tals won't fight. They're toadies of the king, boy. No sense in having young Talrit come spy for his father and uncles. You'll earn us a one-way ticket to the king's dungeons. Know how many people survive his dungeons?" He walked away, shouting over his shoulder, "None!"

Arnik inhaled at the cutting words. Now that he was eighteen, just like the other young men, he hated being treated like he was seventeen.

Dyter was right, though. Everyone knew which houses were in the king's pocket, and the House of Tal was one of them. The Tals had a constant supply of food and goods, which in the depths of the hunger meant they were obscenely rich and, as such, disconnected with the plight of the likes of peasants. Why would the House of Tal ever revolt against King Irdeldon?

"Talrit is not a spy." Arnik's pale skin blotched as his temper rose.

Pretty soon he'd be yelling, and the argument would go nowhere. Besides, Arnik needed to leave or he'd run the risk of breaking curfew.

Arnik clenched his fists and leaned forward, gearing up to fight. "We've been friends—"

For two weeks. I grabbed his arm and said, "You'd better go. You're cutting curfew too close." I raised my eyebrows at Dyter, a pointed look meant to tell him to stop. Thankfully, he understood and turned toward the kitchen, mumbling something about grabbing a mop.

9

"Come on," I said, leading Arnik to the door. "You know how Dyter gets when new people come. You can't keep bringing everyone who says they're unhappy."

"But, Cal—"

The elusive Cal, the rebel leader. Everyone speculated he was someone from the late queen's family. Queen Callye died before I was born, but the stories were that she helped the people. Of course, Irdelron killed her and sent her entire family to the front lines of the war to be slaughtered. Even their son was sent off to battle when he came of age. *His own son.*

The rebels had taken up her family name, and the leader was our one hope for salvation, or so everyone older than me said. "No one even knows who Cal is. No one knows what he looks like, not even Dyter. He sends messages by courier and never the same one twice. We don't know if Cal is even his real name."

Despite the rebel meetings Dyter held at The Crane's Nest, my involvement was half-hearted at best. I mean, I wanted Dyter and Arnik to win, and I wanted to catch a glimpse of the mysterious Cal, but I wasn't itching to fight. I'd do my part if it came to it. But it seemed like a hopeless cause. No one could defeat the king's Drae.

I tugged Arnik to the door. "Dyter says Cal will only reveal himself to those he knows are loyal, so you can't keep bringing new people in. If you want to meet him, you're going to have to stop."

I pushed the door open, and the moonlight settled upon my shoulders. My insides shuddered with yearning, a sensation that was growing stronger every day. I longed to step over the threshold into the night. Resisting the urge, I instead pulled myself back to the present. "You don't have to agree, but you should show Dyter some respect. He's higher up in the ranks than you." *As in, you're barely in the ranks.*

Arnik leaned forward and whispered, "All this talk of Cal . . . Don't you want to see him? Do you really believe we can overthrow the entire kingdom because of one man?" He sounded doubtful. "The king has Lord Irrik, after all, and Cal is no Drae."

There was only one Drae in Verald, so that was obvious. I shivered. Talk of Lord Irrik gave me the willies. "Be careful walking back," I said, glancing at the beautiful, silky night. "You heard Dyter. The Drae has been spotted in the skies."

"Do you think he'll incapacitate me with his magic breath and chew on my bones?" Arnik asked.

I snorted and shoved him out the door, but cold terror shot through me at the line from our mothers' stories. If the Drae was flying in the dark sky, Arnik wouldn't even see him until it was too late. Drae could shift from dragon to man, or vice-versa, in the blink of an eye.

Arnik took a few steps and turned back, hands shoved in his pockets. "I won't bring any more friends, but tell Dyter to stop being an old fool," he said, oblivious to my fear of the Drae. "We need all the help we can get for the rebellion, even if it is from the third son of Tal."

I had no desire to do dishes for the rest of my life, so I'd say nothing of the sort. I was getting tired of being stuck in the middle of these two. With a sigh, I shook my head at my friend.

A small, half smile pulled at his lips as he took the few steps back. Placing his hand against my cheek, he said, "I'm sorry, Rynnie."

His skin was warm, and although the gesture was foreign to our friendship, there was comfort in Arnik's touch.

"I shouldn't put you between us," he murmured. Without waiting for a response, he gave me a boyish wink and slipped into the laneway, his dark clothing blending with the thick shadows from the neighboring stone buildings. His golden hair reflected the moonlight, a beacon for only a second before he pulled his dark hood up, covering his head.

I'd heard Lord Irrik could hear a person exhale from a mile away and could see the warmth within a human body when all sunlight was gone. It was unlikely a cap would help, but it made me feel a little better.

I tossed my rag over my shoulder and went back inside.

Dyter had made quick work of the cleanup. The bench seats were all stacked. I suspected the tables hadn't been wiped. They'd be sticky by morning from the ale and stew, but I couldn't lift the benches myself, and Dyter wouldn't shift them a second time tonight. I'd just have to wipe the spots I could get to. *Teamwork at its finest.*

Dyter pushed through the swinging door with a mop and a pail. He grinned, and the scar on the left side of his face pulled his upper lip higher so he looked like he was snarling maniacally. "How worked up was the lad?" he asked with a chuckle. "Truthfully."

I scrubbed at the wood smoothed from generations of elbows and sliding tankards. "You always stir him up and leave me to deal with it."

I stomped past him to the next table, but he laughed, and I had to work to hide my amusement. I'd known Dyter longer than Arnik, as far back as my memory went. The tavern owner was part father, part uncle, and part friend. He'd helped Mum settle in when she'd arrived in Verald—when I was a baby—and he'd been close to us ever since.

We cleaned the bar area in silence, the familiar companionship its own brand of communication. But the meeting tonight was still a burning mystery to me, and when I couldn't stand the silence any longer, I asked, "How did it go?"

Sure enough, he grinned his lip-pulling snarl. "How did what go?"

I threw my rag at his face.

He gave mercy, tossing me the soiled cloth back. "Oh, the rebel meeting? It went well." He paused before amending with, "*Very* well. Now is the time to overthrow King Irdelron and the House of Ir. I feel it. The king is desperate to find something to end the famine, and it weakens him."

"He cares about ending the hunger?" Contradictory, considering his brutality.

"He cares about staying alive and keeping his arse on the throne, Ryn. There are many things you can do to people without them rebelling, but starving them isn't on the list. As cruel and rich as King Irdelron is, he's not an idiot. The situation is nearing a boiling point. More people have joined our cause in the last three months than the last three years."

I thought about the last few months as I scrubbed at the sticky ale. Nothing seemed different. People were starving now, just like they had been last year and the year before that. "How do you know he's desperate?"

"You haven't noticed the extra soldiers?" Dyter stopped his cleaning to raise his brows. "What about the extra beatings?"

I shook my head, averting my gaze. I wasn't really *into* the rebellion, but I should've noticed extra beatings.

Dyter pursed his lips and leveled me with a serious stare. "What about the giant black Drae circling the skies?"

I rolled my eyes. "Of course." *Only, I hadn't.* Mild anxiety pushed the next question from my lips. As much as I liked to tease about Dyter being an old coot, he was like family. "In that case," I continued, "are you sure you should be having rebel meetings here?"

Dyter shrugged. "People meet up here on a day-to-day basis. To the outsider, there's nothing amiss." His face darkened. "As long as Arnik stops bringing pups in."

But there was truth in Arnik's argument, too. "You need the pups, old man. They have young bodies that can fight."

Dyter gave a grudging nod.

I hated upsetting him. "But they can't do without the experience and wisdom of you oldies." I smiled as he puffed his chest out a bit. "So," I continued, sliding my gaze his way, "are you excited to meet Cal?"

Dyter let out a belly laugh that spread to every faded and worn part of the tavern. "You saw the boy by the door. I thought he was going to wet himself with excitement."

I joined him in laughter. "I thought he'd faint from the mere mention of Cal's name." I wasn't about to admit I'd shovel horse plop for three hours straight to be able to meet the leader of the rebellion. Now, *that* would be exciting. More excitement than I'd had since the Tals' donkey escaped their stable and went on a bender about town, kicking the stalls in the market over—I wanted to let it out again.

When the last glass was put away, Dyter held his hand out for my washrag. "You stayin' the night?"

I had a room upstairs, something Mum had insisted on when I started working at The Crane's Nest. Curfew was strict here, and the penalties if caught depended on the soldier's mood at the time. Over the last year, I'd felt a deep pull to be outside in the darkness, and Dyter's thatched roof didn't have a window I could see the night sky from.

Dyter knew I didn't sleep well here, so he never pushed.

"Mum is expecting me. She might already be pacing the floor." The last was said in jest as we both knew she wouldn't be. Ryhl didn't get anxious. She either did something or she didn't, but she didn't waste energy on worrying.

"Al'right then. Best scoot out. Be careful, my girl."

There was a real strain in his voice on the last four words. I gave him a quick peck on the cheek because I knew he secretly loved it even though he always waved me away. I grabbed a piece of brak to nibble on the way home and waved goodbye, stepping out into the moonlight.

"Oh," Dyter called.

I swung around to look at him, mouth stuffed with brak.

He came to the door, his lip lifted in his gruesome smile. "You'll want to be here tomorrow night."

My heart hammered. *What?* "Why? Will *he* be here?" I spoke around the food, spitting some on the ground. If Cal came, I'd probably die of excitement.

Dyter grinned and slammed the door in my face. I listened as he retreated into the depths of the tavern, chuckling at his hilarious wit.

I stared at the solid wooden door. He wouldn't have said anything if Cal wasn't coming here, would he? My gut told me no. *Holy pancakes!* A squeal built inside of me, but I opted instead to punch-dance on the spot.

The rebel leader was coming tomorrow night.

Beaming, I faced toward home and stepped into the caress of the dark shadows.

*I*n the old tales, Verald was the jewel kingdom within the Draecon Empire. Known for its fertile fields, the inhabitants of Verald produced the agriculture for the two other kingdoms in Emperor Draedyn's realm. But Verald's fertile fields were myths, like the legends of the Phaetyn, who could heal anything living. If there ever was truth to either story, it was long gone now.

Each household in the Penny Wheel, the slums of Verald, was allowed a small piece of dirt, a garden of their own, to do with as they wished. Ours did particularly well. Mum'd sit outside and talk to the plants after I'd pulled weeds or watered the garden or shifted dirt to new spots like I was born for it. Somehow, she coaxed the plants to grow with a wildness that *could've* made the neighbors jealous but instead motivated them to keep the abundant harvest a secret—probably because Mum shared her talent, helping others with their gardens throughout the entire Verald kingdom. Mum's green thumb was probably why Seven wasn't as skinny as the rest of the Harvest Zones.

I crept along the alley on my way home from The Crane's Nest, placing my feet carefully as I hugged the lovely shadows of the buildings in the Inbetween, pausing at intervals to listen for anything concealing itself in the night. The temperature was the energy sucking kind, unseasonably warm for mid-solstice. Something about the night kissed my skin, and I welcomed the black tendrils with open arms. If the dark were a person, I'd latch onto him and never let go. This pull to be in the night was a recent thing. Mum said it was a cheap thrill to make up for the monotonous routine of daily life. But for me, when the twin moons were up, the mystery of the shadows provided this spark I craved. The dark could take me away from this wasteland. The dark made me believe I was more than just a girl stuck in a life with no future but marriage and potato stew.

I crept through the shadows until fire lit the black sky in a sudden blazing inferno. I jumped and pressed my back to the wall, heart in my mouth, flashing danger searing my insides. *Mistress Moons. Please tell me that was a series of meteors.*

Making sure to keep concealed, I tilted my head to peer upward. The roaring streaks of red-and-orange flame were a brilliant beacon, painting an image of deadly beauty across the velvet of night.

The fire was no meteor shower. It was Lord Irrik.

I inhaled sharply and receded deeper into the shadows.

Lord Irrik, the king's pet Drae, was right there, in front of my eyes. The outline of his wings and body, and even his serpent-like tail, blotted out the stars. I'd grown up on stories of how the king had bound a powerful Drae to him. The Drae was invincible, and because he was fiercely loyal, his power protected the king.

The Drae circled the skies over the Money Coil and the Inbetween, making no effort to conceal his massive dragon form. He was far too close for comfort. The Drae breathed bolts of fire that extended as long as the main laneway in Zone Seven. My mouth hung ajar as I stared at the streak of lethal heat illuminating the sky.

Several moments passed as I debated my predicament. I couldn't stay here all night— eventually a patrol would pass by—but moving now could alert the Drae to my presence. Of course, if Lord Irrik could really hear someone breathing from a mile away, I was screwed anyway. I glanced back at the sky, and judging by scorching fire, he'd passed into zone eight. I could make it home if I was careful.

I ran to the next corner on my right and ducked behind an empty refuse bin and then took a deep breath as I plotted my route home. This far out from the Money Coil meant the streets would be empty. No one here could afford to bribe a patrol. I had two choices, and neither was very good. But before I could make my next move, the heavy powerful beating of wings and an inhuman roar came from much closer than before. Like, overhead close.

He couldn't be hunting me, though. I was absolutely secure in that conclusion. The king's Drae had more important things to do than hunt a seventeen-year-old. I stilled as I glanced back the way I'd come.

A seventeen-year-old who'd just left a rebel meeting.

Dyter said the Drae had been circling the skies the last few nights. He also said no one would suspect the meetings were at The Crane's Nest.

This had to be coincidence, nothing more. There was *no way* the Drae was bothering with me. Uneasiness tickled the inside of my rib cage as I connected his presence here as something *more* for the first time. What if the king had sent Irrik to find out about the rebel meetings? What if they knew? Was there more to his presence than general intimidation and keeping the starving peasants in check?

Despite the heat, chills danced across my skin. If Lord Irrik wasn't patrolling, he was hunting rebels.

And half-arsed rebel though I was, I'd just left the meeting point for all the full-arsed rebels.

My heart raced, a quick scurrying of beats, like a lizard running over hot sand. I stared up at the night to try to make out the black-winged and horned dragon above, but millions of stars winked back from the darkness, revealing nothing of what shared their space. My mother's hushed whisper from when I was young rose in my memory: *The tendrils of midnight can cling to him, taking him in as one of their own, keeping him invisible in their midst.*

Seemed like that part was true. Sweat broke out on my forehead.

There was something distinctly different between the story my mind told as I snuggled under a blanket and the reality of the night and heat surrounded me, the fear pulsing from deep within. Yet, I didn't feel full of terror. Scared, yes, but his presence had nothing to do with me. It couldn't. I'd never ever had anything to do with the powerful Drae—thank the Moons.

The fire in the sky was gone, and with the sudden darkness, silence fell. On soft feet, I darted to the next corner, through the abandoned buildings, and across the road into the area where the rich lived. Their stone buildings were neatly arranged, and nestled in the middle of their rows was a dry, square space with a grand fountain where a beautiful garden used to grow. Only a couple of the buildings bordering the large square were occupied nowadays, but in times gone by, Mum said it used to be a bustling and happy place, full of people and goods—back when the land healers were still alive. *Stupid king.* Killing the Phaetyn seemed a moronic thing to do, even if you did want to live forever.

I took three, theoretically calming, breaths and studied the dark, shadowed area with the fountain in the middle. Right now, with the invisible monster of my childhood overhead, the uncovered space only meant one thing.

Open-expanse-where-powerful-Drae-could-eat-me-in-one-bite.

"Al'righty," I croaked. I probably wouldn't be the pep talk queen of Harvest Zone Seven either.

Maybe I should go all the way around. It put me at greater risk of encountering a patrol, but. . .

Flame erupted in the black sky far to my right. He'd moved.

Good time to go, good time to go, good time to go. Leaving my protective shadows, I sprinted across the barren garden.

A primal force urged me to go faster, faster than I'd ever run before.

Clearing the area, I pressed against the stone wall of the House of Tals' residence, attuned to every tiny piece of my surroundings, and attempted to regulate my breathing. The chirping of crickets was only interrupted by the mournful whinny of a screech owl. That seemed normal-ish.

An unbearable tickle attacked my throat. I worked to suppress the sneeze protesting the lack of moisture. I brushed my tongue over the roof of my mouth until the sensation passed. *Drak*, imagine that. Making it across the fountain garden just to sneeze.

Thirty minutes later, I'd wound my way back out past the Inbetween to our section of housing.

Peasant homes used to be built from wood, but with the barren land in Verald, that wasn't an option anymore. The wealthy built their homes from stone mined in the Gemond Kingdom. But the quarries and mines there, much like our land in Verald, were barely making quota. Long before I was born, King Irdelron ordered large sections of houses demolished, thinking the land beneath had lain fallow and would produce crops. Unfortunately, that wasn't the case. However, most of the demolished housing materials were useable after, and the peasants of Verald erected hodgepodge houses from stone, wood, and metal.

Our houses in the Wheel were in narrow, parallel rows, with a wide strip of shared dirt between every second row for personal gardens. Our garden spilled into the one behind, belonging to Celyst, and I often cut through from her house to avoid going in our front door.

Our three-room dwelling consisted of a living space with a kitchen and eating area as well as a daybed that also served as a couch.

There was a washroom, too, and a bedroom Mum had insisted was mine a year ago.

I scampered past Celyst's house, through her lush garden, thanks to Mum, and into ours. The growth became increasingly thick the closer I got to our house. I stepped over potato plants, squash vines, and then pushed through the rows of corn, behind which was my window. A year ago, plants reached all the way to the wall of our house, but I'd been trampling the ground beneath the window to my room when climbing in and out, and now a small patch of dirt lay trodden and infertile at my feet.

Gripping the sill, I made quick work of pulling myself up and through my bedroom window onto my bed.

As my heart rate returned to normal, I laughed to the empty room. I was in the safety of our four walls now, not just alive but unharmed and undetected. Tomorrow, I was totally telling Arnik I escaped Lord Irrik—with embellishments. Huge embellishments.

—*Girl from Harvest Zone Seven Escapes Invincible Drae*—

—*Lord Irrik and the Skill-less Peasant Who Outsmarted Him*—

—*Soap Queen Defeats Drae in the Realm's Most Epic Battle of Wits*—

I'd work on it.

My bedroom door swung open, and my meticulous mother stood before me. With a sigh of relief, her shoulders sagged as she greeted me. "Ryn."

"Hey, Mum." I smiled and waved at her, trying to look nonchalant. *Drak*, my hands still shook. I tucked them behind me. I might want to gloat to Arnik about my escape from Lord Irrik, but my mother was so earnest with her warnings I didn't want to risk her wrath.

Her face, illuminated by a lantern, swung into view. Her eyes were wide. "I was worried."

I pulled up short and said, "You don't worry."

She gave a tight smile. "Lord Irrik is patrolling. You shouldn't be out when he is, Ryn. No one should. I'll have to remind Dyter to keep you if the Drae is about."

Dyter was in trrrrouble. "Do you think the king's Drae is here for more than patrolling?"

She shifted her eyes to the window, saying slowly, "Whatever the reason, they've tripled the king's presence in Zone Seven. It isn't good." She frowned and continued, "I'm not sure I want you going back to Dyter's until they're gone. Not with him having those meetings there."

"But they could be here for months," I protested. "Besides, I'm skill-less Ryn. Everyone knows that." *And the rebel leader is coming tomorrow night.* I was smart enough not to tell her that.

My quip made her smile, but she pursed her lips and shook her head. She placed the lantern down and came to sit next to me. "You're anything but skill-less, baby."

"Young lady," I corrected. "We agreed."

"My young lady-baby," she replied.

We smiled at each other.

Her gaze dropped to where my feet were pulled up tight against my body on the bed. "What are you doing?"

"Nothing," I replied quickly.

Everyone knew Lord Irrik could hide under beds at night, or anywhere else that was dark, and if my feet were off the bed, he would drag me underneath and I'd die a slow, horrible death.

"The Drae were once our saviors. They kept us safe from invasion. They were a loyal and honorable race."

Mum had told me stories of the Drae since I was a baby. But they were myths, bedtime stories with lessons mixed in. The Drae were supposedly peacekeepers, self-sacrificing, generous with their skills, and did their best to serve humanity. But the emperor, who was also Drae, was greedy and tried to force them to join his war. He betrayed his own kind, having them slaughtered for their refusal to help him rule the world.

"Don't forget the Drae boy," she said with a quirk of her lips, referencing one such story of self-sacrifice. She then smoothed her expression and said, "We should go work some of the gardens in Harvest Zone Two."

The opposite side of the kingdom. We'd be gone for at least two weeks. "Right," I drew out. I did not want to miss my only chance to meet Cal. "And I'm coming?"

"I got a message from Bratrik. Their crops are failing. They need our help."

I shook my head. "Your help, not mine."

"Fourteen children died last week. There are dozens of gardens to visit. You know I can't do it all on my own. Who else would haul dirt?" she asked with a smirk.

The tension in the room dissipated, and just like that, mother erased my disappointment. I'd help the children. Of course, I would.

"Funny," I chirped, resigned to my fate. "We'll see who's laughing when I'm soap queen of Verald. I won't be hauling your dirt then."

She laughed, and the sound was my absolute favorite. It was delighted and youthful and carefree, and it lifted my mood to match hers. Another talent of my mother's.

"When will we leave for Zone Two?" I yawned.

"I'll need a day to make ready, so two days. Why?"

Yes! Thank the moons she was such a planner. "I need to ready my entourage; that's why."

"Al'right, soap queen," she said with a grin. "It's time for bed." She swept up her lantern and blew me a kiss. "Goodnight, lady-baby."

"Night, Mum."

I kicked off my boots and held my breath as they fell into the danger zone off the bed. *Faster than your eyes can track, with talons that can fell a tree in one swoop.* I didn't dare change into my nightclothes and leave the safety of bed island. Snuggling under the quilt, the adrenaline of the day waned and my eyes grew heavy. I was hovering just barely on the edges of consciousness when my mother's next words drifted to me from the doorway. "I checked under the bed earlier. You'll always be safe."

"Hey, lady-baby, I need you to take a delivery to Arnik's mother this morning, and one to Talryna in the Money Coil. I forgot there are three orders to fill, and I need to stop by Pru's." Mum set a basket on the table next to me and ran her hand over my long, cinnamon-colored hair. The table was set with two plates, two forks, and two glasses filled with honeyed milk. Someone must've paid Mum with it.

"I can lower myself to grant this boon." I tipped my nose up and sniffed. The scent of lavender from the soap basket was stronger than whatever Mum had concocted for our breakfast.

She mussed my hair with her wet hands. "My thanks, soap queen. I've got deliveries all day today, but I'll be back before curfew. We should wash your hair tonight, too." She stepped back toward the stove and flipped the contents of the pan. She pointed the spatula at me and said, "Make sure you're back. No matter what's happening with Dyter, you need to be home before curfew with the patrols out."

I nodded, trying to peek at our meal. I didn't care about my hair. In fact, the stuff Mum used to wash it made it all stiff and gross. No, what was important to me right then were the glasses of milk because if we were having milk, there might be something else tasty.

"We'll leave tomorrow at first light. It'll take us two days to cross the Quota Fields."

"We're not taking the Market Circuit?" I asked. The paved ring road went through all twelve Harvest Zones and was the easiest way to travel.

Verald was shaped like a bull's-eye and split into twelve wedges, called Harvest Zones. In the mountainous center of the kingdom was King Irdelron's castle. The flat band of space immediately surrounding the castle took up the most space in the kingdom and belonged to the dry Quota Fields where the farmers worked. The next band out was the Market Circuit, which was the road running through the twelve Harvest Zone wedges. The wealthiest families lived closest to the Market Circuit in the next band, and their public houses, taverns, and trade shops were here as well. We peasants called the place where the wealthy hung out the Money Coil. The next band out from the Money Coil was named the Inbetween, a space for those who were on the fringes of wealth. And then the uneven very outer band of the kingdom where the rest of us lived was referred to as the Penny Wheel. As a rule, the closer to the king you were, the more he cared about you. That was why his food source was closest and his workers farthest away.

The Crane's Nest was one of the only taverns outside the Coil in the entire kingdom. Dyter was on the very outskirts of the Inbetween, which was why he took payment of any kind, not just coin, like in the Money Coil.

"What's for breakfast?" I asked Mum, trying to peek.

"You'll see if you wait one second."

She brought our plates to the table, and my stomach grumbled.

Breakfast was one potato pancake each and a small serving of sweet apple mash. Better than gruel, at least. Mum set her lavender-flower syrup on the table beside my plate. There was just enough for both of us—practically a feast with the milk.

A feast that was gone in less than a dozen savored bites, but a feast nevertheless.

Eating done, I washed the dishes, went back to my room to grab my boots, which somehow survived Lord Irrik under my bed overnight—not even a chew mark—and swiped up the basket. Calling a goodbye over my shoulder, I shook my head as I watched my mother ladle the dishwater into jars to water the garden.

"Remember to tell Dyter you won't be in for the next two or three weeks!" she yelled after me.

Smiling, I bounced down the street toward Arlette's house to deliver the soap she'd ordered. I was disappointed to find Arnik already gone to the vineyard for the day when I dropped off the basket, but his absence couldn't put much of a dampener on my day for two reasons. First, I was a Drae survivor. And second, we weren't leaving Zone Seven until morning, which meant I'd be seeing a rebel leader tonight. He probably had a scar on his cheek—and *muscles*.

I lifted a hand to my eyes as I scanned the sky for the Drae. Nowhere to be seen.

Facing toward the king's castle in the distance, I darted through the hodgepodge peasant housing of the Penny Wheel on my way to the House of Tal. I went through the Inbetween, and soon the grand stone houses of the Money Coil were ahead of me. I slowed when I reached the Tals' house—the largest of them all. I left the second basket at their door after pounding on the heavy entrance for a full minute.

The barren garden from last night stretched before me, the grand fountain at its center.

This time, with no winged foe above me, I stopped at the fountain that had been dry my entire life. Pausing here was habitual because a tiny welded flower was inlaid in the side of the concrete fountain—

the sole bit of beauty in the otherwise functional and practical space. I don't know how it caught my eye as a toddler, but Mum said I'd pester her from dawn up to dusk about visiting the flower. After checking soldiers weren't around, she would lift me up to trace the petals of the flower and its curving stalk. For years she'd lifted me, until one day I could stand on my tiptoes and touch it myself. Now, whenever I passed this place, I continued the tradition, stroking the welded flower with fondness.

Leaving the Money Coil and my welded flower, I wiped perspiration from my hairline and began retracing my steps to reach the shelter of The Crane's Nest on the other side of the Inbetween. *Mistress Moons,* the sun's rays burned with muggy heat this morning.

At this time of day, the laneways were about the busiest they ever got, and I smiled and nodded at nearly everyone. I'd known them my whole life—seemed rude not to say howdy. Hyrriet from House Hy glared at me, and I pretended not to see her pristine ankle-length skirt and perfectly ironed aketon which she'd drawn in at the middle with a wide leather belt. Hers had been the last potato bush I'd killed. I swear I'd done everything right, but two days later, Mum told me they'd found it shriveled up.

I dodged through the crowd and knocked at the back door of Dyter's, tapping my foot as I waited.

"You're being followed, girl."

I yelped and spun to see a man shift in the shadows two paces from where I stood. He stayed crouched behind the cover of the stacked crates outside Dyter's back door. The stranger poked his head up, and I caught a glance of the speaker from underneath a wide-brimmed garden hat pulled low over his eyes. The young man I'd seen last night; I'd recognize his twenty-somethingness anywhere.

He hunched back over, disappearing behind the potato crates, and said, "Two men are following you. They've been on your tail since you left the Wheel." When I did nothing more than stare at him, he snapped, "Turn around and act like you're waiting for the door."

Numbly, I turned to face the door again. I didn't dare glance over my shoulder to the mouth of the alley to check if this man told the truth. He didn't seem the kind to make stuff up.

"This place has become interesting to the wrong people," he said. "You're not the only one with a tail today. Lord Irrik followed you and several others last night and ordered soldiers to follow you all and report back."

His concerns reinforced the uneasiness I felt in my gut at Lord Irrik's presence. The Drae was here to catch rebels, and so were the king's guard.

"How do you know all this?"

He spoke over me. "Tell Dyter the meeting needs to be moved to another location at a later date. He'll know who needs to be there and how to make it happen. Warn him."

Two men were following me, and the fear pulsing through me became my entire world. The seriousness of what that meant hit me with a force that made my knees weak. If I wasn't on the king's personal radar, I was on the radar of his personal Drae. Which could be worse. Unable to remain quiet any longer, I asked, "Are they watching me?"

"They're hanging back around the corner."

"What do I do?" I didn't know this man, but he was the only adult around, and I needed help.

He paused for a moment. "I wouldn't worry too much. They've set tails on suspected rebel members in the other Harvest Zones, and nothing came of it. Don't do anything suspicious until the soldiers leave the area. Blend in as if your life depends on it because it probably does. Could you leave for a while, maybe go to a different zone?"

For the first time, I wondered if Mum's sudden gardening trip wasn't all that sudden. "They won't hurt my mother, will they?" I asked, trying not to move my lips. To the men watching me, it probably looked as if I was staring at the door. "I need to warn her."

The man shifted back down the alley. "Stick to your usual routine. Unless," he paused, "your mother has something to hide?"

I snorted, gaining back a bit of my lost confidence. The certainty of my mother set the world all right. "My mother? Not a chance."

I POUNDED ON THE BACK DOOR AGAIN, BUT NO ONE ANSWERED, AND I figured The Crane's Nest was busy enough that no one was in the kitchen. After all, that was where I was supposed to be. Too scared to go back the way I'd come, I went all the way to the other end of the alley and circled around to the front of The Crane's Nest to go through the public entrance. I was officially spooked.

Relief washed over me as I stepped into the familiar setting, but the feeling lasted less than a second. The tavern was empty with the exception of Dyter and two men I recognized as members of the rebellion that weren't from around here. One of the men mumbled something to Dyter before the two rebels disappeared into the kitchen.

Dyter rounded the bar with a terrifying frown. "You can't be here today, my girl."

"A man in the alley told me you should move the meeting," I blurted. "I've got two men following me and Mum made potato pancakes and we're leaving, but the man said to tell you."

He dragged me to a tall stool by the bar and sat me down. "Calm yourself, Ryn." Then he yelled toward the kitchen, "Don't go out the back. She's being followed." He took a deep breath and faced me. "Now, what is this? What man in the alley?"

"The blond man that was here last night. The one in his twenties."

A spark entered Dyter's gaze, and he said, "I see."

I stared at him. "That's it?"

He circled around the back of the bar, absently rubbing the stump on his left wrist. "You have two tails?"

I nodded, swallowing the fear clawing its way up my chest.

Dyter closed his eyes. "You're not the only one, unfortunately. I don't know how it happened. We had men check the area for soldiers before everyone left."

I told Dyter what the man had said. "If Lord Irrik can conceal himself like Mum says, then the man could be right," I said. "The Drae was breathing fire all over the place."

"You think it was the Drae's signal to the ground soldiers to follow you?"

I paled. No. I hadn't. But that put a different perspective on last night.

"That certainly explains it," Dyter continued. He heaved a sigh and closed his eyes briefly. "Your mother's going to hurt me for getting you involved."

"We're going away for a few weeks," I said. "She said to tell you."

"That'd be best. I'd never forgive myself if anything happened to ya."

Last night had been scary, but I'd thought myself safe when I got home. I'd even come to think of it as exciting. Now, that sense of security was rapidly burning away. I might've wanted some interruption to routine, but this? This was much too scary, and I didn't like it, not one bit.

Dyter said, "Hold here a bit, love. I'll be back."

He disappeared out the front and reappeared a few minutes later. "*Drak*. Two tails, al'right. One's tall and skinny with a face like a snake, and the other's a fat toad."

"Seriously?" A laugh escaped, my anxiety rising to hysteria. My tethered grip on reality was slipping.

He cupped my cheeks, forcing me to stare at him. "Take a deep breath, Rynnie. It's going to be fine. One is headed around the back now. I just saw him go. I'm going to distract Toady, and I need you to run. Go into the Quota Fields, and then head home. Make sure you go sideways through a couple of zones so you can lose them, al'right? Your mother, is she going to be out all day?"

I nodded.

"Well then, you best stay in the fields until curfew. I don't want you home alone."

"Can't I stay here?" I whispered.

He squeezed my shoulder and shook his head. "I don't know what the soldiers plan to do or how much they know. If they come here, you'd be in harm's way for sure. I don't want that, especially when I might've put you there in the first place."

"I made my own choice," I said, refusing to let him feel guilty over allowing me to work here.

"I know," he smiled, "But you're the daughter I always wanted, and I can't help getting overprotective."

"I . . . I can help." I wasn't sure if I could or not, but I didn't want to leave. Somehow, in my mind, staying here with Dyter was safer than hiding in the fields.

"I appreciate that. I do. But that *no* is firm. I won't have you here."

I scowled at him. A real one. "Shouldn't I warn Mum?"

"Your mother is a lot safer going about her day in ignorance. But you tell her as soon as you see her next. If you need help getting away in the morning, you send word via Arnik, you understand?"

I knew that look, and I'd learned years before that it wasn't worth arguing once his *no* was firm. It was time to dash past the toad and hide in the fields. "Yes, Dyter."

He gave me a tight smile and headed for the door.

5

*T*he workers had left their stations more than an hour ago. The sky was now a convincing twilight, and there could only be an hour until curfew, just enough time to get home if I ran. Mother would be back by now, and I was certain if I wasn't back before curfew, she'd actually worry for once.

I'd spent the day thinking about all the things I should've done if I hadn't been completely flustered by having two of the king's guard following me. Like asking one of the children to run a note to mother, telling her to pack, or how about staying at The Crane's Nest last night instead of taking a moonlight walk and being spotted by the king's Drae and getting into this stupid mess?

Next time I decided to take a moonlit walk, I was going to slap myself. Twice.

Except for now. Because I was taking a moonlit walk now.

From tomorrow onward, if I ever even thought about a moonlit walk, I'd slap myself twice.

The skies had been empty all day, but before I moved, I gave the sky a last anxious scan.

Nerves twisted in my gut, making me eager for the moment Mum could take over the decision-making. Prior to this trouble, I'd thought myself a capable person, but I was learning this wasn't true at all.

I kept low, opting to scuttle through the fields with the high growing vegetables and fruit for extra cover. Snake and Toady weren't following me; I was certain. I'd taken considerable care losing them in the Quota Fields of Zone Six. Then I'd dodged through five before hiding in the fields of Zone Eight for the day.

Thirty minutes later, I was back in the fields of my own Harvest Zone. If I could make it over the Market Circuit and through the fountain garden in the Money Coil, the rest of the way to our house in the Wheel would be easy.

I sprinted across the Market Circuit and all the way to the edge of the fountain garden. I pressed myself to a brick wall as I stared up at the sky, panting hard. The stars were just starting to wink into life, and I took a deep breath before turning my attention across the garden.

My feet faltered, and I nearly had a heart attack when I glimpsed the man standing in the shadows opposite me.

He wasn't a soldier—they all wore the same blue or green uniform with a black trim. This man wore solid liquid black, perfect for sneaking. I blinked several times to get rid of the blur his clothing had going on with the shadows, almost as if the dimness clung to him. My eyes were obviously feeling the strain of the day.

"Psst," I whispered to him across the gap, determined to be a good neighbor. "You shouldn't be out here, mister."

I couldn't see his face, shadowed as it was, but he was tall and muscular. I'd crossed over into Seven, and the thought came to me that this man better not be Arnik playing tricks. I'd kill him.

The man turned to me, just his head, and I gave him a pointed look. "Well? What are you standing there for? The king's Drae is out and the soldiers, too. You need to get on home before curfew."

The man jerked, as if surprised I was addressing him.

I rolled my eyes. This one must've dropped his acorns when he was fighting for the emperor.

"You see me?" he demanded.

Oh, brother. It was sad, really, what happened to men after war, but Mum said manners didn't cost a thing. Using the politest tone possible, I asked, "Are you usually invisible?"

The silence following my remark was drawn out. In only a few seconds, it became awkward. I shifted, debating whether I should leave him, but something about his surprise held me back. His mouth open and closed several times, and then he answered, "Yes."

He took a step toward me, still cloaked in shadows, and my heart stopped.

It wasn't that I immediately connected his single word reply to what it meant.

Not at all.

It was that the insects stopped their chatter and the night became heavy exactly as he took that step.

One step and the world *held its breath.*

I'd been thinking about the night sky and the thing it concealed too often in the last two days to miss the connection. This man wasn't lost. As my bones rattled inside me, I knew. The deathly quiet was confirmation a predator had found me. The king's Drae was right in front of me. The shadows appeared to cling to him because they knew him. My heart sputtered in my chest, and rushes of blood sounded in my ears. I hadn't blinked. I *couldn't* blink. I couldn't breathe . . .

Lord Irrik.

I took a deep breath as a billow of heat pushed against me from where I stood just beyond the center square. The warmth swirled around my legs and caressed my arms, and I felt an urge to flee and stay at the same time. *Play it cool, Ryn.*

"Al'right. You take care now," I said in a hoarse voice. I willed my legs to move, but they seized as the inky darkness melted away and the famed Lord Irrik glided completely out of the shadows. My heart pounded, the thundering loud in my ears. A sliver of rational thought processed the danger I was in.

"You see me," he repeated, stalking closer. But his words were no longer a question. His statement was a confirmation of what we both knew.

Death stood three paces from me, and I couldn't move. My mouth dried as I stared at the man who I knew turned into a terrible beast. My gaze dropped, taking him in. He wore black boots, black breeches, and a sleeveless aketon that hit mid-thigh. His clothing fit like a second skin, revealing a lean build that was nevertheless all muscle. His fists were clenched, and his muscles flexed as if ready to strike.

I was going to die. I knew it as certainly as I knew death shouldn't look so good. Not when it was already invincible. I'd heard Lord Irrik was beautiful, that even knowing he would bring death, looking at him would almost make up for it. My mother left *that* part out of my bedtime stories, but the women here talked.

His dark eyes narrowed, and he asked, "What are you?"

I frowned at him. *Huh?*

The Drae's face didn't change, except for a flicker of annoyance. "Let's try a different question then. Why are you out after curfew?"

As he spoke, he flicked a lock of dark hair away from his face, and I embarrassed myself by flinching in the most horrible way, expecting him to strike me. He smirked again.

My mouth was parched, and it took several attempts before I could voice my almost incoherent reply. "I'm sorry. I didn't realize the time."

It was true. This time. I'd thought I still had half an hour.

He didn't seem to hear. My words bounced off him onto the chipped cobblestone ground. He took one step toward me, and I took three back before hitting the coarse stone wall.

"I won't do it again," I whispered, pressing back. "I promise."

The scream lodged in my throat as he crossed the remaining space in a blur my eyes could hardly trace. I turned my face away, lifting an arm out of instinct. My mother would never know what happened to me. *Mum.* I had to keep him from her.

I straightened but jerked when I saw his face inches away. I tried to meet his eyes but focused on his chin instead. Then he leaned forward, blowing a long breath into my face.

I clamped down on a scream because I knew what that breath would do to me. Why else would he breathe in my face? A Drae could turn anyone into a puppet with a single exhale in close range.

He looked at me expectantly, and I looked back.

His square jaw was covered with a day's worth of growth, but it did nothing to distract from his sculpted lips, the lower slightly fuller than the top. It made him appear sterner, adding to the terror his air of darkness inspired. His nose was straight, and his deep-set eyes appeared to be the same color as the inky night. I couldn't tell if his pupils were dilated so wide I couldn't see his irises or if his eyes were really that onyx black. His hair was liquid coal, like the color of his clothes, and confined at the base of his neck. The sleeveless aketon exposed plenty of his neck, and his skin was warm like the burnt sugar Mum made on Solstice celebrations.

I swallowed and waited for the moment I would lose all control of my mind and body. Had it already happened? Though his breath smelled sweet, I didn't feel like I was losing control. I wondered if I would know when his power took effect. Would I care when I betrayed my people? Would I care when he finally killed me?

"Last night you left The Crane's Nest after a meeting. Who were you with, and where can I find the others who were there?" he finally asked. His voice was different than before, like the warmth of embers on a cool morning, a beautiful rumble that calmed my frayed nerves.

"My friend. She lives just up the road." The key to lying was to tell as much of the truth as possible and keep the important information concealed. Should I be able to reason like this? Maybe the breath thing wasn't true, but then why had he unleashed a lungful on my face?

He chuckled, and more of his sweet breath surrounded me. It was more than his breath, I realized. He smelled good—his body or what-ever—like sunbaked pine and dried sandalwood. I started to lean forward, and he sighed, shoving me back against the wall in irritation.

Get that a lot, do you?

"Who is your friend?" he snarled.

There was no way I would tell him about Dyter or Arnik. "Why? You want to visit her, too?"

He furrowed his brow, and the disinterest on his face lessened for the first time. "What?" He eyed me for a long second and took a deep breath, blowing it in my face again.

I frowned at him. "Can you stop that? It's kind of really, really strange."

He jerked, eyes widening, and took a step back, almost seeming to stumble as he whispered something in a different language, not taking his eyes off my quaking form.

Drak, I should've kept pretending, maybe I could salvage the situa-tion. I smirked at him, feigning unfocused eyes, and said, "I can take you to meet Syla if you'd like?"

"Stop pretending." He growled. "I can tell."

A snicker escaped. As soon as it sounded, I slapped my trembling hands over my mouth. *Mistress Moons!* What was wrong with me?

The intensity with which the Drae studied me cocooned us, and the rest of the world disappeared.

"You can see me. You're resistant to the droplets in my breath." He studied me, his gaze intense and penetrating. In a low voice, almost to himself, he murmured, "It can't be."

He didn't wait for me to babble an answer but brought his hand up in tiny increments, his expression rapt as he circled the back of my neck. His warm palm connected with the clammy skin at the nape of my neck, and I shrieked. Fire licked where our skin touched, the warmth spreading from where his hand tangled in my hair, sending tendrils of pulsing energy all over until I felt like I was crawling out of my skin. I screamed again, but this time the sound was muffled against his shoulder. I'd fallen, or he'd pulled me.

He ripped his hand away and stared at it with what looked like betrayal as I fell to my knees.

He swore long and hard again in the language I didn't know. Some of the same surprise I felt was echoed within the guttural sounds he made. *He* sounded shocked.

"That wasn't in the bedtime stories." I squeezed my eyes closed to rid myself of black spots. *What just happened?*

"Where are you going right now?" he asked in a different tone. Gone was the disinterest. Something very different took its place in his expression. His gaze darted behind as he turned toward the fountain, scanning the dry space. "There are people coming."

"Snake and Toady." If my luck was continuing in the same stream.

"Who are Snake and Toady?" he asked in an urgent tone.

I batted his hands away. Why was my body drained of energy? The back of my neck was pulsing. I moaned, "My tails."

What the hay did he moisturize his hands with? Or was this some other Drae power no one talked about?

His face froze. "Tails? Soldiers?"

I didn't answer.

Anxiety crawled between us, originating from him. Was his magic finally working? There was no sense of compulsion, and I guess if I was able to contemplate lying, I had my answer.

"I was going home," I slurred with fatigue. "Don't kill my mum," I said. "Please show her mercy. I'm just the soap queen. I don't know anything important."

He wasn't listening. In the same way I didn't pay attention to buzzing flies. The darkness reached for him as he grabbed my arm and yanked me toward the other end of the alleyway.

"Hey," voices shouted behind us. "Halt!"

"*Drak*," he swore in a hushed tone.

I stumbled to keep up with his long stride. He couldn't walk me home; Mum was there. "If you're going to kill me, could you please do it now?"

He didn't answer.

I was terrified, tired, but I felt the first strains of anger begin to wriggle inside.

We ducked out of one alley and into another then crossed over into Harvest Zone Six and backtracked to a laneway near the square in Zone Seven before heading toward the Wheel where I lived.

"You need to get out of here."

He spoke for the first time in several minutes.

What the hay was going on?

"Let go of me," I demanded. I tried to pull away from his grip, but he held tight, his long fingers circling the entire width of my bicep with a strength that told me he could break my bone just from losing focus.

Irrik closed his eyes and pinched the bridge of his nose. "Why are you even in this kingdom? Do you want to die? You need to be gone. Right now."

The intensity of his words made my skin crawl, and the burn of his stare made me want to quiver at his feet like a mouse before a hawk. What he was saying didn't add up. "What?"

"The soldiers saw us," he said, his voice low. "I don't know how you're . . . alive. But you need to leave. I'm going to try to fix it, but I can't risk . . ."

He made no sense, yet his warning seemed sincere. I stared into the stone-cold face of the king's Drae and could have almost mistaken the wild look in his eyes for. . . fear.

"What is wrong with you?" The wriggling in my stomach swelled, and anger laced my voice. "I thought you were going to swallow me."

His fear made me furious. What did a Drae have to fear? "Why are you so upset? Because—"

He grabbed my shoulders and said, "Listen, girl." His grip tightened. "I'll give you this warning once. When I let go, run. Run home. You and whoever you live with need to get out of here. Do you hear me? You must never come back." He shoved his face to mine, eyes blazing. "I'll kill you myself if I see you again."

My brain rattled in my head as he shook me. The upheaval of his emotions was too much, and I wrenched myself from his grasp. "Stop. Please!"

He let go, but continued snarling words I couldn't hear through the increasing buzz in my ears. He watched me, his eyes lit with an intensity I'd never seen before.

My nerves were frayed. My emotions were taxed past the point of being reasonable. Something inside me recoiled with a sharp snap. For the first time in my life, I raised my hand and slapped someone across the face.

We stood in the dark, empty alley, staring at each other as I lowered my hand.

My chest heaved with emotion, and he shuddered slightly as though about to explode. The outline of where my thumb and index finger had connected with his skin was visible in a pink welt. "I'm so sor—"

"Get out of here," he gritted out, shoving me toward the next corner.

I took flight, sprinting through the streets as though the king himself was behind me, which in many ways he was.

Eventually, I calmed enough to recognize the outskirts of the Inbetween.

I adjusted my course, and as soon as I was in our housing section, I slowed. I was breathing way too loudly for creeping, so I put my hands on my knees, taking in deep gulps of air while I waited for my heart rate to settle.

The night was warm and dark; this normally brought me comfort. Instinctively, I looked to the sky, but instead of stars and the inky canvas I loved so much, I heard the beating of wings spread wide, far above my head. He was there, I knew, invisible against the sultry night. The beating sound moved in a circle overhead, and my skin prickled with the awareness of his attention as, I assumed, he waited for me to go inside.

The king's Drae knew where I lived.

Comforting. That wouldn't give me nightmares at all.

I gave myself a mental shake and rolled my shoulders back until I stood tall. Doing so was the last thing I wanted to do, but it made me feel better to appear dignified when I'd been obliterated with fear ten minutes ago.

Circling our home twice, and finding no signs of Snake and Toady, I cracked open our front door to slip inside and talk with Mum. I peered up at the night sky one last time, unable to resist, a bolt of fear splicing through me as a set of fiery reptilian eyes burned into mine from the darkness high above.

6

I lay wide-awake in bed, staring at the dark ceiling, blankets yanked to my chin. Four hours ago, my mother lost control. As I'd told her of my day, and I'd held nothing back, she became more and more panicked.

I was afraid. My mother was supposed to make the decisions; she was older and smarter and stronger. But tonight, Mum was just as scared as I was.

My bulging rucksack sat in a corner, ready for tomorrow's journey, and Mum had told me to take whatever I didn't want to be without. I knew what that meant.

I could still hear her downstairs, trying to be quiet as she made preparations, doing the exact opposite of what she'd told me to do. We couldn't do anything out of the ordinary to attract attention before we left, which included smashing around to pack when we should be asleep.

I stiffened as a scream rent the air. The sound was outside, maybe from a few houses away. Mum stopped in her fear-driven ruckus below, and my heart rate doubled as I lay still.

Another scream followed, along with men shouting and the hammering boom of fists on wood. Close. Too close.

I leaped out of bed, already dressed on Mum's orders. The door flung open a moment later, and Mother rushed in.

"We're leaving now."

"What's happening?" I asked, reaching for my bag, but Mum pushed me toward the door and then pulled me back, only to push me toward the window.

"They're coming for you. They've gone to the wrong house."

How was that possible when Snake and Toady knew where I lived? "How will we get . . . ?"

The rest of my sentence evaporated as I caught sight of my mother's face and spun to the window just in time to see Lord Irrik climb through. If this situation didn't leave icy-cold fear in every part of my body, I would have been rolling on the floor with laughter. The Drae even looked mildly disgruntled at being subjected to the indignity of a schoolboy entrance. He was dressed exactly the same, in fitted black clothing.

His dark gaze rested on me, searching up and down. Then it went to my mother. His nostrils flared, and his eyes widened as he gasped a string of words in the same guttural language I'd heard him use before.

Mum didn't budge.

"How. . . ?" he said, staring at my mother as though looking at a specter. "How can you be here?" He reached forward as if to touch her but stopped before making contact. "I was told you all died."

His voice radiated fury, and it was the simplest of self-preservation instincts that had me backing away toward my mother.

Mum *ignored him*, tapped her index finger to her lips, and began to pace.

I looked between them. Did my mother know who this was? She couldn't, based on her inappropriate lack of fear. And how did Irrik

44

know her? Why was he asking questions that didn't make sense instead of killing us?

Mum's shoulders were tense, halfway up to her ears, a sure sign she was stressed. Stressed but not afraid of Lord Irrik, which made no sense. Slowly, her shoulders dropped, dropped past the point of normalcy into defeat.

I'd been so busy watching this happen and keeping one eye on Lord Irrik, who now contemplated me with an intensity that made me want to jump out the window he'd just come in, I missed the moment my mother started crying.

Her eyes were filled and spilling over as she knelt in front of me.

I'd never seen my mother cry, and I ached to make it stop. I winced at her pain, and my apologies spilled incoherently from my lips. I sat before her, trying to dry her tears as I babbled.

"You must go," she said, cutting me off. "You're running out of time. You need to go."

I inhaled shallow breaths. This wasn't what I expected or wanted to hear. I didn't know what I expected or wanted; actually, nothing about this made sense. And didn't she mean *we* must go? "There's a Drae in my bedroom."

The only response to my crazed mutterings was Mum stroking my cheek.

"It should've never happened, but I'm so glad it did, Rynnie," my mother sobbed. "Please know that."

Her heart was breaking. Why was her heart breaking? "Know what?"

"I have no regrets. You're a miracle, my miracle, and every minute with you has been the air in my lungs and the blood in my heart." She pulled me into a hug and kissed my head.

"Mum." I wet my lips. "You're scaring me. Why are you saying this? What's going on?"

She cupped my face in her hands and stared into my eyes, her own eyes taking on a fierce look as she said, "No matter what happens, don't come back here. Go straight to Dyter's, and I'll come get you when I can."

Her words made no sense, but her panic drenched the room and filled me. Her alarm was so raw, it overrode the terror induced by the predator not three steps from where I trembled. I knelt there, struck dumb. Was I missing something obvious? Lord Irrik seemed to know more than I did, and he'd just met my mother. Didn't he? I'd known her my whole life, but I didn't understand. If I did, I'd know why she was saying these terrible things about miracles and . . . I swallowed, struggling to translate the warning my mind was screaming at me.

Mum pushed me toward the window. "Hurry, Ryn. You mustn't be caught."

The rest of her words were lost to the pounding in my ears. We were already caught—Lord Irrik was here, but mother clearly wasn't worried about him. She hardly spared him a glance.

"What about you?" I looked at Lord Irrik and asked in an almost foreign voice, "What are you going to do to her? What's happening?"

He shook his head, but his baffled gaze told me he was still reeling from whatever shock seeing Mum meant to him. His dignified bearing didn't wear shock comfortably, and my stomach twisted as I felt a spark of kinship. My entire world was upside down, and the Drae was just as disturbed.

His gaze darted from me to mother and back to me. Stepping up next to Mum, he pointed to the window and, in a low, hoarse voice, said, "You must go. Now. If they find you here, I won't be able to stop what happens."

He'd said the same thing to me mere hours before. We should have left straightaway.

The screaming cut off, and we muted.

A door slammed. The sounds of a scuffle floated in the window, and while not uncommon on our street, the disturbance was nearer than any I'd heard before.

"Ryn," my mother warned, wiping a tear from her smooth face. "Please, you must go now."

The fact she begged shocked me to my senses. She'd never begged me for anything. Ever. My mother was strong, efficient, direct, not. . .

"I misdirected them, but they'll be here soon," Lord Irrik said, eyes fixed on the door of my room.

I scooted back to the ledge and slung my leg over. "You'll come get me, Mum? When it's safe, you'll come?"

"You need to go, baby. I love you. I'll come get you . . ." She blinked, her vibrant-blue eyes filling with fresh tears. She waved at me, both a shooing motion and a farewell.

Another scream, closer, propelled me out the window. I grappled with the stalks as I slid and fell to the dirt below.

Mum wanted me to hide from the soldiers.

They were after me, so it made sense I had to be gone. A faraway voice nudged me about the presence of another in the room, but my mind zeroed in with tunnel vision on hiding to protect my mother.

I ran, dodging in and out of buildings, in and out of shadows.

I might not be able to go back for months or more. Where would I go?

Lungs burning, I crouched in the darkest shadows of the rich housing by the fountain garden, sucking in long gasps of air. Where was it best to hide? The fields? Lord Irrik would find me if he flew overhead. Nothing could hide from the black-winged beast in the open.

I froze.

Lord Irrik.

Without conscious thought, my head spun to face back the way I'd come. I'd left my mother with the most ruthless and cruel of the king's lapdogs. My blank gaze blindly searched the barren square, thoughts running rampant. As I did so, the light from the twin moons caught at something.

The welded flower on the side of the fountain.

The one my mother had taken me to see most days of my childhood. It was our flower.

Gut-wrenching horror clenched my stomach. I gasped. I'd left my mother all alone with a Drae while soldiers were going door-to-door searching for *me*.

I let my pack fall to the cobblestones and stared at the welded flower, the dark night's heat swirling around me. My skin prickled in chills as anxiety stabbed me in a thousand different places. What had I done?

I abandoned all pretense of hiding, taking the most direct route back to my window and to the woman who had raised me.

There was still time to help her. There had to be time.

I pushed through the stalks of maize and climbed to just beneath my windowsill, pressing myself against the warm stone wall, and listened before entering. If the soldiers already had her, I'd need to formulate another plan to save her from the king's dungeons. I'd be useless to her if we both got caught.

Hysteria rose in my throat, and I pulled myself back from the brink by my fingertips.

"How can that be? What you're saying is impossible." The rumble of Lord Irrik's voice carried out to me. "That would mean—"

"It's why he must never know. You need to protect her. You must swear to me. If there was any other way, don't you think I would take it? If you take me to the king, he will find out." My mother's voice was choked and filled with tears. Before tonight, I'd never ever seen her cry, aside from peeling onions.

"I didn't know," Irrik said quietly.

He'd followed several of us home after The Crane's Nest.

He'd assigned the soldiers to tail each of us.

Even if he'd changed his mind about having me followed for whatever shocked him so much about Mum and me, he'd started this whole thing.

Whatever was happening now, fault rested with him.

I stood to go inside but returned to my crouch at Mum's next words.

"Promise me you'll keep her safe," my mother said in a rising voice.

He said nothing, and I was left to wonder if he had nodded or not.

Mum spoke again. "You must do it now." A moment of silence passed, and then she continued, "This has Phaetyn blood on it. It's the only way."

"How do you even have this?" Lord Irrik said, breaking his silence. He sounded flustered for the first time. "I can't do what you're asking of me. You know I can't."

"Yes, forgive me. I'm not thinking . . ." Mum trailed off. After another beat of silence, she said, "Your soldiers will not stop hunting until they have a head for the king. You tell him I was alone, that I was the one the soldiers were meant to follow. You promise me you'll look after my baby."

Their words made little sense to me, with the exception of the phrase, "head for the king."

I remembered her tears before I'd left, her nonsensical mutterings, and finally, *finally* my mind deciphered what they'd meant.

Goodbye.

Someone hammered on our front door. Several someones shouted. But these realizations came to me as though from a great distance.

She'd lied to me. When she'd pushed me to leave, there had been no intentions or expectations of her seeing me again. The realization was like a punch to the gut, and my mind refused to believe what my instincts told me was happening. Until I heard her gasp. There was something about the sound...as soon as I heard it, I knew.

Lord Irrik swore, and I pulled myself over the ledge in time to see Mum crumple to the floor, the hilt of a golden dagger protruding from her chest.

I screamed.

My mother's eyes widened as she saw me. Her hands uselessly grasped at the hilt buried too deep for her to pull out. Her mouth opened and closed, her words lost in the space between us. Lord Irrik pushed me toward the window, yelling something, but I pushed back, the same fire crawling up my hands as our skin touched. I had to see my mother, and I screeched at him.

"Leave, foolish girl," he hissed, picking me up and flinging me toward the window. "She sacrificed herself so you could get away."

I crashed into the wall, my right side missing the window by only a hair's breadth. The air rushed from my chest, and pain exploded from my shoulder and hip from the impact. My mind couldn't process the chaos surrounding me, and I sat dazed where I'd landed, loud foot-steps pounding closer.

Irrik crossed the floor in a single stride and picked me up once more. He stared down at me in disgust and strode to the window—

—just as several soldiers crashed into my bedroom.

7

"*Lord Irrik*," exclaimed a burly soldier from the open doorway. The soldier wore an aketon similar to Lord Irrik's, but the material was loose and the color navy. Above his left shoulder were twists of gold, a symbol of rank in the king's guard. He held his blade out, as if he'd anticipated a fight, but upon seeing Irrik he allowed the tip to drop to the floor, and his snarling expression smoothed.

"Captain," the Drae said, face blank.

A distant part of my mind registered there were others here, that they were talking. I even saw droplets on the burly soldier's sword, the blood of one of my neighbors, I assumed. But that was all in the periphery, for my gaze was on my mother, my wheezing, crying, strong mother. She didn't look strong now, and as I stared at her, I knew all the other happy times I'd shared with her would be erased and replaced by this one searing image.

A pain impaled my chest, and a scream worked its way up my throat. Lord Irrik released me, and I scrambled to my mother, dropping to my knees on the stone floor. My hands hovered, unsure where to touch. Her chest was heaving, and shallow gasps of air escaped her lips. She blinked, and a large tear trickled into her dark hair.

"Mother," I mouthed, unblinking.

"Must . . . go," she wheezed, but the fear in her eyes said she knew it was too late for me to run.

The worst thing was a part of me felt I was watching a stranger die. Who was this woman who didn't fear the Drae and could shove a dagger into herself? She had clearly concealed . . . so many . . . *huge* things from me.

The heaviness of hopelessness swept through me as her breath began to rattle.

"I'm sorry, Mum. Please." I wanted so much for her to know just how sorry I was. Sorry for not being careful enough on the walk home, sorry for getting caught by Irrik, and so sorry for leading trouble straight to our doorstep.

"Please," I cried out. "Please," I begged, to no one, anyone, to the nameless, make believe person who could save her.

"Who is this?" the soldier behind me asked. "Is this our little renegade?"

I reached to stroke Mother's hair. Her long, cinnamon-brown hair just like my own.

Lord Irrik snorted and pulled me away from my mother. And like a worthless piece of lint, he tossed me across the room. "Stupid girl."

I slammed into the wall above my bed, this time on my left side, and pain exploded in my ribs in a burst of blinding white. My hatred ballooned for this . . . monster. This unfeeling, horrible *monster*.

Revulsion tore through me, but it wasn't enough. It needed an outlet. I needed to hurt him. I rolled off the bed, clutching my sides, and the room blurred as the blood drained from my face. Loathing sharpened my vision, and I lifted my chin only for my heart to stall.

Irrik had his back to me now. His boot on top of the blade in my mother's chest. Mum was facing me, the peace in her eyes at odds to the turmoil and rage in the room.

"Baby," she mouthed.

Mother, I answered her silently.

"This was the one you were meant to follow," Irrik said as he pushed down on the hilt with his boot.

My mother's body jerked before the spark in her eyes went from dazed awareness, to acknowledgement, to acceptance. The spark became smaller.

Smaller and duller.

"No," I screamed, throwing myself at the Drae. We crashed into a heap on the ground, and I drew back my fist, punching him as hard as I could on the chin. I couldn't have been the only one surprised when his head snapped back in response. His gaze returned to me, an intensity in his eyes as he stared at me.

"I hate you," I whispered.

I slid off him and crawled to Mum, even though I could see she wasn't there anymore. I closed my eyes, tears streaming down my cheeks, and opened them to find her still dead.

Blood saturated her tunic. She stared vacantly at my room's ceiling. She was . . . extinguished.

Gone.

But my mind couldn't make sense of this fact or of the sight of her.

Someone lifted me to my feet, and I struggled to free myself from his grasp. I wasn't ready to say goodbye.

"I'm not leaving," I snarled. *Just try to take me away.* I'd never wanted to hurt someone more than in this moment.

"Throw her on the street," Irrik snapped as he brushed a speck of Mum's blood off his aketon. The Drae radiated anger and disgust, and he didn't look at me whatsoever. His tone was a haughty command. "She's upset about her mother, an ignorant child. I won't be wasting our resources—"

"She attacked you, sir. It is an unpardonable offense," the captain countered, stepping up to the guard holding me. The captain grabbed my chin and squeezed until the pain elicited a whimper. "I'd think you would be happy to dispose of her, Lord Irrik. After all, she is the daughter of an insurgent. The apple doesn't fall far from the tree, so they say."

I couldn't look at the Drae. I couldn't look at the person who had kicked a dagger into my mother's dying heart. A scorching abhorrence bubbled up, filling my chest and pushing up my neck, and I couldn't keep my anger contained. I flung the vilest insults and obscenities at Lord Irrik, needing him to know how much I loathed him.

The captain slapped me. Hard. His hand connected with my face with a sharp crack that made white spots erupt in my vision. I slumped in the guard's arms, head stabbing with pain and vision blurring.

"There's no challenge in disposing of one so weak," Irrik said to the captain. "She'll die during the cold season, and I like the thought of a drawn-out death for her." He stared at me, pointed at mother's body, and said, "We'll have someone collect the body to take to the king. I have reason to believe she was high up in the rebellion, so leave her to rot for a day or two. Let the Zone find her so word will spread. He'll be pleased."

So callously said. This man was dead inside.

I didn't want to hear anything he had to say. Ever. He was a liar. No, *worse*. He was pure evil, rotten from the inside out.

I stamped my foot down on the guard's instep and shoved the captain aside, then pulled the dagger free from Mum's chest— knowing the squelching sound as it came out would never leave me— and launched myself at the Drae. He had to die.

He killed my mother.

Irrik grabbed the hand with the dagger, squeezing until it clattered to the floor. I swung my other fist into his gut, but if he felt anything, he didn't react. Instead, he flipped me so my back was to him. With one arm, he circled my waist, and his other arm wrapped high across my chest, pinning my arms to my sides.

My chest tightened both with my grief and the Drae's hold. How had this happened? I needed someone to help me understand.

I killed my mother.

The captain laughed. "She's gone feral. Better subdue her."

Lord Irrik held me close, and his voice wasn't entirely human when he spoke to the soldiers next, "Get out."

His voice resonated through my back, and the three soldiers in the room pushed past one another to get out of the room.

"Just holler if you need any help," the captain said from the doorway. "She's a feisty one. Just the way I like them."

The man let his gaze wander over my body, and I stood numb, unable to care. I glimpsed a horde of soldiers outside before the door closed.

I clenched my teeth. "Let go of me. Now."

"No. Be quiet." His inhuman voice was so soft I wasn't sure if I was hearing it or feeling it.

I twisted to free myself, but his grip tightened. I turned my head and tried to elbow him but couldn't get any force behind the movement.

Lord Irrik pulled me closer still, and this time I was the one who growled.

"Keep that up and you'll only hurt yourself," he said in an emotionless voice.

"You killed her," I ground out between my clenched teeth, staring at her lifeless body. "You said you'd help her and you—"

"I said to be quiet," he growled, putting his hand over my mouth. He turned us, his body blocking the view of my mother's corpse, and put his lips to my ear. "I know you're in shock, but now is not the time to say something that will get you killed. Your mother just sacrificed herself so you would live. You think she'd want you to throw that away?"

My rage erupted. "How *dare* you speak as if you knew her?"

The black in the room drew into him, made his skin tingle against mine. Monster.

He whispered, "You should have listened. It wouldn't have saved your mother, but it would've saved you. Now you'll be going before the king, and I can't help you there. You need to stop. Right now."

I wanted to hurt him so bad. I wanted to curl up in a corner and cry. I wanted to wake up from this nightmare to hear Mum comforting me. He was saying all these things, and I didn't care.

"My breath won't work on you," he muttered.

Subdue. That was what the captain had meant. A tiny thrill of defiant triumph ran through me. Irrik couldn't subdue me.

"Will you pretend?" he asked in the low tone that left me shivering.

"Will you bring my mother back?" I turned to glare at him and had the satisfaction of seeing a tiny crack appear in his impassive façade.

"That's a no," he said. "You won't like the alternative, Ryn. I *can* make you, and I will if that's what it takes. Are you sure you won't help yourself?"

He seemed to know the answer to that without me vocalizing it. Over my dead body would I go along with anything he said. I didn't care if I died right here on the spot. I wouldn't lift a finger to help.

He sighed, his chest pushing into my back. Then he picked me up, still facing away from him, and walked me to the door. In a fluid movement, he spun me so I faced him, and then he gritted his teeth as he held my arms down by my sides.

His body boxed me in.

A new fear unfurled deep inside me as he closed the distance between us. He trailed his nose from my neck to my ear, and my insides melted when he growled, a low, throaty inhuman sound. When he lifted from my neck, his eyes were solid black.

"This could have been easy. Remember that," he snarled. His canines lengthened, and black scales appeared across the bridge of his nose. "Let's hope it works."

Shock silenced me as I watched with wide eyes, and my lips parted as I gasped.

"I'm going to kiss you," he rumbled.

What?

I sucked in a deep breath to scream, and at the same time, I raised my leg to knee him in the groin. But he anticipated my move and pushed his body against mine, pinning me to the wall.

With a glint in his predatory eyes, he covered my mouth with his.

Fire exploded between us. I tried to turn away, but he nipped my lip as he raised his hands to hold my face immobile. I pushed uselessly at his chest. But as the kiss went on, I struggled to remember why I wanted to end it in the first place. His tongue brushed against my lips, and I sighed, returning the tender caress languidly.

He growled again, and the kiss became soft, like the first shadows of dusk. Irrik threaded his hands into my long hair and pulled me to him. I went willingly, wrapping my arms around his neck as we continued our intimate dance.

Warm lassitude spread like heated honey from my head to my chest to my feet. A part of me was livid, but that small part had little voice now. As the kisses continued, the voice disappeared altogether. I wanted to crawl up into the Drae's lap and kiss him forever.

He sighed, and I smiled in triumph. Though why I should feel triumphant was anyone's guess.

I laughed at the thought as the door opened behind me, making me stumble forward. Irrik was the most handsome man-person I'd ever seen. How had I not seen it until now? So handsome and so sad. He'd tried to help Mum and me . . .

"Why are you sad?" I said on a sigh, reaching out to touch his face.

Irrik's countenance shifted, and a cold mask dropped over his features. But I could still see the sadness in his eyes. He took a step back, and I followed, wrapping my arms around his waist and leaning my head against his firm chest.

"You got her good," the captain said with a chuckle. "We thought you were losing your touch there for a minute."

Lord Irrik pushed my hands away, grabbed the captain by the front of his aketon, and pulled him into the room from where he lingered in the doorway. The captain's face met Lord Irrik's fist with a resounding crunch. The captain fell to his knees, amid shocked murmurs from the soldiers who had a clear line of sight inside. Irrik wrapped his arm around my waist and pulled me from the room, shoving the king's guard aside.

I opened my mouth to tell him something. I wanted to say . . . something, but my mind was so fuzzy, like I'd been drinking the brew at Dyter's. I knew what I wanted was in my brain. I just couldn't access it. I looked up at Lord Irrik. His jaw clenched, and his eyes flashed fire.

He pulled me out into the night air, and I sighed as I looked up at the dark sky. So beautiful. I wanted to tell him how the night was my favorite. The warmth that filled me brought comforting peace. There was something particular that should be bugging me, but the feeling continued to elude me. Instead, a deep sense of security settled.

Lord Irrik was helping me.

I wanted to kiss him again.

"Where are we going?" I asked, snuggling closer. My arm was around his waist, my hip pushed to his as we walked side by side.

He looked down at me, and his eyes seemed to pulse with energy. He shifted his body, increasing the distance between us and said, "To the king."

I furrowed my brow, something nagging at me. "Why?"

"A woman from your house was seen roaming the streets after curfew the last two nights. There have been rebel meetings, and the woman was seen leaving the suspected site of these meetings. There were several persons of interest captured tonight. The king is not ignorant of the revolutionaries." He scrubbed his face with his free hand. "King Irdelron has asked anyone connected with these rebel peasants be brought in for questioning. You're coming in because you were too stupid to listen and have forced my hand."

"Will he hurt me?" Why did Lord Irrik feel so good? I tried to wind closer to him.

He glanced behind us, and I followed his lead. Two soldiers followed, and behind them, two more were half dragging the unconscious captain down the dry, dirt road.

"If you're lucky, the king will see you're not a threat." Irrik studied me, his gaze flicking to my lips and then back to my eyes. "Because you're not a rebel, right, Ryn? You know saying that will get you killed?"

The darkness of night cocooned us, and I knew Irrik had blocked us from view of the other soldiers. He tipped his head down and pressed his lips to mine. His warmth pulsed through me again, and I stood on my tiptoes to prolong the kiss. When we pulled away, I beamed up at him. "You don't want me to die?"

"No," he said in a quiet voice, eyes sad again.

"I don't want to die either. Don't worry. I'm not a rebel. I'm not a threat. I'm not a woman."

He grumbled something under his breath about too much.

I reached up and patted his cheek. "You're so much more handsome when you're not scowling. You shouldn't be so grumpy."

Lord Irrik pulled away, pushing my arm down to my side when I reached for him.

The darkness dissipated, and the two soldiers dragging the

sleeping soldier caught up to us. They were scowling, the same grumpy look Lord Irrik wore.

The three soldiers were like triples. I should ask the triples. "What happens if the king thinks I'm a rebel?"

The short man wearing a navy aketon raised his eyebrows. The one wearing green laughed. "You are dead."

Irrik snarled and backhanded the young soldier. Then Irrik grabbed my arm, pulling me down the road with him. "Don't ask them anything. If you want to know, you ask me."

I swatted at his hand. "Don't yank on my arm like that. It doesn't feel good."

He loosened his grip and said, "Come on. We're nearly there."

"Do you want to be happy?" I sighed.

We came to a stop outside the castle gates. I looked back, surprised we'd come so far in such a short amount of time. I didn't remember passing through the fountain garden or the Quota Fields after leaving my house. Guards lined the top parapet, their bows drawn and trained on me.

"You know nothing of happiness. Your life was a lie," Irrik said to me.

The words were a slap. Like my mind was snapping back into itself. How dare he? He dragged me across town, after kidnapping me, stealing me, and Mother . . . Horror doused me as pieces of memory came back, one image at a time.

He'd done something. I tensed as my mind rattled, still in the throes of his kiss fog.

In a much louder voice, Irrik yelled, "Open the gate."

He turned back to me and grabbed my wrist as I shifted my weight to run. What happened to me? I felt my lips. How did he do that? Change my thoughts like that? Make me act like I was drunk. I . . .

"Ryn," he said in a voice that brokered no argument. "Look at me."

Yeah, right.

"*Drak*," he swore. "How are you doing this?" He pushed his hand into the hair at the nape of my neck as he pressed his weight into me from my chest to my knees. Tingles crawled over my skin, and panic pounded in my chest. I desperately wanted to avoid him. Fear at what was to come bubbled within. Trapped between him and the stone wall, I tried to turn my head. I did not want him to kiss me. I raised my hands to claw at him, and he released my neck to grab my wrists. He pulled my arms up above my head, trapping them in one hand, and threaded his other hand back into my hair.

"Please don't," I begged, tears dripping from my eyes.

"Shh," he whispered. "I only want to keep you safe." Fiery urgency pulsed between us. Irrik's kisses were harder this time, and I could taste the saltiness of my tears on his lips. He kneaded my back, and his teeth grazed my lower lip.

My will seeped away until it disappeared. I gripped his arms as my legs decided they were done for the day. But he didn't stop. His lips were wet and warm, and his tongue teased me, pushing and tangling with mine in a passionate embrace. He drew my lower lip into his mouth, and I groaned with pleasure. Colors and stars burst behind my eyelids. I craved more, some primal instinct urging me closer to the man kissing me, and I pushed into him, pulling him to me.

Nothing else mattered but this right now. Just him and me.

"Lord Irrik," a woman said. "I see you've found some prey."

8

I rrik jerked away, holding me at arm's length, and my body screamed for him. My mind streamlined through the haze. Lord Irrik was all I saw.

"I need to report."

"She's too pretty—lavender eyes and that long hair," a woman said with a shake of her head.

I didn't care about her.

"Yes," Irrik said, jaw clenched. "Can you get her ready?"

The woman sighed and tugged at my sleeve. "Come with me, missy. You can't go to the king looking all 'innocent harvest girl.'"

The young woman had mousy brown hair drawn back in a low ponytail that accentuated ghastly scars on both her cheeks. Her face was splotchy and her eyes red, like she'd been crying before coming to get me, but the brutality of the scars had me transfixed. Like I was reading a map of some horrific journey she'd endured.

"Quick now," she said, pulling me up the courtyard, toward a side entrance into the king's castle. The way was a blur I knew I'd never be able to retrace.

I blinked, trying to make sense of her tears. "Did the king do that to you?"

Her eyes widened, and she darted a glance behind her and then past me before whispering, "Shoot, missy. You don't know nothing, do you?"

I shook my head slowly, and my bottom lip trembled as a deep sadness assailed me. What I was sad for eluded me. I only knew that Irrik wanted to help.

Irrik!

I whirled, searching for him.

"He's gone to report to the king to give us time. I saw that kiss. I've never seen him kiss a girl before, just the breath usually. Probably why you're wavering like you've spent three days on the brew. Don't be angry at Irrik, though. He tries to make it hurt less, and having you look so pretty could make it worse, especially if one of the guards takes a fancy to you. Come on now. Let's hurry and see what we can do. Won't be long before the king loses patience, and then no one's safe."

The girl tugged me up two flights of narrow stone steps, squeezing past several other scurrying people. We climbed more intervals of winding stairs before arriving on a long, narrow landing. She ushered me into a small room with a chamber pot and a large shining square object where a girl who looked just like my escort stood next to another girl with hair the same as mine. "There are two of you?"

The scar-faced girl barked a short laugh. "Never seen a mirror before, have you? Well, don't fall in love. You won't look that way for long, but it's all for your own good."

She extracted several jars from an old set of drawers and opened them. Dabbing her fingers into one, she rubbed an ointment on my cheeks and then another one in my eyes. My eyes immediately burned and watered.

"*Mistress Moons*, missy. You're one of those people who look decent when they cry. No good," she muttered. The girl returned the ointment and grabbed another one.

This time, my vision blurred and the burning was so fierce I couldn't open my eyes because of the pain.

I felt her grab a fistful of my cinnamon hair, *Mum's hair*. My heart clenched, and emptiness swirled deep inside. When I heard the sawing of a knife, I tried to twist away.

"Don't be moving now. I don't want to nick you in the neck. Whatever you use to dye your hair has left it a clumped mess."

I wiped at my eyes, tears streaming as they tried to clear whatever noxious substance the girl had rubbed there. Something about it smelled like the soap Mum used for my hair, and I wanted to tell the girl about the soap because she was mistaken, it wasn't dye. Suddenly, my head felt lighter on my left side, and I watched as the heavy strands fell to the floor.

The stone room stole my attention as I wiped at my blurry eyes again. Despite being a servant's quarters, it was finer than our house.

She grabbed another handful of hair so hard my scalp tingled. Confusion overtook the numbness, and I whispered, "Why are you doing this to me?"

The girl sniffed and continued her snipping. I didn't for one second think she was feeling sorry for me.

"What did Irrik drag you in for?" she asked.

"I'm not a rebel."

The woman came around to stand in front of me and lifted my chin, pinching it. "Listen to me, and listen good. There is a one-way path from here. There's no happy ending for you now, but there are ways to make your life less painful. So, you better get smart quick, missy, or he'll break you before you can blink." The girl's fierce stare turned inward. "He breaks everyone in the end."

"Even you?" I mumbled.

She stepped to the side, revealing the reflective surface. The girl staring back at me had only tufts of brown hair standing in uneven chunks. My eyes, a purple-gray that people described as lavender, were rimmed and puffy, the color now resembling a watery gray. My skin was now the same splotchy color as the girl standing next to me, but mine was still smooth and unmarred.

The girl studied my appearance with obvious disapproval. Then she answered, "The best you can hope for is to find a place they can't touch and know the rest isn't necessary for survival. Your body is a shell. Your skin—the wrapping. Your will, theirs. But somewhere deep inside you, there is a place, whether you see it as the corner of your mind, your heart, your soul, whatever, and that part is yours. *That* is the difference amongst the people here. Figure out what's necessary, and let *everything* else go."

She had to be younger than I was, but I felt like a toddler in her presence. Even so, something deep within protested what she said. To give up everything I was *except* a sliver of my soul? I didn't think I could live that way. How would I determine what was necessary?

The girl placed the scissors in the drawer and dusted off her white apron. "I've done the best I can with what I've got. Now, we need to go. I'm only showing you to the throne room, mind you."

My mind felt as though I was clawing out of a fog. It felt . . . familiar.

The girl continued her morose chatter as she led me from the washroom. "Most days, I don't know why I don't just give up and become fertilizer for the fields like everyone else. Did you know that King Irdelron heard decomposing matter nourishes the soil? The bodies are piling up out there now; my friends, my family. Beats me why I keep trying, but I do. I think it's just habit. Ain't that awful?" She smiled sadly at me, her scars pulling tight. "Maybe it's because the crops ain't gotten no better for it. I could never abide waste."

A gruesome image of a field of dead bodies flashed through my mind, and my stomach churned. Then an image of my mother flashed across my mind, dagger in chest, and I searched blindly for a wall to support me. My mind experienced the same snapping sensation of an hour before as it cleared.

Kiss fog. My hate for Lord Irrik returned and multiplied until I was shaking as memories assaulted me once more. I wiped my lips. How long had I been out of it? Minutes? Hours? I could've been escaping this whole time.

"That bastard," I hissed, and then I scrubbed at my lips.

"Shh," she hissed, glaring at me. "Don't even think—oh, you're talking about Lord Irrik?" She chuckled then whispered to me, "Don't be upset with *him*. He didn't mean nothin' by it, 'cept to help. Usually, he doesn't even bring anyone in. He's not the worst of the two. That's for sure."

Not the worst of the two. Was that meant to be a recommendation? I'd claw his eyes out if I ever got a chance. A part of me saw that my bitter hatred for the Drae was incased by large doses of my own guilt and self-hatred, but whatever my role had been in Mum's . . . death—I pulled in a ragged gulp of air—he'd definitely played a part by signaling the king's guard to follow me in the first place. We hustled through a passageway the size of my entire street, and my heart began to thud as the last of Lord Irrik's kiss wore off. Guards lined both sides of the hall as we neared a huge set of double doors, which extended to the ceiling and were covered in gilded designs.

The guards were dressed in their navy aketons with black trim, each holding a spear with a sword strapped at his side. They didn't look at us as we passed. But I felt their complete attention on me and picked up my pace.

What would happen beyond those doors? I scrambled to make sense of what had happened thus far: Irrik had followed me, set tails on me, and when the guards came, Mum . . . I squeezed my eyes shut and saw her blood everywhere. She'd taken my place. There was something I was missing, and it made me want to pull out what remained of my hair.

On the surface, the king thought I was a rebel, and what I said next would determine if I lived or died. I knew that. But there was something *more*, a whole other importance that mother was terrified to have the king know, something she was willing to die for. Or she could've tried to run with me. She'd been trying to keep me from notice. She'd had a blade with *Phaetyn* blood.

As we reached the gilded doors, I forced my legs to move, certain I was about to die.

I wished there was a way to get a message to Dyter. To Arnik. To anyone. I didn't want to die without saying goodbye. They'd find my mother's body and would never know what happened to me. I chewed on the side of my lip and ran my hand through my hair—what was left of it—and a few long strands, which must've been missed when the girl cut it, came off in my fingers.

Two huge guards, nearly as large as Lord Irrik, broke from the lines and hauled open the doors of the throne room of King Irdelron.

The girl beside me whispered something, but her words were lost in the terror of my mind. With a last shove to get my feet moving, she retreated with the door, keeping out of sight.

My feet took me into the room, stuttering just like my heart.

Long tables, twice the size of my bed, lined one entire wall, and were laden with food. Roasted birds with golden skin sat atop platters loaded with root vegetables, the rich juices of the birds soaking into the potatoes, carrots, and turnips. A hunk of meat, at least the size of my torso, was cut into slices, revealing a tender pink center to its dark seared crust. There were plates of breads in every imaginable shape and size, and next to the piled rolls were ceramic crocks. Bowls of greens, containing fresh leaves of lettuce and cooked beans sat beside an entire pig with an apple in its mouth in the very center. There was roasted orange squash and a platter of grilled corn.

A table with dainty finger cakes, cookies, and pies the size of my palm sat beside it. There was so much food, enough to feed several Harvest Zones, and the air was rich and sweet with the scents, but no one was eating.

I glanced through the room. There were two dozen other empty tables, and the opposite side of the room was barren, except for the raised dais where King Irdelron sat on his throne, a gilded monstrosity. The back of the throne was a handspan taller than the Drae standing next to it. *Lord Irrik.*

Next to the king, on the other side, was a smaller throne, much less ornate and also empty. How many queens had sat on that chair? He'd had many wives during his life, extended as it was with Phaetyn blood. How many queens had he murdered when he tired of them? How many of his own children had he slain to ensure he remained king?

King Irdelron appeared nothing like I'd expected. First, he looked far too young for his alleged age of one hundred and thirty, more like forty. His hair was like maize, so golden and fair it didn't seem natural. His eyes were a vibrant green, the color of the leaves on Mum's pea vines. And his skin was smooth and fair, like he and the sun were unacquainted. I couldn't believe the rumors. How could he be over one hundred? And then my gaze landed on the gilded vial that hung around his neck.

"You've kept me waiting, girl," King Irdelron said from his throne. His voice was calm and quiet, but there was a thread of something cold underneath.

I glanced at the Drae, but Lord Irrik's face could've been carved from stone where he stood in the shadow of the throne.

The king raised his eyebrows and said, "I don't take kindly to waiting."

9

The doors creaked open behind me, but I couldn't take my eyes off this man. The girl had been right. The Drae was a monster, but the king . . . The sickness pouring off him was warning me to run and hide. He wasn't particularly tall, nor his features sharp or twisted. He didn't have the physical prowess to give the impression that he could fell me in a sweep of his sword. He radiated something much worse.

The girl who'd cut my hair was shoved beside me. A guard towered over her. She fell to her knees and scrambled back to her feet as I watched from the corner of my eye. Shame filled me at my cowardice, but I didn't dare help her.

The king fixed the girl next to me with a pointed look. "What happened to Lord Irrik's friend, dear Madeline?" He fingered the chain from whence the small flask hung then ran the bottle back and forth on the chain. "You haven't been doing things you oughtn't, have you?"

The girl replied in a wooden voice, "She went berserk, Your

Majesty. Said she had to use the pot, but the next thing I knew she was trying to kill herself." She curtsied and said, "Sorry, sire."

Her gaze flitted to Lord Irrik, but the Drae watched me, his mouth curved down in disapproval. I glared back, trying to convey my disgust without the king mistaking the glare as meant for him.

"Madeleine, it pains me to see you lie," the king said with a kind smile. He extended his hand and waved toward the door. "Jotun, at your hand."

Madeleine sucked in a deep breath, and at the same time, the soldier nearest to her drew his sword. In one fluid movement, he swung the sword in an arc, slicing through the young girl, eviscerating her from one hip clean through her rib cage in a diagonal line. Her lower half crumpled to the ground, and her top half almost seemed to float in the air momentarily before falling to the gray stone floor. She landed on her side, and blood gushed from her gutted torso, her heart still beating, pumping the blood out of her system and onto the floor. Her eyes widened, and she ran her hand over the stump of her body as she watched her life spill out before her.

"At last . . ." She sighed before her head fell back on the floor.

Bile burned the back of my throat, but I was learning I could only feel so much and go through so much before all the screams and tears were gone. That was where I was right now. I stared at the body of the girl who had tried to spare me some of the king's wrath by cutting my hair and rubbing ointment on my face.

My mind told me she was dead now, but even though I saw the truth of it before me, I couldn't process the perpetual horror I was experiencing.

I'd never seen brutality like this before. I'd seen cruelty from soldiers but never the river from whence the streams came. This man was the namesake. His savage inhumanity sat underneath his average face and average height and mild manner. I'd have to be a fool not to quake in fear.

There were different rules in this place.

This was not a game I knew how to play.

The king cleared his throat, and I looked at the fair man. He licked his lips as he closed the bottle. His gaze returned to me, and his eyes glinted with the first pieces of hardness I'd seen.

"You are to curtsey before your king, girl. Or did your rebel mother not teach you manners?"

His words were a trap, and I peered down, my gaze falling on the bloodied hem of my tunic. My mother was dead because of his orders. He didn't kill her with his hands, but what he'd done was worse. The king had no idea who he'd killed with his instructions to his guards. I doubted he cared. The girl, Madeline, lay on the floor at my feet.

I curtsied. Low. And waited.

"Hmm. You may rise." Turning in his seat to face his first, King Irdelron asked Lord Irrik, "Does she not speak?"

Lord Irrik stared through me to the back of the room. "Mostly nonsense, sire. She hasn't been coherent in my dealings with her, limited though they've been."

His voice was emotionless, but another glint ran through the king's expression as though he heard something I did not in the Drae's voice.

He leaned forward. "She's truly worthless?"

"That is for you to judge, sire," the Drae said in a disinterested voice. "I followed a woman from the rebel meetings to her house. When I questioned the girl's mother, she pulled a knife."

"Your mother was a rebel, girl?"

I kept my focus on the king, and my tongue twisted before I managed the words, "If she was, Your Majesty, she did not include me in her plans. I had no idea she was anything more than a mother until tonight."

It was true.

The king's gaze slid to Lord Irrik, who was still as a statue. "She's pretty, don't you think, my Drae? Is that why you lowered yourself to kiss the daughter of a rebel? Three times, according to reports from others in my guard? Once in her house, once on the street, and once at the gate to my castle?"

Three times? I felt violated.

"She was hysterical. She came into the room as I killed her mother and started screaming. Her screams irritated me."

I gritted my teeth but remained silent as I processed what Lord Irrik had said. He killed my mother? No, she'd asked him to, to protect me. He'd refused, and she'd stabbed herself. But then he stepped on the blade to finish her off. The images flashed through my vision, twisting and distorting in my memory.

"Is that so?" the king mused. He tapped a finger on his jaw and propped his chin on an elbow to one side. He glanced toward the Drae again. "Have we apprehended any other rebels?"

"Three others. The rest have gone into hiding. I don't believe the same strategy will work again. They are fast learners."

What others?

The king's face twisted, and the mask he'd kept in place until now slipped. "Peasants," he sneered, turning his attention to me. "Trying to kill me and take my throne? Do they think I will ever let another take it, girl?"

I jerked, heart hammering. "No, King Irdelron."

That was the truth as well. They knew he was a power hungry, selfish sod. If he'd kill his own children, it was no surprise he'd kill the peasants.

The king glanced over my head and raised both brows before setting his eyes on me once more. I heard twin sets of footsteps march up behind.

The Drae to the right of the throne twitched, nearly imperceptibly.

Cold realization settled heavily in my chest. The king wasn't going to let me go. He was going to kill me. My eyes slid to Madeline's corpse; she'd said there was only one way out of here, hadn't she? The seconds stretched, and I contemplated my fate. I had accomplished nothing of significance in my life, and I didn't want to die here.

I tensed as the footsteps halted beside me. If the king thought I wasn't going to try to run he had another thing coming. I waited for the order that would seal my fate, muscles coiled to escape.

Lord Irrik spoke, "Perhaps it would be wise to question the girl. If she knows anything, she may be able to corroborate whatever the other three prisoners disclose. She'll be easier to break than the others."

I shifted my eyes to the Drae, furrowing my brow.

The king still watched me with his assessing gaze, and I hoped I hadn't betrayed anything.

A slow smile twisted the king's features. "Lord Irrik, what an excellent plan. You echo my own thoughts. Though I must ask, seeing as you've kissed her several times, is your lust for her going to inter-fere with the interrogation?"

Lust! What the hay?

King Irdelron leaned back in his gilded throne, and studied me over his steepled fingers.

The Drae's face remained impassive. "I am bound by oath, sire. And I would never lust for a human."

Irdelron laughed, a cruel barking sound. "Then you will be alone for eternity." He raised his hand and waved me forward. "Jotun, take this wisp of a girl and find out what she knows. Feel free to show her your brand of *hospitality*, but don't kill her. I want her alive—for now." His eyes slid to Irrik, then back to the guard. "When you're done, find suitable accommodations for such an esteemed guest."

His words were all courtesy, which was enough to convince me I wouldn't be getting hospitality whatsoever.

Dyter told me of the king's dungeons. Just the other day he'd told me how many people escaped them.

None.

Madeline's blood had seeped across the ground and was nearly at the outer edge of my left boot. *At last*, she'd said—the girl who'd made me feel like a toddler with the wisdom in her eyes, wisdom I was convinced was forged from haunting experience. Was it so bad here that death *like that* was preferable? The girl had told me she was uncertain why she hadn't given up, that it was just habit to live. She'd told me to do whatever was necessary to stay alive. To find my corner.

Yet she'd welcomed death in the end.

How long would it take me to become like her? Would I welcome it, too?

Jotun, the guard who murdered Madeline, crossed to me. His features were nondescript, from the muted color of his hair and eyes, to the color of his skin, neither light nor dark. His expression was blank deference to his master. He moved forward without a sound, despite the weapons he carried. He was one of the big guards, the ones close in size to Lord Irrik.

"What are you going to do to me?" I asked.

The king laughed. "Oh, it's no use talking to Jotun, girl."

The guard grabbed my arm, his thick fingers circling my bicep in a loose grip. It was useless to fight him. I'd seen his earlier speed, and now I felt his strength.

For no other reason than in this dark room I knew him best of anyone, I lifted my eyes to the king's Drae. His lip curled into a sneer, and I knew whatever "help" he'd offered was officially at an end.

I was on my own at seventeen. I'd wished for excitement, and it brought me this. My heart was broken, shattered. My chest was empty. I had no one.

I followed the soldier out of the king's presence, past the rows of guards, and down an endless staircase. This one was damp with fewer torches. Small windows spaced farther apart and up out of reach offered the only light. The first rays of the morning sky penetrated through.

I stumbled, and only Jotun's hold on my arm kept me from tumbling down the stairs. He said nothing as he yanked me upright.

"What are you going to do to me?" I whispered. Now that we were out of the throne room, my attention turned to what was coming next with exhausted acceptance. Maybe if I knew what to expect, I could prepare.

Jotun remained silent, and I couldn't be sure if he was ignoring me or hadn't heard.

Swallowing my pride and fear, I raised my voice and asked again, "What are you going to do to me?"

The guard didn't stop walking. He didn't turn to look at me. He didn't even glance my way. He just continued propelling us forward with his grip on my arm.

The windows stopped as we descended, and the distance between the weak light of the torches grew. We reached a stone landing on the stairway, and an ear-splitting scream tore through the air. Stagnant, fetid air clung to me, pushing its rank odor into my lungs. A gust of cold rot blasted me as we passed an open doorway, and I instinctively reared back, bumping into the guard.

Jotun pushed me away, his grip on my arm tightening as he increased the distance between us with just the extension of his arm. I'd never met anyone so strong, aside from Lord Irrik.

We passed several wooden doors, all closed. From the gaps in the slats came muffled sobs or pleas for help. The sound of metal grinding came from behind one door, and a sharp scream was cut short by a wet gurgle.

So many doors, and behind at least three of them were people I knew, according to Irrik. Were they being tortured? Were any of them my friends? Dyter? Arnik? The thought of one of them being severed like Madeline made my knees weak, and I discovered I wasn't as completely soul numb as I'd thought.

Maybe there was a fist of fight left in me.

My eyes were gritty and ached with the need to close. More than that, my mind begged for a chance to sort through what was happening. I needed to close my eyes for a few minutes, to fill in the hole in my heart that throbbed; every part of my mind, body, and soul yearned for a moment of peace. I wanted them to leave me alone.

"Please?" I begged, pulling on my captor, resisting him with all my meager strength. "Just give me a few minutes."

But Jotun didn't even deign to look my way, speeding up instead.

One look at his face, and the obvious futility dried up my pleas. His previously dull eyes were alight with anticipation that made my stomach roil.

Without breaking his stride, he flung me forward. My legs tangled, and I landed on my knees. The top layers of skin from my palms and knees disappeared into the rough stone floor, and I yelped as I rolled off the painful abrasions.

The beast grabbed my forearm and dragged me over the sharp stone ground.

My shoulder screamed in protest, a new pain overriding the burning of my knees, and the searing pain tore through my shoulder, my back, down my side, and into my chest. I gasped and sobbed, tears spilling from my eyes. The stone clawed and sliced through my tunic and then my skin. A loud keening carried from one of the chambers, the sound swelling louder and louder as we seemed to follow it to my doom. The wailing intensified, and my soul echoed the sound of grief and pain. When Jotun stopped, I couldn't do anything but sag in a heap of grazed pain at his feet. The person's weeping waned to whimpers, and I wondered if the terrified woman was as tired as I was. She sounded like she was. Had she suffered a similar torture?

Jotun pulled a ring of keys from his pocket and unlocked a door.

He kicked me savagely and I scampered into the room, not needing any more of his vicious encouragement. I was willing to make this easier on myself. What was happening was beyond my understanding —the hurt, the unkindness, this entire situation. The deepest recesses of my soul couldn't make sense of why someone would hurt me this way.

The sound of a key twisting in a lock echoed in the room, my mind, my heart, and my soul. The scrape of metal on metal undid the last of my courage.

Jotun rounded on me, smiling for the first time.

I watched him draw closer with burning eyes, already searching for the place inside me that Madeline spoke of; The place that would help me survive when I woke from this terrible nightmare.

10

*T*he tang of blood and charred meat singed my nose, and my dream for a dungeon cell evaporated before my eyes. This wasn't the accommodation I'd hoped for. This was no quiet cell with dirty straw in a corner and a promise of solitude.

In the center of the cramped room was a thick wooden table, similar in size to the ones in the throne room. The table filled most of the space, leaving enough room for a man to pass on either side. Heavy leather straps hung from the table's sides, the ends fastened around a metal buckle, the perfect contraption for holding someone to the table against their will.

The woman's screams began again, her voice expressing the horror in my soul. I scanned the rest of the room, and fear trickled into my pores, making my skin crawl.

The walls were lined with metal hooks, spikes of various materials and in various sizes, as well as thick mallets and heavy hammers. Ropes of barbed metal wound into loops hung from pegs and boxed contraptions.

I ran my tongue over my lips, and the high-pitched keening

stopped. Understanding dawned on me as I noticed my sandpaper-dry mouth for the first time. *I'd* been the one screaming. That terrible wailing had been me.

Jotun grabbed both my arms and lifted me to the table.

Panic ran through me. Adrenaline I'd thought gone flooded me with a desperate need to escape before he could employ any of the atrocious tools of torture on the wall. I writhed, trying to escape, and he released my right arm. I flailed, hitting his arms, chest, and face several times before his hand circled my neck and slammed my head against the table.

Bursts of light blinded me with the impact, and I gasped for air as his hold tightened. The explosions of white stars increased, and I clawed at Jotun's hand, trying to get him to release me. My vision tunneled, and I knew it was over. I'd lost.

I AWOKE TO SHARP PAIN DIGGING INTO MY BACK. I TRIED TO ARCH AWAY from the pain but couldn't. I jolted to full consciousness and shifted in desperation, testing my arms and legs. My range of motion was only a hair's breadth in any direction. I was strapped to the table!

My lips were wet but my mouth still parched, and I instinctively licked at the moisture and gagged at the oily substance coating them, its taste foul and rancid.

"It's funny how licking the lips is always the first thing people do when they wake," a man said.

I cracked open my eyes and stared at the king.

"In this position, if you vomit, you'll choke. If you're dead, you become useless," the king said in a flat tone, his face illuminated by the weak light from the single window.

The sharp pain from my back disappeared, and the king waved a bloodied needle in front of my face before setting the tiny weapon down. "I'm surprised you passed out so quickly. Jotun wasn't even able to welcome you properly. I should have told him that extracting information quickly didn't mean killing you—yet."

It didn't seem kingly to be down here in the dungeon, amidst the evidence of my torture. Yet Irdelron seemed more at home here than on his throne.

I said nothing, afraid if I spoke, I would have to swallow. Instead, I stared at the ceiling and let the saliva pool in my mouth until there was enough to push the foul substance out with the collected drool. It trickled down the side of my face and neck and into my sawed-off hair, crawling along my skin, a disgusting trail of vileness.

"Well now, it seems that you are revived enough for my attention," Irdelron said and moved into my line of sight. I flinched from the cruel pleasure lighting his fair face. He was in a white aketon, fitted much like the one Irrik wore, tight to his torso and sleeveless. Gold thread embroidered the edges in a filigree to highlight his muscular build. He smiled down on me as if he were my savior. "I'm so glad you will be with us. I'm most curious to see who has my Drae wrapped in knots. This is the first time in one hundred and five years he's shown any interest in a prisoner. It's quite interesting to behold, especially because it seems you hold some power over him. It's good to remind my subjects of where they stand now and again, don't you think, girl? Even a Drae." His eyes grew distant. "Especially a Drae." He straightened. "And a rebel, too." He leaned over me and whispered, "You'll help me crush the rebellion and remind Lord Irrik he is a subject, not king."

I gritted my teeth and closed my eyes.

"Tell me, girl. Who conspires against me? Give me names, and I shall end your suffering with mercy."

Right. Everyone knew King Irdelron had no mercy, and probably never did. Besides, I'd never let Arnik or Dyter suffer on my account.

The king's breath was warm on my face. "Last chance."

I refused to answer. As the king withdrew, a heavy dread settled in my stomach.

A hot sting sliced across my nose and cheek with the crack of a whip. I tried to turn my head away from the source of agony. I screamed as my cheek burst into searing pain, and I thrashed in my restraints, unable to avoid what was causing my anguish. The burning spread across my face and down my neck to my chest with successive lashes.

"No more!" I begged.

The burning waned, and a dull throbbing took its place. Tears leaked from my eyes, and snot ran from my nose through the substance on my lips and into my mouth. I retched, but my stomach was empty, and I spit the bile and snot and poison out as I coughed.

"You've deluded yourself. You think this is as bad as it will get?" Irdelron shook his head in mock sympathy as he leaned over me, the gilded vial of Phaetyn blood dangling from his neck. "I already know you'll give me the answers I seek," he whispered, caressing my face. "Everyone does. This? Jotun and I do this for fun. I have an odd . . . *obsession* with besting mortality. Have you ever noticed how easy it is for one life to end? I *own* that power. It's my life's work."

He reached for the vial, his eyes losing focus.

I was being foolish. I knew it before I acted, but his fake sympathy was too much. I spat at him, that vile mixture in my mouth. My spittle sprayed his chin, neck, and the top portion of his pristine aketon.

In an instant, the fake kindness was gone, and white-lipped fury took its place. Irdelron slapped me, the force of his hand jerking my head to the side. He spun, his back blocking my view of what he was grabbing. Then he seized my hand and smashed it flat. He held the object high, and I pleaded with him as the stake glinted in the weak light. But he only laughed. He brought the weapon down, splicing it through my left hand.

I screamed in agony as the pain exploded. I writhed, but every movement made the pain worse, and I attempted to hold still. I tried to wiggle my fingers, but even that sent excruciating waves of anguish up my arm. The rest of the world melted away, and my entire universe was the brutal torment crushing the bones and veins in my left hand.

Jotun's impassive face came into focus when the initial pain diminished, leaving an almost unbearable throb. I glimpsed the door swinging shut out of the corner of my eye, a flash of white aketon showing as it did. Irdelron was gone. I whimpered in relief.

Jotun turned to the wall, to his weapons, and my heart fell.

He came to my side, a thin needle pinched between his thick, now gloved, fingers. He set a clay container down on the edge, by the hand that was nailed to the table, and removed the lid.

I swallowed, clenching my jaw, tightening my core in anticipation of more pain. I closed my eyes, not sure if it was better to remain in ignorance or see the next means of torture.

He pinched the inside of my elbow, and shards of ice crawled up my arm toward my heart. I opened my eyes, and the room fractionated into tiny slivers that shifted and twirled, preventing me from making any sense of the countless pieces in front of me. I had a single moment of relief before the torment began.

The tiny ice pieces surged inside me, ballooning as they morphed into insects and arachnids. They coalesced in purpose and descended, gnawing and clawing at me, shredding my skin and burrowing deep to lay their eggs. They climbed under my ragged tunic and into my hair. I tried to turn my head, but there was no way to prevent them from digging into my ears. I forced air out my nostrils again and again, trying to keep them from my nose, but the number multiplied, and I had to close my eyes as a second wave descended.

The bugs pinched at my lips, and I folded them in between my teeth to prevent the insects from getting into my mouth, but as they filled my nostrils with their clawing, crawling legs, I was forced to open my mouth so I could breathe. The eggs under my skin started hatching, and the new creatures tore their way out. I screamed, chomping the bugs and spitting them out as fast as I could. Their legs stuck to my tongue, and I spit and chomped while trying to suck in enough air to stay alive. But I was slowly losing. A slithering centipede with millions of feet crawled across my cheek toward my mouth. I whimpered in horror, gagging as I tried to chomp the creature so I could breathe. But the pieces of the one became dozens of smaller invertebrate, and their segmented bodies wriggled into my throat and then into my lungs. I screamed, my voice raw from the overuse, and then I retched.

Pain shot up my arm as another creeping beast gnawed through the rest of my hand, the dead fingers discarded to the ground for other crawling things to eat.

They were in my ears, in my brain, eating away at everything that made me, destroying me until there was nothing left.

*M*y arm flopped forward, stirring me from the escape of unconsciousness. Someone was here, shifting through the space, back and forth, silently.

I floated in and out of awareness, and each time, the person was in a different place.

Working from left to right. Methodically. Curiosity forced one eye open—the other was too swollen to cooperate.

The person stopped and turned toward me. His height and broad shoulders bespoke his gender as well as his square jaw, which was shaven clean. His downturned lips were visible, but the rest of his features were hidden beneath a dark hood pulled low over his face.

His lips thinned to a meager line, and he draped me with a cloth. Then he turned his back to me and continued wiping and storing the instruments in the room. Jotun's cleanup crew. I couldn't have done a single thing to protect myself if I tried.

I slipped away into oblivion.

THE PUTRID STENCH OF FECES AND SULFUR WAS MY FIRST INDICATION I was still alive. But I was warm. I had to be dreaming. *Or dead*, I thought, remembering the bugs and my torn throat and mind. How could I be alive after that? Were the bugs real? Or did the injections cause me to hallucinate? I shifted and inhaled sharply as I realized I had *moved*, unrestrained.

Not only was I warm and unrestrained, but nothing hurt. *Nothing.* Not my face, my skin, or my left hand. I clenched my left hand, it was heavily bandaged, but I could feel my fingers. Someone had tended to me.

I opened my eyes just enough to see I was no longer on the table in the torture room but on a stained mattress on a stone floor, buried in a mound of blankets.

I was alone. *At last.* The words flashed through my mind before I remembered them as the dying lament of the girl, Madeline. I rested back on the lumpy mattress, staring at the ceiling and wondering how much time had passed since Jotun injected me with . . . Horrible shakes raked my body at the memory of the bugs under my skin. They continued for an indiscriminate amount of time in the destitute darkness of my new home.

I was alone.

Mum was gone, and the bit of fight left in me before Jotun strapped me to the table was non-existent now. I could hardly recall I'd had the notion, and I couldn't remember what it felt like. That piece of myself the girl told me to keep, the place that separated survivors from victims. I didn't know how to find it or if I had one to begin with.

A tear leaked from the corner of one eye and ran into my hairline and around my skull onto the mattress.

Another followed.

And more, until I was sobbing, face pressed into the filthy mattress to conceal my breaking point as best I could from the other prisoners.

My mother was gone, and I might have killed her.

My mother was gone.

My mother was gone.

Each time the thought circled around, it was more frantic and higher pitched. My chest clenched so tight it hurt as I cried for my mother, and my guilt over leaving her, for the girl Madeline who might've been me. For myself because I was not the innocent girl I was before and knew I could never return.

I'd heard stories of Irdelron's cruelty, but I had no comprehension of his brand of evil. I had no idea such brutality could even exist.

The girl I'd been couldn't understand it.

Had been.

The girl I was now . . .

I saw the way Irdelron clutched his vial of blood. I now understood the king's determination for power, no matter the cost or depravity. He'd slaughtered the Drae and the Phaetyn to secure his throne. He drank the blood of the Phaetyn. He enslaved his own people, and reigned with brutality.

But that one person would do such things; *that* knowledge threatened to overwhelm me. My heart could not accept it.

Staring blankly out of the thick metal bars into the darkness, I sobbed until every ounce of my waking strength was gone.

THE NEXT TIME I AWOKE, IT WAS TO THE CLANG OF METAL.

I jerked up, pushing my hands into the bed to lift myself. No more sound came, and I slowly relaxed. I lifted my hand. The bandage had been removed since the last time I awoke, and I stared at my hand in awe in the dim dungeon light.

My jaw dropped. Whoever bandaged me had to be a magician, because my hand was whole, completely unmarred from the stake. I pushed the blankets aside and looked at my legs. I felt . . . so much better.

I glanced around the room, taking it in for the first time. The damp square space was mostly empty. A chamber pot sat in one corner with straw scattered around. The rough floor was dark stone, uneven and jagged. Three of the walls were solid, no windows or breaks to allow for light or ventilation. The air carried the weighty dank stench of wet rock and rat droppings. There was space to take three large steps in each direction. I turned in my bed and faced the last wall. Bars spanned from the rock ceiling to the floor and from wall to wall. On the other side of the bars was a narrow, stone hall.

I stood, my tender bare feet protesting the uneven surface, and my knees buckled as I straightened. The room spun, and I put my hand on the wall beside the mattress to stop my collapse.

Balance restored, I gingerly inched my way toward the front of my cell. As I approached, I noticed a bundle on the ground, a dark rag holding a hunk of bread, a wedge of cheese, and a flask I prayed was water. I unstopped the cork and sniffed. The sweet smell was foreign to me. The food and water could be a trap, or poison, but neither of those mattered anymore. I took a sip, and a glorious sweetness danced across my tongue, encouraging my thirst to flee.

I had no idea how long I'd been out, but my stomach didn't even rumble at the food, so I knew I had to be well down the path of starvation. It wasn't like I'd had fat stores beforehand.

My tummy churned when the fluid hit, but instead of protesting, I craved more. I sipped the fluid and nibbled on the bread, relieved when I kept it down. I stashed the remaining food back in the cloth and wrapped the cloth and flagon in a blanket before depositing it on the corner of my mattress.

I returned to the wall of bars and peered left and right down the hall. I could only see a few feet in either direction. The dark and narrow hall outside my cell extended past my limited vision. If there were other cells, or other prisoners, I couldn't see them, and I wasn't foolish enough to call out.

I sighed, both disappointed and relieved to be alone.

"Who's there?" a scratchy voice whispered from my right. "Is there someone else here?"

I froze, dropping into a crouch.

Who was that?

I inched away from the bars. On tiptoes, I returned to my bed and lay down as quietly as I could.

I waited, tense, ears straining for a long while after. Maybe I hadn't heard a voice at all. My mind was on edge and probably playing tricks on me. Though, if someone else was down here, they could be one of the three prisoners Irrik mentioned to the king.

I just hoped Arnik and Dyter weren't captured. My heart ached with the thought, and I hoped against hope they were safe. No one deserved to be in here, except Irdelron and Irrik. And Jotun. I shivered.

I imagined seeing Arnik's expression when he realized I was gone. He'd be worried sick about me. I probably would have married Arnik when I was eighteen. Not because he had ever kissed me, but because he was the obvious choice. I wouldn't marry now. I wouldn't have children. I wouldn't need to worry about my lack of skill. I wouldn't live a life outside this place.

In these walls, I would die.

Dyter, he'd be beside himself.

I winced as I thought of him finding out what befell me. Did he know Mum was dead? Had he seen her . . . like that? I hoped not. This was all assuming Dyter still roamed free. I had no way of knowing if the soldiers captured him, too.

Heat sparked in my chest, and the warmth was so stark against the cold inside me that I couldn't help noticing the emotion.

Defiance.

The urge to protect Arnik and Dyter rose within, the only emotion other than despair I'd had since Mum died.

Madeline's words about survivors clicked in my mind, and I realized I'd found my corner of necessity.

My corner was my people, Arnik and Dyter. That was where my strength came from. I'd do anything to save my friends. Now, more so, after seeing what would happen to them if they were caught. Jotun's torture hadn't dragged their names from my lips, and I was determined to keep it that way, no matter what.

I'd waited too long outside my window the night Mum died. I hadn't joined the rebels, nor fought the Drae or the king. I'd done nothing. Now, all I could do was keep my lips sealed and not betray Arnik and Dyter. I still had control over that.

The king's face swam in front of my mind's eye, my throat tightening as the sensation of bugs scuttled over me, and I saw my earlier error.

Spitting in the king's face was unnecessary. I'd felt the need to show him what I thought of him, but doing so hadn't helped me protect anyone or myself. It made him hurt me more, making me less able to protect myself later.

As I lay here, this new world separated into an altered list of what I would and wouldn't do. I understood what Madeline meant by necessary.

I wouldn't laugh in his face.

I would bow, even grovel, if required to.

I wouldn't tell them what happened between Mum and Irrik.

I would lie.

I wouldn't betray my friends.

I would let the king and Jotun hurt me.

I wanted to be brave, but here, in this damp cell with smatterings of moss, I wasn't. Bravery was for stronger people, or people ignorant of the things I'd been put through. Being brave was easier before I'd known the depravity in the world.

I pulled the blanket tight, rolling on my side.

Bravery was for someone other than me.

I'd do what was necessary to protect my friends from this fate.

*T*ime passed. My food and drink were gone. My strength had improved from careful rationing, at least enough that my legs didn't tremble when I stood, but if I didn't get more food soon, it would be over. I'd accept dying of many things, but dying of starvation felt too personal, too much like giving up, too much like acceptance of what the king could do to his subjects.

Ironically, I cared more about the ideals of rebellion now than ever before. If I could go back to Harvest Zone Seven with this knowledge, my input would be much different. All-consuming.

Should have, could have, would have.

This was the trap my mind went to in the dank fetidness of my cell.

The uneven ground poked at my tender feet as I paced. I'd learned which areas of the dark stone were the sharpest and avoided them.

I hadn't seen or heard from anyone down here after that single time when the man in the cell next to me spoke, and after a while I couldn't be sure the voice wasn't a desperate attempt of my mind to alleviate my isolation.

My stomach gave a loud rumble, and I wrapped both arms around my middle over the filthy tunic that displayed the recent events of my life in splatters and splotches and stains. My hair was stiff and matted, and my smell bothered me—not the lavender soap scent I smelled like before.

How I'd run through the freshly overturned dirt of the Harvest Zones beside Arnik, avoiding new crops, and laughing as farmers shouted after us.

How I'd made jokes of my future to Mother while gazing at the clear blue sky, bird song floating down from the roof to where we sat in the garden.

My chest tightened . . . I had to survive.

"I need food," I said as loudly as I dared.

When no one answered, I raised my voice. "I need food."

With increasing volume, I yelled my need for water, but only silence met my pleas. Perhaps this was a different type of torture meant to break me. Perhaps I'd been left here to die, useless and wasted. The king thought I possessed information crucial to taking the rebellion down, and he'd confessed I was a pawn in his power play against the Drae. I had no idea what the king saw in Lord Irrik to be convinced the Drae favored me, but I knew the king was irrevocably wrong.

The Drae was the bane of my existence.

I rested my head on the bars, closing my eyes. A trickle of scent wafted past. Something less offensive than the rest of the air down here, and fear and hope warred within.

Necessary. Water was necessary. "Who's there?" My voice cracked. "I need food and water."

A cell opened, followed by a muffled thump. A man cried out, his wail like a wounded animal, and the clank of a door closing with the click of a lock ricocheted through the low underground space.

Someone was here, and that someone could give me water.

"Water," I whispered. Only half the word came out.

I sank to my knees by the bars when no one answered.

That was when I felt his presence. Lord Irrik stood outside my cell, staring down at me, anger pulsing from him in waves. I lifted my tired eyes and silently told him how much I hated him. I didn't bother moving. If he wanted me, nothing I could do would stop him. Scrambling away was *unnecessary*.

I was so busy directing my hate at the Drae I didn't see Jotun until he announced his presence by reaching through the bars with his torture gloves on and grabbing the front of my tunic. The guard yanked me forward, smashing my face into the bars, repeatedly, and bursts of white exploded across my vision.

The two of them took turns in their abuse. I gasped as searing agony pierced my arm and climbed up to my shoulder. Nausea hit me in a crashing wave, and I gagged, falling onto my hands on the uneven stone.

"No more," I pleaded.

Mercifully, my vision returned, and I saw the hall was empty of Lord Irrik and Jotun. They were done with me for now.

"*Drak*," a man said, his voice hoarse and low. "What did you do to piss off the king?"

His words registered slowly, my mind trying to push past the fog of desperation and pain to make sense of his question. I just needed . . . "Water."

"Water? What did you do to the wat—Oh! *Drak*, sorry," he said. Something crashed against the stone. "Hang on, lad."

Great, and now I was apparently a guy. Way to kick a girl when she was down.

Something scraped against the stone.

"That's as far as I can reach. But if you put your arm out, you should be able to reach around the lip of stone and grab it. It's not water, but it's the closest thing I've got."

He had water? Or something like it, and he was sharing? I was far too desperate to care if this was a trap. I hauled myself over and stuck my arm through the bars and around the rock wall protruding into the hall. The structure ensured prisoners couldn't see into the next cell.

My fingers grazed something, a sharp piece of ceramic, and I stretched to hook the edge. I pulled the container back and blinked back tears when I saw a curved shard of a flagon filled with several measures of clear liquid. The broken flagon was just small enough to fit through the bars.

I lapped the sweet liquid up like an animal, afraid to lift the makeshift bowl for fear of spilling any of the treasured contents. The fluid coated my tongue and then slid down my throat. The nectar seemed to absorb into my system before ever reaching my stomach, replenishing me immediately. Queasiness roiled through me but settled quickly as a wave of relief claimed me.

"What's your name?" the man asked. His age was hard to place, his voice odd, like a series of blades chopped up his words. He spoke with the inflections of someone from the Harvest Zones, however.

I was too tired to explain, but I didn't want to be rude, either. Not after he shared his drink with me. As I drifted back into the land of dreams, I simply said, "Ryn."

He said something, but whatever it was fell unnoticed out in the hall between our cells.

"So you're from Zone Seven?" he asked in a parched voice.

The question was just the latest during our on-and-off conversation of the last indiscriminate period of time in the shadows. These shadows weren't my friends. But this man might prove to be.

"Born and raised," I said. This wasn't strictly true. I was more at ease talking to the man, Ty, now and more certain of the kind of person he was, but who knew what he'd repeat under Jotun's thumb. Better not to impart anything that could be shared. He was probably doing the same.

First rule of torture club, don't talk about torture club.

"Here, I got more food yesterday," he said in his husky voice.

Yesterday, or hours or days ago, I'd asked him what happened to his voice. He told me King Irdelron poured acid down his throat. One of the king's favorite torture techniques, something he did regularly. Explained why Jotun couldn't talk, as well as most of the king's guards, I guess. After that, I wasn't sure I had the right to complain about bugs under my skin.

I was sitting against the conjoining wall already and shifted to reach my arm through for the goods.

"Are you sure?" It belatedly occurred to me to ask if he could spare the food.

"You're still in the early stages, Ryn," he answered. He knew I wasn't a boy by now. "They only do routine torture on me. You need your strength."

"Oh, goodie," I said. "Routine torture. Something to look forward to."

He chuckled. "Here."

Our fingers couldn't quite touch, and he had to push whatever he was passing to get it all the way to where I could reach it. Was it wrong that I longed to touch his hand? That even the tiny human contact of our conversation made me want to curl in a ball and cry like a baby?

"Why do they feed you double what they feed me?" I scowled—not at Ty but at the unfairness of an unfair situation.

Ty said in a hard voice, "Jotun seems to have taken a particular dislike to you."

"Why?"

He paused. "You know Lord Irrik?"

This time a real growl rumbled from my lips. "I do."

Ty began to ask more but then cut off his question, saying instead, "Jotun thinks the Drae favors you. I'd guess that's why he attacked you. Usually he sticks to his torturing schedule like clockwork."

I snorted.

"Lord Irrik dragged him away when Jotun smashed your head against the bars."

"Really? I thought he joined in." I frowned, trying to remember.

"Next time you see Jotun, take a look at his face. I hate the Drae as much as anyone here, but it was one of the better punches I've seen," Ty said with a dark, rasping chuckle.

I quirked a brow. The Drae had acted strange at our first meeting, then violent, then strange, then he'd finished off my mother, then strange, then kissed me to take control, then emotionless. Which led me to his visit here. He hadn't prevented a single bad thing from happening. The opposite, actually. He had another reason for doing these things, and I didn't want to get caught in the games of the Drae and the king. I'd always had a clear set of rules for my life. Emperor Draedyn ruled the realm from his lands in the northwest. Within the realm were three kingdoms—Verald, Gemond, and Azule—their sovereignty given to the Drae emperor. We gave him all our capable men over twenty years for his war; we gave him and the other kingdoms some of our harvest. We worked each day to get enough food and to keep the guards' attention elsewhere.

But those rules didn't matter anymore.

"I'd rather Lord Irrik didn't come down here again," I said. "If that's what happens."

We fell into a heavy silence, and my eyes closed.

"Of course, me having more food could be because Jotun has a crush on me," Ty quipped. "He's a great admirer of good looks."

His remark dragged a real laugh out of me, brittle though it was.

"Now it's all coming out. How long has your sordid affair been going on?"

Ty's wheezy chuckle echoed through our cells. "It's one-sided. I hold out hope he'll move on. I get the willies when he pulls on his gloves."

The willies. I grinned. "How old are you?"

He paused. "Twenty."

Huh. I sat back, unwrapping the parcel he'd passed me. Flat bread. Hard, flat bread. Yummy. Ty was a lot younger than I'd pegged. He was almost my age.

"I thought you were my imagination the first time you spoke," I confessed. I leaned against the wall, my head resting on the stone. "I called out for you when I ran out of food and water, but you didn't answer."

"It happens in cycles," he explained. "The torture. They'll go through periods of starving you, too. The key is not to take anything for granted. You have to store enough food and liquid so you'll have it when they don't give you any."

I wanted to ask him how that was possible, but I didn't want him to know where I hid it, just in case. "Al'right."

We fell quiet again.

"Is there anyone on your other side?" I asked.

"No, you're the first—the first one to survive. There are other prisoners in other wings, however."

"Why are we separated?"

"Who knows," he rasped. "Maybe we're just special."

Another horrible thought occurred to me. "How long have you been alone here?"

I heard Ty take a sip and wondered what he looked like, what had happened to him, and what would happen to me. I don't know what my state of mind would be if he hadn't been here to talk to.

He spoke again. "It is better now that you're here, Ryn. Please stay alive."

THE RATTLE OF KEYS AT MY DOOR WOKE ME, AND I SAT UP, DISORIENTED. Sleep had been peaceful, like *before,* and for a moment I thought I was home with Mum. But Jotun stood in my doorway, and the reality of my situation struck just before his hand connected with my face.

My eyes watered, but I bit my tongue, refusing to let a whimper escape my lips.

The guard grabbed my arm, a method he seemed to favor, and hauled me from bed. I scrambled to stand, but he yanked me one way and then another, throwing me off balance. I tumbled to the ground, only to be yanked back up and then out of my cell and down the stone hall.

I tried to get a glimpse into the cell next to mine, but all I could see was a lumpy mattress with heaps of blankets. Ty was likely buried in that mass, and his warnings drove thoughts of him away. There was only one reason Jotun would come to get me.

I thrashed, screaming and clawing at him. But Jotun didn't flinch. When I fell to the floor, he dragged me over the unforgiving stone until my skin was raw and bloody and my shins battered and bruised.

He climbed the stairs, and I scrambled to keep up with him, deciding it was better not to inflict pain on myself. Each step was more difficult than the last. The screams of victims being tortured assaulted me as we crossed the landing, and I couldn't help the sob that bubbled up my chest and out my lips.

"Please," I begged. "Please, Jotun. You don't have to do this. Please. Please!"

He didn't even glance in my direction while I cowered at his feet. The tall guard unlocked the door, and his lips flattened as he stooped over to pick me up. He scooped his hands under my arms, like a mother picks up a child, but instead of pulling me to him and offering comfort, he slammed my body to the table, dazing me with the brutal impact.

He tilted his head to the side, waiting.

I knew what he wanted, and I gritted my teeth. "I'm not telling you anything."

Time lost all meaning. I screamed until I had no voice. I was sure my skin was flayed. I was sure I was going to die. I wished I would.

*J*awoke in Jotun's playroom, still strapped to the table. A hooded figure leaned over me, and my eyes widened in a silent scream. He shushed me, putting his fingers to his lips, and moved away. The person strode around the room with confident steps despite the dark. He was tall, just shorter than Lord Irrik, but his clothing didn't fit nearly as well. He wore a black aketon, but his was sleeved, and he wore matching gloves. The fabric was plain cloth, much rougher than Lord Irrik's clothing or even the guards'. This man's aketon also had a hood, which was pulled up, covering most of his face and casting the rest in shadow. He wore black leggings and black suede boots that extended almost to the hem of his aketon.

He glided through the torture chamber, wiping down the tools Jotun had used on me. The hooded stranger was methodical, first the tools, then the table. It must be his job to clean the tools of torture between victims.

I'd seen him before, though I'd forgotten him from the first night.

He turned and I started when he began working on me. Shock held me immobile. His gloved hands were gentle, whatever material he used to cover them was supple, and he washed and then dressed my legs.

I whimpered, and he stopped. Shaking his head, he put his gloved hand to my mouth as if to tell me to be quiet. Either he wasn't supposed to be here, or he wasn't supposed to be helping me. I nodded my understanding and did my best to be silent.

He dipped a white cloth into a clear liquid that cooled the fire of my wounds on contact, returning the now stained cloth back into the ceramic pot again and again as he cleaned the wounds on my abdomen, arms, chest, face, and even my head.

By the time he finished, my senses had returned, and I recognized the smell of the salve he'd applied to my injuries. My mother had used a similar ointment on me, one she went to great lengths to procure. We had to travel to the far corner of Zone Twelve every month to get it, and the gray-haired woman who made it always glowered at Mum when we picked it up. I always thought the exchange was odd, even when I was a child. We didn't pay in gold or even goods. Mother would hand her a small opaque bottle no bigger than a thimble.

Why would this hooded man waste this balm on me?

His silence and the relief of my pain lulled me in and out of consciousness. When done, he helped me sit and offered a simple shift to replace my shredded tunic. There were only pieces of bloodied fabric left. How was I even alive?

"What's your name?" I croaked. Wary gratitude drove me to ask the question despite my raw throat. Was he friend or foe? I desperately wanted to know.

He glanced back from where he'd chucked my tunic and the evidence of my torture into a pail. The hooded man tapped his throat and shook his head.

My brows rose, and I winced as the motion pulled at a cut on my cheek. "You can't talk?"

He nodded. Straightening, the hooded man strode to me and wrote three letters on my palm.

"Tyr," I deciphered. "Your name is Tyr?"

A sad smile showed beneath the rim of his hood.

I swallowed, pushing back my fear, and tried to crack an answering smile.

He was at the castle, which could only mean he was employed by the king, right? So then, why was he here? Why was he helping?

"Do you work for him?" I whispered. I didn't want to say his name aloud. Not ever again. I'd add it to my secret corner, along with my people.

The man shook his head. His lips moved in silent explanation, and I wanted so badly to know what he was saying. Without thinking through what I was doing, I reached out and touched his jaw with my hand.

—*I want to tell you, but I can't.* His voice spoke as clear as day in my head. *You wouldn't understand.*

I dropped my hand and stared at it. "I . . . I just heard you in my head."

His lips parted.

Was this a first for him as well? "How can I hear you in my head?" I whispered. "What wouldn't I understand?"

He shook his head, backing away.

I swallowed, glancing at my hand again. Was it me, or was it him? Or was the reason I could do that connected to the reason he bandaged me and cleaned me? Had he taken care of me after each beating? "Why are you helping me?"

His lips pulled down in a deep frown over his clean-shaven jaw as he curled his hand into a fist and raised it before him, squeezing tight.

What did that mean? Guessing, I rasped, "You're strong?"

He shook his head and pointed at me.

"I'm strong?" I asked in disbelief.

He nodded and placed a hand over his heart, bowing slightly.

The hooded man thought I was . . . strong? His honor humbled me, and I mumbled, "I don't feel strong."

The rest of his face was covered. I ducked my head to try and see his eyes, and his lips curved into a wry smile. He lifted his head to show me. There was nothing. Just empty blackness.

I reached forward to touch him again, but he pulled back with a shake of his hooded head. He went to the door, opened it, and looked out, his head turning as he scouted the hall. He returned and offered me his hand, his gloved hand, to help me off the table.

I scooted to the edge, and my stomach roiled with the movement. I accepted his offer for help, but when I stood, my legs buckled. He caught me and scooped me up in his arms. Out of respect for what he'd done for me, I kept my hands to myself although they itched to touch his face again.

With another search, he strode out the door, down the empty hall and damp stairs to my dungeon cell.

Heat radiated from him to me, a warmth that seeped into my skin and into my soul. Having arms around me, arms that hadn't hurt me, made me feel human again. Hesitantly, I rested my cheek against his shoulder as he carried me, and I closed my eyes, listening to his heart.

Nothing about this man scared me. I'd never blindly trusted, even when I was light-filled Ryn. I *should* be scared of this man, that I heard his thoughts and that he was helping me without giving any explanation. Yet something in his gentle demeanour made me want to lean on him.

"Why are you helping me?" I mumbled against his hard chest.

He pulled me closer, holding me tight as we entered my cell. He set me down on the bed and knelt next to me.

"I don't want to be alone." I hung my head at my confession.

He gathered me in his arms once more, stroking my hair which he'd painstakingly washed the majority of the blood out of. After a few minutes, he untangled himself and took my hand, pressing it against his cheek.

You are strong, he said in my mind. *You haven't betrayed anyone. You are still kind and good. Don't confuse humanity for weakness.*

A lump of emotion clogged my throat, and I tried to swallow back my burning urge to cry. I hadn't betrayed my friends. I would be strong.

He gave a brittle smile and turned my hand over, kissing the back of it before he stood to leave.

I lay down in the bed, more mobile than I should be after Jotun's treatment, though I felt a deep cut on my thigh that would take a long time to heal as well as what felt like cracked ribs. Whatever Tyr did to heal me had saved my life at least twice.

"Thank you, Tyr," I whispered.

"RYN. *RYN.*"

I moaned and rolled onto my side as someone urgently called my name. My eyes flew open. I'd rolled onto my side . . . with cracked ribs. Sitting up, another thing I shouldn't have been able to do, I pushed down the blanket and unraveled the bandage on my leg. The gash that had been there was a scabbed cut, and most of my other cuts were gone.

"*Ryn,*" Ty shouted, snapping me out of my bafflement.

"I'm al'right," I said. I wasn't certain how or why or what it meant. But I was alive. "Are you okay?"

"Fine," he said. "Nothing that won't heal."

I bit my lip, unsure whether to tell him about the hooded man. The warning in my gut was only slightly uneasy, but I decided to heed it for now.

He growled, a deep gravelly sound that sent chills down my spine.

In his raspy voice, he said, "I could hear your screams from here, Ryn. Why do they hate you so much?"

I shrugged, my silent response lost to him. The problem was, the king and his Drae *didn't* hate me, not really. I was insignificant to both and somehow stuck in the middle of their power play, destined to wait until one of them emerged the victor.

"Are you al'right?" Ty's voice was strained.

"As al'right as anyone in here," I answered. Arnik and Dyter were still safe, I hadn't betrayed them.

"I hate that they're doing this to you. I wish I could get you out."

Why would he wish that? He hardly knew me. Yet as the thought crossed my mind, I saw it wasn't true. Our dependence on each other for food, but mostly for companionship in this terrible place, had forged something between us.

I would lie for Ty. Things that weren't necessary to do for him when I first got here now seemed necessary.

"You, too," I whispered. And I meant it.

He inhaled sharply and, not for the first time, I wondered what his face was like. "Why are you here, Ty?"

The scuffle of him moving toward our wall spurred me to sit up and join him. I rested back against the stone wall, only the solid rock between us. These days, I felt most grounded when I talked with Ty.

"Same reason as you, I gather," he finally replied. "The king's guard slaughtered my entire family. He wants to know what I know."

His tone was closed, and I didn't pry. It's not like we were desperate for time down here. I hadn't told him anything about why I was here, but it didn't surprise me he'd read between the lines. "They killed my mother. Lord Irrik killed my mother. He pushed the dagger in anyway."

"I'm sorry. I'm so sorry. His soul is dead inside and has been for a long time."

"I hate him," I said, seething with vehemence.

We sat there, not talking, the repetitive dripping in some far corner our only company.

"How many rooms are down here?" I asked.

"In this wing of the dungeon, ten cells. This is the lowest dungeon; there are only three people with keys that get this deep. Lucky for us, no one else is here at the moment, though there are prisoners in another wing."

"There are?" I turned my head toward him, wondering if they were from Zone Seven. "Are they alive?"

"From what I saw when Jotun took me to his fun room, yes. But I'm afraid that's all I know."

The tip of my tongue burned with the urge to tell him I may know them. That could get the prisoners in trouble though, and if it was Arnik or Dyter or even the hunched old Syret, I couldn't risk it.

"So what do you want to do today?" he asked.

I laughed under my breath. "I thought we could go out and pick strawberries in Zone Two."

"I've heard they're huge this year."

"Unusually so," I said brightly. That was where Mum and I would've gone. She would've made it so the strawberries were big and red and delicious.

He chuckled in his razorblade voice. "Perhaps afterward we could hire some horses and go for a gallop to the Gemond Mountains."

"How delightful."

This time he laughed. The hoarse rattle echoed through the dungeon and slowly faded to silence. "It is kind of a holiday today," he said. "Jotun has Tuesdays off."

I frowned. How did Ty know it was a Tuesday?

A door opened, and I hushed, hearing Ty do the same.

The air shifted, and the scent of pine and soap and steel floated by. My stomach clenched, and I inhaled the smell if for no other reason than it was the only freshness in this rotting world. I scrambled away from the bars and crept back to the bed in the dark, burying myself in the covers.

The outer door clanked, and I stilled as a blade scraped along the bars of Ty's cell.

Lord Irrik sneered, "Don't get comfortable, Ty. Jotun is anxious to visit with you tomorrow. He's devised a new solution he'd like you to sample."

Irrik laughed, but Ty didn't answer. Three people with keys to this level of the dungeon, and Irrik had to be one of them.

My stomach churned as Irrik taunted Ty. Wasn't it enough that Jotun tortured him? Now Ty had to put up with this, too? Irrik's cruel remarks made me angrier than anything had since the monster killed Mum. I said nothing, both because I didn't want to draw the Drae's attention to me, but mostly because I knew I couldn't do anything. Right now, I had no chance. But another time, I might.

Necessary. Opposing Irrik was a luxury I couldn't afford to indulge in.

The clack of metal on metal rang out as Irrik dragged the blade across the bars again, but as he came into view, I cracked my eyes open and saw it wasn't a blade but one of his talons. There'd been nothing in Mum's stories about Drae partially shifting.

"Good morning, little Ryn," Irrik said, his dark presence looming outside my cell.

Don't come in . . . don't come in . . . don't come in. Maybe he'd assume I was still passed out from Jotun's beating. Should I pretend to be worse than I was so the hooded guard didn't get in trouble?

"Good try, human. I heard you talking with Ty," he said, his voice dropping into a low growl. The key clicked in the lock, and the door opened. My heart pounded in my chest like a caged bird.

"I know the hooded Tyr comes here to help you when he thinks no one will notice, but I notice, Ryn," he whispered, crouching next to me. "I'm watching you," he continued, tracing the tips of his fingers down my arm. "And I'm not the only one." His eyes burned into mine.

Was he . . . warning me? I couldn't think because everywhere he touched was like fire. The magic that covered his skin was warmth traveling to my heart and pumping out to the rest of my body. I closed my eyes to try to shut out the searing sensation.

"Has Jotun even been working on you? It doesn't look like it, but Tyr is good at what he does." He traced my face, first along my hairline and jaw, then my eyebrows and the sensitive skin below my lower lashes. He trailed the pad of his finger down my nose, and my breath hitched when he outlined my lips. I would never let him kiss me again.

I pulled away, unable to tolerate his proximity.

"I have a treat for you," the Drae said. "Would you like to know what it is?"

I gritted my teeth.

Four guards came in, all dressed like Tyr with dark hoods and simple black aketons, dragging a large copper tub over the rough floor. As soon as it was in the room, they left, standing outside the cell with their backs to the inside.

A young girl, who looked to be the same age as Madeline, sauntered into my cell, her full lips curled up on one side in a smirk.

She bowed to Lord Irrik and turned to me. Her features morphed, and she grimaced as she drew close.

The girl threw Irrik a helpless look. "She's disgusting. One tub of water isn't going to be enough to get all that filth off her. She's been down here how long?"

"Three weeks," Irrik answered, eyes narrowed. He grabbed the front of her shift and pulled her close. Pursing his lips, he blew in her face, released her, and drew back a step.

Her eyes glazed over, and she swayed on her feet. Her disgust dissolved, and she stared up at Irrik with a dreamy smile on her lips.

"I love you," she said. "I wish you would kiss me." She began untying her apron.

I scrunched my nose. *Drak*, I better not have done that.

Lord Irrik's gaze flitted toward me before zeroing in on her. He scowled, a growl slipping between his teeth. "Keep your clothes on. Clean up the girl."

He cursed under his breath as he stepped aside.

The thin young woman stared at him as she sauntered across the stone floor to me. I leaped from the bed and backed away from her.

The girl pouted at the Drae, crossing her arms.

"I'm not going in there," I said.

His black brows arched. "You don't want to be clean?"

I was desperate to be clean, not that I'd admit that. The thought halted me. I *wanted* to be clean. What did it matter that the bath came from someone I loathed? Maybe I should accept the offer. Who knew when I'd get the chance again?

With a growl, Irrik traversed the space in two strides and reached for me.

I pressed my back against the wall. "Fine, but leave me to do it."

The Drae halted right in front of me, and the intensity of his gaze made me rethink my plan. I wanted a bath. Truly I did. But not if he was anywhere in the vicinity.

"Leave me to do it," I mumbled and then forced out the next word. "Please."

"Guards, outside," he snapped after a second. "Lydelia, help bathe her. There's a clean garb . . ." He gazed around the room then shook his head. "Delio, go grab her something to wear."

One of the men turned and disappeared down the corridor.

"Are you allowed to do this?" I asked.

His face firmed. "I'm a Drae. What do you think?"

I stared at him, at his cold face and cold eyes and where, if he had a heart, I'd surely be able to see it. "I don't want to be part of the game you're playing with the king."

"That game is the only thing keeping you alive," he sneered. "I'd think you'd want me to use you as a pawn, if only so you saw another week or month."

I scoffed and gestured. "You call this being alive?" *I will never help you. I will do everything I can to kill you.*

His eyes flashed.

"If you know about Tyr, why haven't you told *him?*" The name of the king wouldn't pass my lips.

Lord Irrik's lips thinned on his beautiful and horrible face. The Drae's eyes searched my expression, seemingly growing angrier by the second. What did *he* have to be angry about? So his oath to the king was a collar, boo-freakin'-hoo. Why did he make it in the first place if he hated the king so much?

"You coming here will only bring me pain," I said. "Yet you knew that because of Jotun's reaction last time. This is why you've come. The bath, the servant—" I broke off, breathing heavily, *sick* inside from how flippantly these people were playing with my body and mind.

His face didn't change, and my fury swelled as it reminded me of the first time I'd seen him, cloaked in the shadows of the fountain garden. A burning began behind my eyes, and I hoped he saw it in my gaze—how much I wished I'd never stopped, never met him.

"Get out," I said.

With a cruel twist of his lips, astonishingly, he did.

14

"*R*yn?" Ty's hoarse whisper called me from sleep.

The deepest, non-injury related sleep I'd had since my mother died.

I shifted on my bed, wincing when my face grazed against a blanket. I brought my fingertips to the previous gash on my leg only to find my skin was smooth and unmarred after my bath.

The girl had been right. One bath wasn't enough. The water had kept flowing even though Irrik hadn't returned. The girl had changed my bedding, brought me fresh clothing and a blanket, plus more food. All while telling me what a grand lover Lord Irrik would make. Sick.

I'd rather marry a donkey with one and a half legs.

Ty called louder this time, his voice tinged with worry. "Are you al'right?"

I blinked through the last dregs of my amazing sleep. I kind of felt like a person today and *would* have if I didn't have the monster to thank for the way the warmth of the bath had defrosted some of my soul.

I also felt guilty I got a bath and Ty didn't.

"I'm fine. Sorry, Ty. I'm right as—" My mother's expression caught in my throat. Right as rain.

"I'm fine. I was allowed a bath yesterday." Ty had probably heard my groans and splashes. Blood rushed my cheeks at the thought. I supposed I should be well past caring about that now.

"Yes," he said, drily. "I heard. It was a different kind of torture for me."

If he'd been in front of me, I wouldn't have let the grin cross my face.

I rolled over on my bed and grabbed a hunk of bread, nibbling on the edges. "Do you have any food left?"

Ty cleared his throat. "Not much. A mite of cheese and maybe a crust . . ."

"I have some. Let me share with you. I was only asking so I could give you some to replenish your safe store."

I tore the rest of the loaf in half then did the same with the cheese and dried fruit. I wrapped the portion in a strip of cloth and pushed it through the bars toward him. "Here. I know it's not as much as you gave me, but it's something to fill your belly tonight. Or today."

I gave it one more push, hoping I'd wiggled it far enough into the hall for him to reach it. My cheek was smooshed against the stone wall.

"I'm sorry there's not more," I said.

"Don't be," he said in his husky voice that was now more comforting than any other sound.

The rawness in his voice squeezed my heart in a vice, and I had to swallow back my emotion. "How did you do this all alone?"

"Now that I know you, I'm not sure."

My chest constricted with loss. I wanted my mother. I wanted Dyter. I missed Arnik. I wanted someone to hold me, to hug me, to tell me things were going to be all right and mean it.

"I miss my mother," I said, and a fat tear slipped down my cheek and landed on the sharp stone I sat upon.

"I know, beautiful. I know."

I choked on a cry, forcing it back, not wanting to place more burden on this man.

"Tell me about her," he said, surprising me.

I closed my eyes and thought of her soft, familiar face. "She took us away from my cruel father and started a new life in Verald," I said. "Back when I was a baby. Then we settled here, and she discovered she had a knack for gardening."

My memories of her loosened, and I told him of her kindness, her humor, her strength, pausing short of recounting the night she'd died.

"She sounds incredible," Ty said.

I let more tears flow, whispering, "She was."

THE LOCK TO MY CELL CLICKED, AND I LAY IN MY BLOOD ON THE SHARP ground, too weak to move after another torture session—this time with a leather belt, right here in my prison cell. The king had briefly joined Jotun and me and had been displeased to find me so functional —and so clean. Bile rose in my throat as I noted my earlier prediction was correct—Lord Irrik did bring me more pain, and I, like a fool, accepted his dangling carrot, the nice warm bath, knowing the game he played and *knowing* the king would be watching.

I'm a fool.

The cell door was pulled open and a person strode towards me in confident steps despite the dark.

Tyr dropped to his knees beside me, and I couldn't help sobbing like a baby as soon as he reached a hand to my hair. Dried blood caked a chunk of it to my cheek, and my body was covered in welts from Jotun's treatment.

I choked back tears as he stroked my hair. "How long was I out?'

He held up three fingers.

"Hours?" I asked.

A nod was my answer.

There were a few scuffles as he arranged the objects he'd brought with him in a row. Without moving me to the bed, he made quick work of washing me. It showed how far gone I was emotionally that I didn't feel one iota of embarrassment. His movements were quick and clinical, which helped. After that, he helped me change into a fresh tunic and threw the other in a bucket before carrying me to my bed. He lifted my arms and began rubbing the same ointment onto my skin in careful strokes. The ointment soothed me instantly, and I sighed, earning a smile from him.

"Is it daytime, Tyr?" I asked.

He paused and took a deep breath before pressing my hand to his jaw. *The color of the sun was reflecting off the freshly plowed fields this morning. It reminded me of your hair.*

I closed my eyes, pressing my trembling lips together, and tried to draw up the image he'd created. "Thank you." My voice broke.

I couldn't help the welling emotion in my chest. In this dungeon-hole, Ty was like my sun, and Tyr was my moon. The circumstances accelerated the bonds between us, and my feelings couldn't be rationalized away.

Next, Tyr massaged the ointment on my face then the bruises around my neck. He shoved off the blanket and worked on my legs for a while. I tried to stay still as he lathered my skin in the stuff.

After the ointment, he wound bandages around the worst of my injuries and pulled the blanket back over me.

There was a scrape of pottery and plate on stone next to my head, and then he turned toward a bucket of water he'd carried in. He reached into it and drew out a scrubbing brush, but he stopped shy of bringing it to the bloodied ground, lifting his head as something caught his eye by the bars.

Striding over, he crouched in the corner where I sat to talk to Ty.

"What is it?" I whispered.

Tyr returned and knelt next to me, holding out his fist. He held a handful of moss. It looked spongy and—well—green. The only splash of color in this gruesome place.

"That wasn't there yesterday," I said in confusion. "I sit there all the time. My butt would know the difference."

He held the moss closer to my face and shook his head.

"I don't understand," I said helplessly.

Voices echoed down the corridor toward us. In a blur of movement, without saying goodbye, he collected his two buckets and clicked the lock after himself. I held my breath for the sounds of discovery, but they didn't come.

And after that, neither did Tyr.

"Ty," I whispered after clawing from sleep. It's all I seemed to do in here. The dark messed with my clock mojo, although thanks to Lord Irrik I knew three weeks had passed. "You awake?"

No one answered. He hadn't answered my calls after Tyr left either.

"Ty?" I held my breath for his husky reply. Nothing. I squeezed my eyes shut, working through the fear that he might be gone for good. I wasn't sure I could take being alone down here. I'd known the alternative now, and a large part of me doubted I'd be able to do without Ty, or some human company.

With the pain gone, the need to eat before I lapsed into exhaustion swelled.

I worked on my body, wiggling my toes, fingers, bending my

knees, and drawing my hips up before rocking side to side. After an age, I made it to sitting and stared at the food and drink Tyr had left.

The bag was like the burlap kind Mum would take when she went to trade at the Market Circuit, and it was stuffed full of cured meat, cheese, seeded bread, brak, and dried fruit. Stuffed full. A feast.

Next time, I would demand Tyr tell me why he was helping me. I mean, Madeline had helped me when I first came, but what Tyr was doing was a whole new level of danger and self-sacrifice. The king killed Madeline for trying to trick him. What would he do to Tyr?

What if Tyr *was* a part of the rebellion? I hadn't considered this before...

What if he had contact with Dyter and Arnik? Despite my best endeavors not to let it, hope took root within me.

I was a moron to even have the thought. Would they fight their way past hundreds of guards and then kill the king's Drae? Would I invite the same people into the castle that I'd been trying to keep out?

At least Irrik hadn't been back. There was one blessing in all of this —because I'd been seriously planning on kicking him in his Drae face. He was probably lucky he hadn't been back.

—Beaten Girl Turns the Tables on Jerk—

—Drae Bursts into Tears After a Punch to the Throat—

—Ryn Throws Seeds in Drae's Eyes to Win Fight—

"Ty?" I called again. There was something wrong with me to be laughing at my own jokes in the king's dungeon after the worst experiences of my life. Especially as Ty could be lying there half dead for all I knew.

Ty's words came back to me about keeping my food safe, and I searched for a spot to hide a portion of my feast treasure.

I nibbled on brak—Dyter's specialty, a forlorn part of me reminisced—and studied my small cell. All stone, and the only place I could find to hide anything was by my bed and under my blankets. I sat on my bed, munching on bread and brushing the specs of grain off my lap and onto the stone. I regretted wasting the seeds, as small a food source as they were. A quick feel told me the grains were lost to the cracks in the stone floor. And actually, on second thought, my blood was still splattered all over the cell from Jotun's belt whipping.

The soap queen had not fallen that far.

I grimaced, scanning every stony brick of the cell. Even a toddler would know by simply looking at my room that anything of value would be stashed by my bed, which made it a terrible hiding place. The only other object in my entire cell was the straw and the chamber pot. I'd long since moved the pot to the front of my cell so I could dump the contents out into the hall instead of having to deal with it in my room. It had been the only option when the receptacle was full several days ago. The smell was atrocious, but by the next morning, the hall had been rinsed clean.

Tyr's handsome smile flashed in my mind, and I seriously hoped he hadn't been the one to clean up the mess.

I was desperate to keep my food bounty, but the only idea I'd had, besides hiding it by my bed, was repulsive. Maybe repulsive was good. I thought of the oiled cloth from the first time someone had left me food, and fingering the material under my bed, I hoped the cloth would be enough of a barrier.

I scattered the smelly straw around the chamber pot and took the wrapped package of food and the flagon of nectar and put them in the darkest corner of the room, the space I'd initially used as a bathroom. The pot was several paces away, but the very idea made me cringe.

Hopefully my hiding place would make anyone planning to take my food cringe, too.

The victory was small.

But for the first time, I felt like I might be starting to play the game.

*T*y didn't return that day.

I couldn't tell if it was Tuesday or not, but Jotun didn't return for me either. I'd overheard Lord Irrik say I'd been here three weeks. Did that mean I'd been here a month now?

A month since my mother died. Moons, but I missed her. Ty filled the hole somewhat, but no one could ever replace my mother.

Somewhere in the middle of wondering why Jotun opted to have Tuesday off out of all seven days, I must have drifted off again in a sleep that wasn't sleep at all. I tossed and turned, imagining Lord Irrik in my cell, and the king, and then both of them laughing at me. Dyter appeared, and even Mum, her face in anguish as she tried to comfort me. The knife was pushed into her chest. Then the king's Drae pulled it out and handed it to me.

When I awoke, someone was brushing my arm in a cool caress.

"Tyr," I mumbled.

Keeping my eyes closed, I relished the gentle contact, but my arm was stiff from being flung up over my head. My aching muscles screamed to move, and I withdrew my arm from his attention. As I moved, the brush of his fingers tickled, and I giggled, opening my eyes.

My lips parted, and it took me a while to understand I was still in my cell.

A dark circle, almost as big as my face, hovered right above me, and there were pale petals of yellow surrounding it. I blinked, and the anemic sunflower came into focus. The giant flower had fallen over and hovered directly over my head.

Inhaling through my nose, I almost choked on the smell of fresh vegetation.

In. My. Dungeon. Cell.

I pushed the sunflower away and sat up.

I'd finally broken. It was the only explanation.

Surrounding me was a tiny garden. Barley grass, wheat, and a small stalk of corn had sprouted from the meager dirt layer between the stones. Other plants I didn't recognize had begun a doomed life cycle, wilting in the darkness of the cell. Not believing my eyes, I ran my hand over the spikes of the barley, and the thin plants tilted and fell, their roots in the stone of the dungeon cell inadequate to sustain them. I picked up a shoot and bent the tender stalk.

What made them grow?

Yesterday, I ate bread with these exact seeds on it. Today, the same seeds were full-grown.

I stood in the middle of my cell, spinning on the spot.

The moss yesterday. The patch hadn't been that big the day before, not even a patch at all. Now I was sure of it, though I'd been puzzled when Tyr held it out to me. There was something wrong with this dungeon cell.

"Ryn?" Ty rasped, making me jump. "You still alive?"

"I'm here," I answered, looking down at my shredded shift. "Are you al'right? You've been out for a long time."

He coughed. "I'll live. Jotun found out we're sharing food."

"He won't move you away, will he?" I asked, holding my breath.

"I can't say," Ty answered. "I told him I wouldn't share with you again." He paused. "Do you have any food?"

I laughed under my breath. "Such rebellious tendencies."

"It goes with my rugged, dark looks."

"Is that what you look like?" I asked. "Dark hair, dark eyes, a beard?"

He was surprised. "Yes, how did you know?"

"I have powers you wouldn't believe." I glanced at the garden in my room.

Crossing to the chamber pot, I could just see the outline of the flagon of nectar.

I unplugged the cork and drank several gulps before forcing myself to stop. I found the oiled cloth behind the clay flask and unwrapped it and the burlap cloth beneath. The cheese was salty and dry, and the dense, nutty bread dissolved in my mouth, leaving several whole grains to grind with my teeth.

My gaze landed on the plants by my blanket as I chewed. Pumpkin. Barley. Kamut. Pursing my lips, I shook a few of the seeds from the loaf I held into a far corner, not touched by the current crop.

"Do you want some cheese and bread?" I asked Ty. "If you have an extra container, I can pour you some nectar."

"Some what?"

"Nectar. The fruity drink we get. I don't know what else to call it. It's kind of like mead." Dyter had never served anything like it, nor had Mum.

He chuckled. "No, but thank you. I have some of the drink left. Do you have enough?"

I sighed, looking at my dark cell. The phosphorus glow cast an eerie light, and the fronds and leaves looked sad and pathetic in the dark.

"Someone left more for me," I answered. "A friend, I think." It was as close as I'd come to telling him about Tyr.

Awareness of my situation struck me. Besides the obvious ongoing torture-and-death problems, I was in serious trouble right now.

As I crouched to pass the food to Ty, I said, "Hey, Ty? Have you ever had plants grow in your cell?"

He snorted. "What?"

"Like, you go to sleep and wake up with a sunflower by your head, that kinda thing?" I asked. "It's just, how would they grow in here? It's so dark and . . ."

Holy pancakes. I sounded crazy. And sounding crazy when I had several friends was okay but not when I just had one.

At least he was caged in and couldn't run.

"What do you mean? You're wanting to grow plants? Are you sure you're al'right?"

I didn't answer, just stared at the growth at my feet. "Um."

"Ryn?"

I touched the tip of the sunflower with my toe. The leaves and stem were scratchy on my bare, sensitive skin. Regretting my next move because the sunflower was the first bit of beauty I'd seen in here, I bent the stalk to rip the flower head off.

"What are you doing?"

"Hold on," I worked the stalk back and forth. Turned out, sunflowers had really thick stems.

"What—?"

"Nearly there," I huffed. The flower ripped off after a full minute of bending and twisting, and I glared at it as I crossed to the bars. "I'm passing something to you. And . . . well, here."

I stretched as I passed the sunflower head, shoving it through the gap in the bars. I felt the tug as he took the thick stem from me, and I listened as he pulled it into his cell.

Then nothing.

I raised my brows. "Ty?"

"W-where did you get this?"

I settled back against the stone. "Funny story, actually. Yesterday, I brushed sunflower seeds onto the floor, along with some other grains. Then, I wake up today and there's this mossy oasis in my dungeon cell."

It was true. I'd crossed the cell several times, only feeling spongy moss underfoot instead of sharp stones.

"Seeds," Ty said.

I frowned. He wasn't being very quick on the uptake. *Shock*, I realized, mentally hitting my forehead.

"I know it's really strange," I said. "That's why I was wondering if it's ever happened to you? Is there magic in this castle?" I knew nothing about such things.

There was a lengthy pause. "There must be. I have no other explanation for it."

"To the library I'll go," I quipped.

Ty was still silent.

"What happens when Jotun comes and sees a garden in my room?" I asked. This was my real problem.

Ty cursed. "Ryn, you need to get rid of everything. Right now."

The urgency in his voice spurred me to standing. "Al'right. But why? It's not my fault."

"I know," Ty said. "But I can't predict how Jotun will react. I've never heard of anything like this. Who knows what he'll do."

Drak. He was right. I stared at the garden, hating what I had to do to stay alive here. Gripping the corn stalk, I ripped it up.

The barley was next, and the rest of the sunflower stem, then the moss. But the moss clung to the rock and resulted in bleeding knuckles and torn feet from doing my best to scrape it away.

"Someone's coming. Under your bed," Ty urged. "Put it under your bed."

"Who is it?" I hissed, heart pounding because I hadn't heard the door open. My hands grew slick with trepidation. *Please be Tyr . . . please be Tyr.*

A cold voice answered me from the front of my cell. "Who would you like it to be?"

A sense of doom sank into me as I turned, hands full of leaves and stems, to face Lord Irrik.

I'd never seen him truly angry before. As I backed away from where he stood radiating fury on the other side of the bars, it astonished me that there was a more terrorizing level to this man than I'd encountered before.

"They just appeared," I blurted.

His eyes were slits—he'd partly shifted to Drae—and he studied me with his reptilian eyes. "What have you done?"

My chest rose and fell as I hyperventilated. As he unlocked the door and entered my cell, I dropped the plants, and clasped my hands together. "Please, it wasn't me. I have no idea what happened."

"No idea?" he asked, his lip curling in a sneer.

The door clanged open down the hall, and Irrik's eyes widened. He grabbed me in an iron grip and threw me from the cell. I rolled across the stones of the outside passage, crying out as my hip struck solid rock.

The Drae was on me in a beat, gripping me by the back of the neck. He directed me past a few empty cells before he shoved me forward to the ground and snarled to someone over my head, "Make it good."

Gingerly getting to my knees, I tilted my head to look at Jotun.

"Why do you help me, Tyr?" I slurred.

He wiped the tear trickling down my cheek then bent over me and kissed my forehead in answer. I felt the warmth of his feelings for me radiating from his tender touch.

"That doesn't tell me anything," I complained as he lifted one of my arms.

A wry smile showed under his hood, but it was tight and lacking in humor. I must be a sight, so I could hardly blame him. Jotun had taken Lord Irrik's command to heart. By now, I'd learned Jotun obeyed *all* the king's orders, except when it came to Irrik-related matters. The mute guard seemed to hold an all-consuming hatred towards the Drae. I had no idea why. Maybe Jotun was jealous of him. More likely, there was politicking I'd missed while in the torture chamber. One thing I did know: Jotun's deep-set grudge did not bode well as long as he believed Lord Irrik favoured me because that made *me* an Irrik-related matter.

Games. Always games.

I groaned as Tyr reset my dislocated shoulder, and then I asked, "How long will I live?"

My question was rhetorical, directed to the universe that allowed such atrocities to occur, not the man caring for me.

When Jotun dragged me down here, I never expected to live longer than a week, and I couldn't bear the thought of this abuse going on endlessly. The game between Lord Irrik and the king surely couldn't continue much longer. Soon, the king would realize I was worthless to him. . . If he even recalled he'd put me down here.

Either way, I was dead. It may take a week or a month or a year, but I was dead.

Maybe it would be better if Tyr stopped healing me, if the healing only put off the inevitable. How much could one body take before it simply failed?

Tyr paused, and I realized I must've said at least part of this aloud. As I looked around, I saw the room was now back to its stony, plant-free self. *Too little, too late.* I hoped the plants didn't come again.

A drop landed on my arm, and I startled, glancing up at Tyr's hooded face. His strong jawline wasn't clean shaven, not like it usually was, and his full lips were twisted as if trying to contain . . . A tear trickled from his cheek to his chin and then dripped.

"Tyr," I whispered.

He was crying. For me.

My heart squeezed, and my throat clogged with emotion. He held one of my hands gingerly, stroking his thumb over my palm. Instead of pulling it up to his face, he brought his face to my hand.

Ryn, he thought, full lips pressed together. *I'm going to get you out of here. I swear. Please hold on.*

I'll get you out of here. I swear . . .

The words tumbled over and over in my head, even after I fell into an unquiet slumber. At some point in my dreaming state, my learned terror twisted the errant hope I'd felt at Tyr's promise, morphing it into a nightmare of fear and pain.

Hours later, I stared at the low stone ceiling, heart thundering in the aftermath of a horrific dream I couldn't recall. I took deep breaths, closing my eyes to the dreadful reality that was my living nightmare.

Tyr was going to get me out. I'd be free from Jotun, free from Irrik, and free from Irdelron. I dug my torn nails into my palms and tried to imagine what my life could be like if that happened. I tried to picture what that would mean, but there was a solid barrier in the way of that dream— cold fury.

I wanted to kill the king. I wanted to kill Jotun. How could I leave without making them pay for what they'd done?

I squeezed my fist tighter, the pain in my hands nothing compared to the pain in my mind, until warm blood oozed between my fingers. A drip rolled over the pad of my thumb before falling to the floor. The idea of revenge was even more dangerous than the hope of escape. Those were dreams I couldn't have.

With a groan, I rolled onto my side and sat up. "Ty? You there?"

The silence that met my question filled me with guilt. If Ty wasn't answering, it meant he was being tortured, and he'd endured more frequent torturing since I arrived. This was the second time . . . this week? I still couldn't tell time in the dungeon. Around five weeks had passed, by my guess, but I couldn't be sure.

My frustration solidified my determination. If Tyr snuck me out, there was no way I'd leave without Ty. Second rule of torture club: Don't leave friends behind bars.

I circled my shoulders in an attempt to relieve tension and moved my neck side to si—

No!

I gasped for breath as I stood. My blood pooled with the sudden motion after being supine for so long. I sank back to the mattress in response, but my mouth hung open as I stared at the far corner in disbelief.

This couldn't be happening.

I blinked, trying to clear my vision, but the three huge pumpkins still remained, sitting there by my chamber pot, ensnared in the voluminous green tangle of their vines.

I lifted trembling hands and covered my mouth. Pumpkin seeds . . . from my bread yesterday. This time it took no effort for my mind to connect the dots, but the how, or more accurately when, of the new growth had me stumped. The pumpkins hadn't been here when Tyr was in my cell. Or maybe they hadn't been here *before* he'd been in the room, but they'd grown immediately after.

I'd fallen asleep straightaway, hadn't I?

I shook off my daze. Because *the how* mattered less as the moments passed, and hiding the large squash became increasingly urgent.

"Ty?" I choked out and then called louder, "Ty!"

I crawled to the corner, at a complete loss over what to do. The vegetables were up to my knees and bright orange, though, like the sunflower, the green of the vines was pale and unhealthy, a sure sign the plants shouldn't be growing in the dark.

How could I possibly hide them?

"Ty," I begged, moving to our wall. "Please. Please, wake up."

The only answer was the weighty silence, a clear message that no help was to be found next door. If he'd answered? What could he, a prisoner as I was, do to help? Would he hide the pumpkins for me and incur another beating on my behalf when the ruse failed? Impossible. I couldn't even get the pumpkins out through the bars.

Dread blanketed me, swallowing me whole. As I settled deep within the beast's belly, I knew there would be no escape.

I returned to the pumpkins and sank to my knees in front of the largest one.

And awaited my fate.

I DIDN'T MOVE FROM MY KNEELED POSITION IN THE FAR RIGHT CORNER of the cell as the rattle of the lock drifted down the damp hall. When the dungeon door creaked open, I didn't even shift my position. What was the point?

I had a fleeting hope the person wouldn't be Jotun, but his heavy tread announced him as he crossed the room.

At least my mind had broken partially free from stunned disbelief. The time spent gazing in astonishment at the pumpkins had unlocked one truth.

I knew why this had happened. Rather, I knew *who* made it happen.

I knew what Tyr was.

He'd healed me more times than I could count. Brought me back from the precipice of death. Not only that, in the last week he'd begun to heal my heart of its wounds, too. At least it felt that way.

Tyr was a Phaetyn, a healer. His powers could be used on land or mortals. He could halt death in its tracks. He could make plants grow. He'd done something to the seeds. Unwittingly, I assumed. I knew he'd never intentionally hurt me, not after experiencing his meticulous care firsthand.

Tyr was a Phaetyn.

Phaetyn weren't dead.

Jotun wrapped his hand around my upper arm, hauling me upright. My gaze stayed on the pumpkin, even as my hated guard ripped one of the orange squash from its prickly vine. Then Jotun hauled both me and the pumpkin from the cell.

The dark, rough dungeon walls blurred into the dark, rough walls of the stairwell, but we kept going up past the torture floor, and then the dark, rough walls blurred into the smooth, gray walls I hadn't seen in weeks. The windows became more frequent and larger, and light—glorious, blinding, vibrant light—slapped me to my senses. I threw my free hand in front of my eyes to shield them from the onslaught of the sun. After so long in the dark, the light was unbearable.

Tyr was a Phaetyn.

I kept up with Jotun, knowing he would simply drag me to our next destination if I didn't, but as my eyes adjusted to the light, I began to recognize the grand furnishings. Blood pounded in my ears as Jotun directed me into the one place I feared even more than the torture chamber.

Rows of the king's guard lined either wall of the magnificent, dreadful, *deadly* hall. I stared at the ceiling-length double doors ahead and readied myself for what most certainly lay beyond.

I would not betray Tyr. My hooded protector's secret would not cross my lips. He was a person I owed many times over for my life, and—as I remembered his tender kiss on my forehead—someone who grew more important to me with each passing day. The king *drank* Phaetyn blood to stay young, I could only imagine what he'd do to Tyr after discovering the truth. *I* would take his secret with me to my grave. No matter what.

Jotun dragged me and the pumpkin to the entrance, and when the two guards closest to the looming doors failed to anticipate his desire, Jotun struck the smallest guard with the pumpkin, the gourd cracking on the man's head. The guard on the other side surged forward to open the door as the other guard slid to the ground, unconscious.

I lowered my gaze to my filthy tunic and the scabbed skin of my legs underneath as we crossed through the hall, the voices inside silencing as we passed the mountains of food, and stopped in front of the king.

"Jotun, to what do I owe this pleasure?" the king's mild voice rung out.

Roughly translated, I guessed this meant: There better be a reason you're wasting my time, or you'll pay for this interruption.

I couldn't help peeking at Jotun, but I wished I hadn't. An eerie smile spread across his face.

Jotun dropped the pumpkin at my feet.

I fidgeted on the spot. The absence of sound was dreadful, and my palms itched with anxiety. Deciding to risk the king's wrath, I took a quick peek in his direction.

Irdelron's eyes were wide, and his lips parted in a look of shock that rocked me to the core.

"Look at me, girl," the king whispered.

The hoarse command slithered over my skin and turned my insides to quaking jelly. I hesitated, fearing what more he would find to torture me with.

"Now," he shouted. He pounded down the dais steps, making me quake.

Inhaling, I obeyed.

The king stood at the base of the raised platform, his gaudy throne extending several heads above his crown. One bejeweled hand was raised to his chest, adorned in silk layers, with a gold chain stretching between his shoulders, holding a cape in place.

But none of this grandeur distracted me from the nausea churning within at his expression.

His mild face wasn't mild anymore. It wasn't angry or mocking, or drenched in cruelty.

His complete attention was fixed . . . on me.

"Out," he shrieked, making me jump. "Get out!"

A wave of servants washed past us in a mass exodus, leaving Jotun and me behind.

When the room was cleared, Irdelron closed the distance, circling me like I was prey.

"Phaetyn," he breathed.

Wait. He thought *I* was the Phaetyn?

I kept my face smooth, impassive, or so I hoped. Inside, I frantically replayed the last few seconds. How had he come to the conclusion of Phaetyn so quickly? Jotun had only thrust me in front of him and held up the pumpkin. I was missing something here.

"The pumpkin was in her cell?" Irdelron asked, his eyes bright with excitement.

Jotun inclined his head.

The exchange made no sense.

The king stroked his chin and the blond patch of growth there. "How was this missed?"

But he didn't seem to be asking me or Jotun, and we both remained silent.

My gaze flitted around the room. The king's rapt attention only increased my anxiety. A quick peek told me the Drae wasn't in his usual position behind the throne, and I wondered if he was off terrorizing innocent people.

That was the least of my worries. Jotun's assumption I was a Phaetyn was understandable. He'd found me in my cell, kneeling in front of a trio of full-grown pumpkins. If I saw someone in a similar predicament, I'd make the same assumption. That wasn't what bothered me.

If they assumed I was Phaetyn, they would soon discover I was not when I couldn't make anything grow. Worse than that, they would want to know who had made the plants grow. Which meant they would discover Tyr.

"It was Irrik," I croaked. "He put them there. I'm sorry he—"

"Irrik?" the king asked. "You're trying to tell me my Drae made a garden grow in your cell?" He shook his head, bestowing an indulgent smile that made my heart thunder.

I dropped my gaze. If I could convince Jotun and the king that Lord Irrik had done this, it would keep Tyr safe. Despite the slight disquiet I felt at letting the Drae take the blame, I banished the feeling as best I could. I was finally a player in this game, minor player though that was. I would lower myself to the new set of rules forced upon me without hesitation, and that included throwing Irrik off the cliff to save Tyr's life.

The king looked me in the eye and continued, "The girl who cut her hair . . . she used dye to disguise her eyes, or I would have known straightaway. Such a lovely shade of violet. It has been almost two decades since I gave up on seeing that shade again. My girl," the king said, navigating the space between us, the silk of his garments whispering across the smooth stone floor, "why did you hide this? Did you not know I would exalt you?"

"I don't know what you're talking about," I managed. "It wasn't me. I'm telling you. I can't even grow potatoes."

With iron fingers, King Irdelron gripped my chin and, tilting my head, examined me. "The game is up. You can't hide what you are. It's as obvious as Jotun's muteness." He didn't let go of me as his gaze cut to Jotun. A dangerous awareness settled over him as thick as the cape he wore. "You could have ruined everything."

With a quickness I hadn't expected him capable of, the king back-handed Jotun. The guard's head rocked to the side, and blood oozed from his split lip.

The king grimaced in disgust as he watched Jotun wipe at the blood, smearing it across his chin. In a mild tone, the king asked, "Did the color of her eyes never alert you?"

The king again dug his fingers into my chin, and my eyes streamed from the pain. A whimper escaped from my lips, in spite of myself, but the king did not stop.

"Did you not wonder that she was alive and well after the torture you've put her through?"

I had no confusion in regard to that. Tyr had healed me. He'd rubbed the ointment and bandages on me for weeks. My insides relaxed. For a moment, I'd actually thought the king was—

"You—" the king blinked at Jotun. "Imbecile!" The king's voice escalated, and he yanked the whip from Jotun's side and struck Jotun again and again with it, dragging me along using the vicious hold on my jaw. "You nearly killed a Phaetyn. Do you realize what she could mean?" He continued beating Jotun. "You are not so great that I won't dispose of you, Jotun. I've sent my own children to their deaths . . . *Drak*, I even killed several of them myself. Don't think you're safe to make stupid decisions."

Jotun fell to his knees, hands outstretched, imploring his master. He took every single strike the king delivered, and then when Irdelron was done, Jotun lowered his forehead to the ground and stayed with his hands out to each side.

The king released me, and I grunted as the blood pounded into the spots he'd held, bringing with it a throbbing pain. *Five more bruises.* I brought my hand up to rub the tender spots.

The king watched, breathing heavily after his exertion. His lips turned up in a smile. Sweeping back some fallen strands of hair, he chuckled with glee. "A Phaetyn in my dungeon."

I didn't dare make a sound. Soon the king would realize I was not what he thought. Whether now or when I was put to the test. I only hoped Tyr had time to escape before it happened. By the crazed tinge to Irdelron's eyes, it was clear he'd never stop until the person who *had* made the pumpkins grow was found. But if I could hold him off until I got word to Tyr, maybe he could escape.

The king reached for my hand, and I overrode my impulse to wrench away. This time his grip was soft, almost tender, which was scarier. He flipped my hand, palm up, and inspected the dried blood from where I'd cut my nails into my skin not even an hour ago. He rubbed the pad of his thumb over my palm, and I focused on the skin beneath the cracked blood.

The scab flaked off, and I sucked in a breath.

The skin beneath was smooth. Whole. Uncut.

My eyes widened, and I raised my other hand, frantically. It was bloodless and also smooth. I returned to the other hand, and the impossibility of what happened hit a solid barrier of disbelief and was prevented from going further.

I knew without a shadow of doubt the blood had come from me. I'd felt it leave the cut and roll over my palm.

Where was the cut?

The truth I'd clung to, that Tyr had been the person keeping me alive this entire time, had no substance because he hadn't healed me this time. I'd healed myself.

"My dear girl," the king's voice barely registered. "My dear *Phaetyn.*"

Mouth dry, I blinked at him and caught the anticipation fluttering over his face like a shiver of joy. He stepped in close and whispered in my ear, "I have something I'd like you to do for me."

17

For the first time in my entire life, I wasn't hungry. I sat at the enormous table at the front of the throne room, surrounded by platters of food I'd only dreamed of, and had no desire to even stick out my tongue for a taste.

"Eat up, dear girl," the king said with a wide smile. "You'll need your strength."

To heal the land. That was my task.

He frowned when I didn't obey, but I was numb with shock over the abrupt turn my life had taken. Not the food and cushioned seat on the chair. They thought I was Phaetyn, and now I was beginning to believe it, too.

How?

"Are you going to drink my blood?" I whispered.

The king laughed and gazed at me fondly. His look didn't fool me. That's how I viewed food.

"No, dear Phaetyn. I have stores to keep me alive for a while, *but,*" he smiled at me, "when my stores run dry, we can reassess your value. For now, you need to make everything grow again."

I closed my eyes and took a shaky breath, attempting to gather my bearings.

"Feed her, Jotun," the king ordered. "I must confer with my foreman and see where our girl should begin."

Jotun brought me a plate of food and tossed it before me, splattering my tunic with gravy. The scalding liquid seared my skin, and I bit my lip as I pulled away from the stiff garment. I stared at the plate in front of me, stacked with slices of roasted bird swimming in glistening brown gravy, mounds of whipped potatoes, and buttered vegetables, and my stomach turned. "I'm not hungry."

The two guards pulled the doors closed after the king with a click.

Jotun tilted my chair back and drove his gloved fist into my gut. The chair fell to the ground, me with it, and I rolled into a ball, gasping for air. He disappeared from view, and I scrambled to stand, lurching my way toward the door. Before I could get there, Jotun grabbed a fistful of my hair and dragged me back to the table. My scalp burned, but my aching abdomen churned from the blow.

"I'm not eating it," I spat.

He looked directly into my eyes, and though he had no voice, he didn't need speech to convey his hatred.

"It's not me you hate," I whispered. "I'm just the only one you're not too weak to fight."

Jotun shoved my face into the plate of food.

Scalding gravy burned my lips and filled my nostrils. The potatoes scorched the sensitive skin covering my eyes. I flailed, my hands clawing at his, as I tried to free myself from his grip so I could breathe.

I fought on and on until I felt myself weakening, hands slipping as they sought purchase on the edge of the table.

The doors were thrown open with a crash.

"Jotun," Irdelron said with a chuckle. "What are you doing?"

The hand holding my neck twitched in surprise.

A menacing growl filled the throne room. The Drae was here. There was an almighty crack, and I heard Jotun's painful exhale a split second before his pressure released from my nape. I turned my head to one side, gasping in a sagging heap against the side of the table as crashes sounded around me. I slid off the chair to become a panting heap on the ground.

"Irrik," Irdelron said, "you surprise me."

"Jotun lost his temper again." Irrik's cool voice slid through the room. "He gets less reliable by the day."

"I rather think it was you who lost your temper, my Drae."

I couldn't see any of them, but I could hear the smile in the king's voice. I wiped weakly at the potato mash in my eyes.

Bracing myself for the next battle in the endless war, I pulled myself to my knees and scrubbed at my face, using a square of linen next to the mess of what used to be my meal.

"I know why you kissed her now. Your breath alone doesn't work on her," Irdelron said, stopping next to me. He pulled on the uneven tufts of my hair, rubbing at the bits closest to my scalp. "Such a lovely, lovely color, silver. Wouldn't you say?"

What was he talking about? My hair was cinnamon brown, like Mum's.

He swept past me to his throne. "I'm surprised you even tried to subdue her that way. Dangerous, I should think. Her cries must've been quite dreadful for you to risk yourself with your natural enemy. Or were you wishing for death?"

Jotun stood, brushing the front of his navy aketon, smearing the moisture of whatever he'd landed in onto his uniform. He glared past me to Irrik and kicked at the toppled wooden chairs, some of them broken from whatever Irrik had done to him.

I turned to face the real threats in the room.

Irrik stood frozen behind my chair. The weight of his presence held me immobile. I glanced down and noticed his hands, covered in black gloves, were clenched, causing the veins in his arms to rise with the tension pulsing through him. Black scales popped up on his otherwise smooth skin. He flexed his fingers and rested his hands on the back of the chair.

"My king?" Irrik inquired in the same guttural voice.

Irdelron shook his head. "Oh, come now. I'm not going to punish you. I understand why you hid what she is, but such a risk to kiss her. Should I question your fidelity?"

Irrik clenched, and the wooden chair groaned with the force of his grip. "It's only her blood that can harm me, sire. And neither of us were bleeding."

"Always calculating, my Drae." Irdelron focused his attention back on me. "Did you know?" he asked. "The only way to kill a Drae is with the blood of a Phaetyn? You are Lord Irrik's weakness, dear girl. Not the weakness of heart I expected, one far more useful and . . . immediate." The king smiled indulgently at Irrik. "No more secrets, my Drae. How long have you known?"

Irrik frowned.

"Come now, Irrik. You can either tell me willingly, or I can compel you through the oath. Would you really prefer that?"

Irrik bowed his head, and the back of the wooden chair in his hands broke into shards and slivers. "When I saw her eyes."

He'd known? This entire time?

"And have you been visiting her cell? Have you been pulling up plants?"

Irrik ground his teeth. "Once. I hid them once. I wanted to see how strong she was before I made a hasty declaration without knowing her true worth. I checked on her to make sure Jotun didn't kill her. He tortured her to such a degree, I knew you would want me to check."

Shock sucked the moisture from my mouth, and I sunk into a chair. He admitted to helping me? I needed a drink. I reached for the nearest goblet and gulped the red liquid. It burned my throat, and I coughed and sputtered.

"That's not juice," I said with tears in my eyes.

Irrik huffed behind me and, reaching over my head, grabbed a glass of water and set it on the table near me. He always made me feel the fool.

The king tsked. "Don't lie to me, my Drae. You killed her mother, something I'm most put out about. Why didn't you kill the girl, too?"

I inhaled sharply but kept my mouth closed. I wasn't going to share anything else. Let the king think whatever he wanted.

"Ah," the king spoke. "You were thwarted at the finish line by my soldiers, were you? Do try for honesty next time, Irrik. You know I deplore lies."

It made perfect sense now. Why Irrik had appeared to help me while so clearly hating me. Why he'd brought the bath, new clothing, and bedding. To wash away anything that could give me away and therefore give the king power over him. The sunflowers grew where my blood spilled, and the pumpkins grew after my chamber pot toppled over. My body fluids were the key to making things grow. He hid my identity not to help but to protect himself from the king . . . because my blood could kill him. Lord Irrik wanted to keep the knowledge of the single weapon effective against a Drae *secret*. I'd heard others talk of the Drae's oath to the king, but I'd always assumed Lord Irrik held the same corrupt ideals as our ruler. I'd just glimpsed evidence of the opposite. Or was this part of their game? Trying to understand the twisted relationships in the castle made my head spin.

"I commend you for keeping your enemies," Irdelron waved first at Jotun and then at me while continuing to talk to the Drae, "close."

Irrik took a deep breath, as if resigning himself to something distasteful. "You misunderstand—"

"No, I think not." King Irdelron chuckled again. His gaze came to rest on me, and he reached to the vial of Phaetyn blood around his neck, touching the glass fleetingly as he watched me. "Jotun, you are dismissed. Irrik, the Phaetyn is now your charge. She is the most precious resource we have, and you will make sure you keep her alive and safe while she works the land. I bind you to this by your oath. Tomorrow, she will start in the potato fields, and we shall see just what our Phaetyn girl can do."

A terrifying and unruly sound burst from Irrik's chest. "Sire—"

"It wasn't a question," Irdelron snapped. "Now get out of here before I decide to punish your disloyalty. Take her back to the dungeon."

Irrik barely made a sound as he appeared at my elbow, cold-faced, and grabbed my arm. His fingers wrapped around so tightly pins and needles filled my hand. Just like Jotun. Perhaps they had required training on how to grip people and maximize discomfort. Maybe they got a medal when they successfully demonstrated mastery. I bet Irrik taught a class on it.

Irrik led me from the throne room, easing the brutal pace once we'd left the rows of guards behind us. His grip lessened, too, and he sighed long and hard, sounding weary. With a veiled look toward me, he guided me back to the stairs that led to the dungeon.

As we marched down the steps, I tried to process what had happened. My mind was drowning in information, and I didn't even know where to start categorizing. Jotun hated Irrik, and vice-versa. Irrik hated the king, and vice-versa. Irrik hated me, and vice-versa. Conclusion: Irrik was an A-hole.

"I could really kill you?" I asked with anticipation for ideas that would surely come to mind. I had no idea how my blood was lethal to him, but if it was, I'd happily spare however much it took to destroy him.

"Just try it," he said, not even deigning to look my way. His jaw clenched, and his pulse feathered in his neck.

The scales I'd seen on his arm earlier were gone, but there was an entire patch of black reptilian skin on his shoulder. The scales disappeared under his sleeveless black aketon and then reappeared on his neck.

"Whoa, are you losing it? Are you going to shift?" I asked, reaching up with my free hand to touch his scales. My fingers brushed the small black semi-circles covering his shoulder, and I could *feel* his anger and hatred.

"Don't," he snapped, pushing me away.

I stumbled more from shock than the force of his shove. Had he not held my arm, I would've toppled down the stairs.

"Do that again and you'll regret it," he snarled, black scales covering both arms now.

I followed alongside the Drae-man mutely, reeling. I hadn't just felt his anger and hatred. I had heard him speak, too. Like I did with Tyr.

I'd heard the words *kill her.*

As soon as I heard the outer door close, I counted to twenty. That would be plenty of time for Irrik to disappear up the stairs. If he flew, it probably took less time, like three seconds. *Stupid Drae.*

When he chose, Irrik seemed to be able to work around the king's oath, which told me I'd better do my best not to incur the Drae's wrath, especially when it was only me and him and the potatoes. Whatever power I had over him was lost to me until I understood how to use it. Whatever power he had over me was already being set in motion.

He lacked none of this knowledge.

Which meant I needed help.

I wiped my face on my tattered shift and turned to my best source of information. The wall of knowledge.

"Ty," I called. He hadn't answered me in what felt like days. I couldn't handle another blow today, and terror at him being dead briefly froze me on the spot. I stood at the corner of my cell, holding onto the bars as I called to him again. *Please be alive.* Stretching my arm through, I tried to reach his cell, but my hand met only rough stone. "Ty, are you there?"

"Ryn?" he croaked. "*Drak*, what happened? I saw Jotun drag you out of your cell two hours ago." His already hoarse voice was even raspier. "What's going on? Are you al'right?"

Just hearing the compassion in his voice made tears spring to my eyes. My throat constricted with emotion, with *feeling*, for the man next door to me, who cared.

"I'm al'right. I . . . I just . . ." How could I even tell him without sounding mad? "Where have you been?"

Ty sighed, and I heard him shifting closer. "Unconscious for the most part. Jotun was worked up well and good this time."

I rested my head against the bars. "It's my fault he's doing that to you, Ty. I'm so sorry."

"He does it because nothing makes him feel pleasure, except pain. I don't regret a thing. In fact, I may've mentioned that to him once or twice. He didn't seem to appreciate it."

"You didn't!" I gasped. "No wonder he did a number on you."

"Not my smartest idea, I'll admit." He slid down to the spot by the bars on his side. "So, how've you been? Made any new friends?"

Not quite.

"Let's see," I mock remembered. "At some point, I nearly drowned in a plate of gravy."

"I can think of no better way to die."

I scrunched my nose, contemplating that. "You might be right. I shouldn't have fought back."

"Wait, you're serious?"

Oh boy, was I? I settled into my spot on the ground. "Remember that sunflower I showed you? The one I thought was magic?"

A beat passed before he said, "Do you know how that happened?"

I considered my words. I'd treaded lightly to this point, feeding him only the barest of details, at first because I didn't trust him and then to keep him safe as much as myself. But I was leaving in the morning, and I didn't know when or if I'd be back. I wanted him to know.

"The king says I'm Phaetyn, Ty." The cork was popped, and the story blurted from my lips until I was rambling in the aftermath, attempting to piece it together. "I don't know how. Mum said . . . She said the shampoo was for nits, but she had to have been dying my hair a different color. The king said my hair is *silver*. What the hay? And she kept me out of the gardens all those years, telling me I killed everything. Was she killing everything? Because it couldn't have been me. And if she was doing all those things, she had to know exactly what I was. She hid it, even from me, and Irrik has been hiding it while I've been down here so the king won't use my blood to kill him. Or rather Irrik was *trying* to hide my identity. The king found out, and he's going to send me to work the land. To save it."

I had no idea if what Irdelron proposed was even possible, but I couldn't contest the growth that happened here in my cell, sprouting out of seeds overnight.

"Your mother was Phaetyn?" Ty asked. "She was Phaetyn living here?"

"She could make anything grow," I said. "I guess I know how now."

"It makes sense that Irrik would kill her if she was Phaetyn. I'm surprised he didn't kill you too."

I listened to the drip in one of the other cells and thought back to the conversation I'd overheard between Mum and Irrik.

"Ty," I hesitated before plowing forward. I needed answers. "Would Phaetyn blood kill a Phaetyn?"

"No. Phaetyn blood only kills Drae blood. Everything I know says it would heal another Phaetyn. But I'm no expert."

My heart dropped. I must've made a sound because Ty asked, "What is it?"

"My mother was killed with a Phaetyn blade, though." I floundered. "I don't understand. She wasn't like Irrik. She wasn't Drae."

But why else had he killed her with that specific blade? I was a Phaetyn. If my mother was a Drae, that meant. . . "She wasn't my mother." And if I was the only Phaetyn, then it had been *my* blood on the blade that killed her.

"What do you mean she wasn't your mother?" Ty asked.

I rested my head back, closing my eyes. "I don't know. Y-you don't think my mother was Drae, do you?"

"She hid that she was Drae all those years? Seems . . . impossible."

I shifted on the floor now covered in moss in this corner.

"Well then, I have no freakin' idea about anything," I gritted out in frustration. Ty remained quiet, and I pushed down my temper after a second, adding, "Irdelron mentioned the oath, that he could compel Irrik with it. Do you know anything about that?"

"Irrik was not always as black hearted as he is now. My family was once quite friendly with the Drae race before Irdelron had them slaughtered. Before my parents were killed, my father told me the story of the Drae boy who'd tried to save his people."

I nodded. "I know this story."

"You do?" he asked in his scratchy voice.

It amazed me that after weeks of talking with Ty, I could tell, just by his inflection, what he meant. "About the Drae boy who didn't want to help the king. The one who hid and watched as the king gathered the Drae, killed the alpha and the males, and then threatened to slaughter them all unless a Drae would bind himself to the king."

Mother had told me the story. But I'd never put stock in the story about how Irrik came to be with the king. Because how could a powerful Drae not escape if he wished?

"The king swore the Drae boy could always be loyal to the Drae first and the king second. The boy believed him, what else could he do?" Ty coughed.

"I dunno," I answered. "Sounds like a crock to me."

"A Drae cannot break an oath, Ryn."

"Really?"

"As real as Jotun's dead heart." He coughed again.

I turned my head to the bars. "Are you sick?"

"No, I'm fine. I'm just worried about you." His voice grew hoarser still. "You don't deserve this, Phaetyn or not. I wish I could get word to my friends. But I'm powerless in here. I can't contact anyone."

I stilled. "What friends?"

"I've never told you why I was captured, have I?" Ty asked. "Since we're sharing, I may as well tell you. I was part of the rebellion. High up. Have you heard of Cal?"

My mouth went bone dry, and I worked to moisten it and reply, "Everyone has heard of Cal."

Ty was part of the rebellion?

"There is a man here in Harvest Zone Seven. One who holds a similar position to me, or the position I used to hold. If I could get a message to him, I know Cal would send a team to save us."

"Against the king's guard and a Drae?" I asked doubtfully.

"For a Phaetyn? Yes. I am categorically sure."

"I worked for Dyter," I admitted.

"You know him?"

"I do." What's more, if Dyter was still alive, I knew someone who might be able to get a message to him. But was he alive? For sure, he'd been captured if Irrik had followed us home from The Crane's Nest. "I might have a way to get a message to Dyter." Maybe Tyr could go.

All I could hear was Ty's raspy breathing on the other side. "Tell your messenger to get Dyter to pass this information to Cal: If the rebellion can kill King Irdelron, they'll free Lord Irrik from his oath. The oath is the only thing binding Irrik to Irdelron's will. Without it, Irrik won't stand in their way. He may even join them."

That would shift the balance of power. "How do you know that?"

146

"My ancestors lived by the Drakonia desert. We knew a lot about the Drae, even their blood oaths. I've been a prisoner in this castle long enough to pick up certain things. Irrik hates Irdelron. He doesn't want to be bound to him. Trust me."

Before any of this happened, I wouldn't have believed Ty. Now, I'd seen enough to wonder if he was right.

espite my fatigue, sleep refused to wrap my weary mind in its repose. Ty and I said our goodbyes with plans for me to make contact with Dyter. Silence fell between us after that. I ached to escape into the repose of slumber. I was bone tired, but my mind wouldn't rest.

I was on the edge of the precipice of why. I yearned to understand why Mum had been killed. Why I'd been brought here. And how the puzzle pieces fit together. Yet I was unfailingly sure there was no way to achieve this understanding without losing a piece of myself, or learning something I'd later wish to unlearn. Namely, that my mother was not who I thought. That she'd lied to me my whole life about who and what I was. That she'd made me feel inadequate under the guise of keeping me safe.

For hours, I stared at the crumbling ceiling, listening to the drip down the hallway and wondering when the hurt would stop, or if it would eventually kill me. My cup was full, and one more drop would see it overflow—losing Tyr, having my hope dashed, calling to Ty to find him no longer there.

Where would the last drop come from?

The clank of a key in the lock announced the arrival of a visitor. I was safe, if only because the king had bound the Drae to make it so. I yearned for familiar arms and a familiar smile. Even if it was wrong, I wanted Tyr.

As if he'd heard my call, Tyr glided through the darkness and into my cell.

I rolled to sitting, my heart pounding with emotion I had yet to name.

He knelt next to me, and for a moment I stared at the familiar slope of his shoulders, the curve of his jaw, and my gaze flitted to the bow of his lips. I reached for him.

He didn't ask questions but simply pulled me into his arms and held me close, pressing his warm cheek to mine. Any touching between us in the past occurred after my torture sessions, when I was physically and mentally exhausted, not before. Tyr's kindness had always been a comfort or boon of compassion.

This . . . was different. Like the hug of a friend. But when I thought of hugging Arnik, it was nothing like this.

I heard what happened, his voice echoed in my mind, rough with emotion. *I'm sorry.*

His words carried a weight of meaning. Until then, I hadn't even thought about his involvement. He had to have known to have been so meticulous about cleaning up my blood.

"You knew?" I asked in a whisper. Confusion plagued me as I tried to understand. And then the answer occurred to me. "Irrik was sending you."

The Drae was the only person who'd known before.

He pulled back, and not for the first time I longed to see his eyes. To see into those depths, I was certain, would mean I'd get a glimpse of his soul.

At first, it was by Irrik's order. Then, I saw your strength.

149

Tyr touched my face, and my skin warmed under his fingertips, his hands were ungloved for once. My eyes fell to his lips, and I shook off the direction of my thoughts, though my heart still thumped against my ribs, eager to escape.

"And now?" I asked, glancing into the darkness shrouding the area above his mouth.

He rested his hands on my shoulders. *I come because I need to.*

The air between us tightened, and I inhaled his scent, a combination of sandalwood and something more. He drew closer, and there was no trace of a smile on his face.

Did he watch me from the depths of his hood? Did he look at me with the same wonder I now felt?

"Tyr," I said after a beat. "What's happening?"

The loaded question was not just referring to my bad situation. Something in our dynamic was shifting, and I was uncertain if this was me or him or us. Did I want it to be us?

He looked at me, head tilted in silent question. His hands slid down my arms, and he entwined his fingers with mine.

"Do you . . .?" My insides quailed, the questions battering at me from within. What if he didn't feel the same? I chickened out, choosing the easier option. "I might have found a way to get out."

He released my hands. *What do you mean?*

"There's a man in Harvest Zone Seven," I related. I wrung my hands, unable to let them remain empty. "His name is Dyter. He has connections to Cal. I never thought to contact him," I admitted. "I didn't think the rebellion would care about my capture. I thought Dyter might have, but he isn't the leader, so . . . anyway, my dungeon buddy, Ty, said they'll come if they know I'm Phaetyn."

Tyr nodded slowly, but the rest of him was oddly still, and he kept his hands by his sides.

I took a deep breath and pressed on. "Would you be able to get word to Dyter, the owner of The Crane's Nest, if he's still there? If not Dyter, there is a boy my age named Arnik who might be able to help."

Tyr rested his long fingers on the back of my clenched hands. *They'll be able to contact Cal?*

"I don't know, but it's all I've got."

He grimaced, the corners of his mouth turning down. *Which is more than I have at the moment. Surely, this rebel leader has ample resources at his disposal and will be able to help you.*

I frowned. But the warmth and excitement I'd felt moments ago, churned with confusion. "Help *us*, you mean."

Tyr withdrew his hand, but nodded.

"Tyr?" His very name was weighted with my question. Was he saying he wasn't going to come with me?

He sighed but did not move as I stepped closer. I reached for him again, this time filled with prophetic dread at what I would hear.

There are things which tie me to this place, and . . . I cannot be sure I'll be able to get away.

I opened my mouth to protest but then closed it. I barely knew Tyr, yet, I *did*. He'd cared for me, brought me food and water and clean clothes, but none of these things accounted for the twinge inside at the thought of leaving him behind. Twinge didn't even describe the feeling. No, the idea of leaving him behind gnawed at me, leaving a hollow ached in my chest. Escaping without Tyr would be a mistake and something I'd regret. If not immediately, certainly later. "Please?"

I want to leave, his voice spoke in my mind, and I both felt and heard his earnestness. *But I cannot be sure, and I will not give you false hope.*

"Please, promise me you'll try. I don't . . . I don't wish to leave you here." No one deserved to live in this way, let alone someone as gentle as Tyr.

He brought his hand up to my face, his movement slow, as if giving me time to pull away if I wanted. But I didn't. I stared into the darkness beneath the hood, the air around us charged with emotion.

He brushed his fingertips over my cheek, and I heard him promise.

I give you my word.

"LOVELY DAY FOR IT," I REMARKED, TIPPING MY FACE TO THE SKY.

My new clothes made me brave. That was the only reason for saying such a thing to the Drae in front of me. My new clothes: breeches, a tunic cinched at the waist, and *shoes*.

In addition, the glorious, joyous rays of the sun touched my face for the first time in five weeks. If I wasn't sarcastic about it, I might burst into tears.

"It is a lovely day, considering it's not night," the Drae agreed, in a voice like the embers of a fire.

My insides chilled. I hadn't expected him to reply, let alone agree. Did it mean something?

We trudged down through the dry castle ground. Well, *I* trudged. He was so graceful it looked like he floated. My insides twisted with anticipation as the call to raise the gate was shouted. The gate rose. Just like that, I was out. I couldn't believe it.

"It's not real, you know," Irrik said. He raised his eyebrows as if questioning my sanity.

"The sunshine is real. The fresh air is real." I gave him a derisive look up and down. "I'm here. Seems pretty real to me."

He rolled his eyes and continued his predatory glide on the path. "You know what I mean."

I did. He meant it wouldn't last, and I was painfully aware of that fact. Yet, with only one *person* guarding me out here, and the castle gates growing farther away with each step, pretending was easy.

Overall, this was a step up in my eyes. If I had to be a prisoner, at least I'd be one who had clean clothes and got to go outside.

The thought pulled me up short. There was something utterly wrong with that. To accept the scraps Irdelron sprinkled out while I did his bidding was sick and pathetic. I might be setting out to heal the land, but while I wanted to do this for the people of Verald, Irdelron wanted to do it for himself; For the same reason he did everything—power. More food meant happier people which meant less rebels. The king's goal and mine might be temporarily aligned, but I shouldn't, *couldn't*, lose sight of what Irdelron truly was.

With a heavy sigh, I glanced at Irrik and said, "You're right." To enjoy this day was to be victim to the sickness of what the king was doing to me and to Verald's people. "None of this is real."

Something flashed in the Drae's eyes, and he looked around at the wilted gardens in disgust. "I hate sunlight."

It hates you right back, nightmare man.

"Where are we going?" I asked, taking a huge lungful of beautiful air as we moved down the mountainside towards the flat Quota Fields below.

He tensed as I let out a grateful and long-winded exhale.

"You're much less like a cowering rat in clean clothes," he said.

The barb stung. A lot. Mostly because of the truth therein. I couldn't imagine anyone would want to experience the cruelty that created *cowering rats*. I was equally certain that some people would rather die than become a cowering rat. But I wasn't one of those people. An ugly and sharp shame settled squarely on my shoulders, seeping into my very being. I was alive after a horrible experience, so I knew the answer to the question no one ever truly wanted answered: what kind of person was I at my worst?

Cowering rat.

"You're much less a cowering rat than others I've met in your situation." He scowled. "I'm not sure how you're alive."

He'd meant the words as an insult, I was certain, but nothing else could've made me feel better than his begrudging acknowledgement.

"I'm not sure either," I said gravely. When his scowl deepened, I couldn't help adding, "I'll try to lower myself to your expectations in the future. And you never told me where we're going."

"To the potato fields."

Right. The king had said as much yesterday. *Always potatoes.* I snickered inwardly. "What exactly am I meant to do while I'm there?"

He snorted. "You are asking the wrong person, Phaetyn. Do your plant dance, I guess. I don't give a *szczur*."

I cracked my knuckles. On my own then. He could've just said. *A-hole*.

How hard could it be?

VERY HARD.

I puffed, running up and down the field. I'd already connected my bodily fluids possessed the magic goodness. The king drank the blood of Phaetyn, so it made sense. Of course, he could've used his stores of Phaetyn blood to save the land, but pigs would fly before that happened.

I had no urge to slice my arm open, so I tried fake crying to no avail. I walked around barefoot until I stubbed my toe on a rock. There was no way I was popping a squat with Lord Irrik watching. Spitting seemed to go okay until I used up the moisture in my mouth.

I was hot, tired, and frustrated. I mean, shouldn't I be able to sense the land's feelings . . . or something? But it was just me standing on top of the soil. Ryn vs. dirt, round eight million and fifty-six.

So, sweating it was.

Lord Irrik watched me do field laps from the shade of a wilting willow tree.

"Drae jerk," I wheezed.

"I heard that," he called.

I was too sweaty to care. Places that shouldn't be sweating were sweaty. *Ew. So much ew.*

Giving up for the time being, I zigzagged between the limp potato bushes to the willow tree, hoping the nightmare man would share the shade with me. I rested a hand against the shrunken bark and asked, "What's the penalty if there isn't a field of huge potatoes by tomorrow?"

He sat with his back against the tree, legs extended, rolling a pebble in his hand. His focus remained fixed behind me, but he answered, "I would say you have a week to show the king your skill is worthwhile."

That seemed reasonable. For a person who might have skills.

"Do you think it's working?" I asked after a brief moment, jerking a thumb at the field.

He tilted his head and gave me a flat look before returning his attention to the potatoes.

"I've been sweating," I whined. *Drak* it was hot, and I wasn't relaxing in the shade like he was.

Irrik replied, "Your clothes soak most of it up."

"I've been making sure to shake my body every three laps to get rid of the droplets."

"I saw."

My eyes narrowed at his strangled tone. "Fine. I don't hear you—"

The Drae moved so quickly the cock and swing of his arm was a blur my mind had to later dissect. A muted thunk, like a rock hitting a tree trunk, came from across the field. I whirled and just managed to catch sight of a king's guard falling to the ground. Dead. A hole in his forehead.

My heart tripped for several uneven beats as I put together what had happened. I glanced down at Lord Irrik's hand. Empty. "You—"

His black brow rose. "What?"

I stepped back and glanced to where the dead guard's brown hair was visible over the gentle slope of a mound. My mouth opened and closed several times before I could string together my words. Finally, I said, "You just threw that pebble in your hand and killed a man."

"Yes," Irrik said. "The king instructed me to protect you."

My brain had a difficult time wrapping itself around Irrik killing the guards. Shock made my response slow, and with raised brows, I asked, "Do you think he meant against his own men?"

The Drae curled his lips, and scales briefly appeared, rippling across his chest. In the daylight, they had a different hue, like a neon-blue flickered deep under the surface. "He should have been more specific."

"Is that the only one you've killed today?" I hushed as he stood and dusted off the back of his aketon.

He scoffed and began walking back across the potato field with a silent tread.

I take that as a no.

With a sigh, I made after him in a hobble, but my muscles seized, and I stopped to stretch my calves. Muttering to myself, I said, "I suddenly see how you find wiggle room around your oath to the king."

He was on me with the same speed he'd displayed with throwing the pebble. The Drae snapped his shifted fangs in my face, hissing, "You think the guards are here to protect you? Would you like to wait and see next time? Don't be naive, Phaetyn." Lord Irrik pulled back, and his fangs disappeared. The scales receded, and he spun away, resuming his walk—if predatory stalk could be called that.

My feet remembered how to move before my body remembered how to breathe. I released a shaking exhale, knowing the Drae could hear my fear. He could probably hear my heartbeat anyway, thundering in my ears as it was.

I trudged after the Drae, muscles cramping, but as the sun set and dark descended, fatigue melted into a blissful lethargy that made me feel the closest thing to peace since Tyr left last night. The freedom of being outside at night pulled at me with a need just as strong. No, that wasn't accurate. This need, it was stronger. Undeniable. The dark of the dungeon was no comparison to the tendrils of the twin moons reaching into my chest and soothing the cracks in my heart.

"Do we have to go back?" I asked. "Can . . . can we stay outside . . . Please?"

Lord Irrik stopped his stealthy glide and turned. "You can't escape. Just because it's dark, you won't be able to sneak away."

I rolled my eyes. Everyone knew the Drae was stronger in the dark. I'm sure there was a bit about being able to see super well at night in Mum's story.

"I wasn't thinking about it," I told him, which was true. "I just like the night."

His eyes blinked from human to Drae and back again. "If you make the potatoes grow," he said in his guttural voice I now associated with his partial shifting, "the king will allow it."

I bent over and pulled off my shoes, delaying the trip back as long as I could. *Classic trick.*

"I'm not falling for that. Put them back on."

Muttering darkly, I dragged my grubby feet up the castle path toward the gate, hating the thought of going back inside and down to my cell of torture. I stared at the stars one last time. Our moons hung heavy and pregnant with their glorious silver light. I drank it in, breathing the night air like a starving woman. I closed my eyes and relished the moment—the warm air's caress, the soil on my feet, and the peace in my heart—knowing it wouldn't last.

Lord Irrik's gloved hand circled my arm in the dreaded grip, and I instinctively flinched as the terror he exuded washed over me.

"If we're not back before curfew, Irdelron will punish us both," he said. "Don't ruin your faux freedom on the first day."

While I was certain he was only telling me to hurry because he wanted to avoid punishment, I recognized the comment was more kind than cruel. For once. Maybe Ty was right and there was more to this nightmare jerk than met the eye. With a sigh of resignation, I allowed the Drae to lead me back to the castle.

As we crossed the stone floor, Jotun stepped from the darkened stairwell that would lead to my dungeon cell, as if he'd been waiting for me. His eyes gleamed, and my fatigue became fear at what I knew was coming.

Irrik brushed by the mute torturer, but instead of taking me into the bowels of the castle, he angled us up.

The king had not lied about exalting me.

Irrik didn't return me to my dungeon cell, bringing me instead to a tower room at the top of a thousand steps. Well, maybe fifty, but it felt like a thousand as we climbed higher and higher. My legs were like jelly after my field laps.

"You're not serious," Irrik growled as I stopped for a rest on step thirty. He muttered under his breath, and I caught the words "weak" and "Phaetyn."

Exhausted and a smidgen ashamed of that fact, I stooped over, panting when we reached the top. Irrik shoved the door open and pushed my weakling butt through into a ginormous but sparsely furnished room.

The ceilings were thirty feet high and the room at least that wide. A large bed sat in the far left corner with a sitting area in the opposite far corner. The corner couch was a guesstimated one million times more comfortable than the lumpy mattress I'd slept on until now. There was a rectangular table in front of the velvety sofa, and the only other furniture was a solid dark-wood wardrobe and an empty book-case tucked against a wall. The only wall without any furniture was one made of intricate, interlocking panels that looked like they could open. The rest of the room was large empty space. Because I clearly measured in dungeon cells now, I'd have to say there were at least six cells worth of free space. Double doors near the wardrobe probably concealed a washroom, and the glory of that privacy seemed like the greatest luxury here—but after sweating all my moisture away, I only had eyes for the bed.

Irrik pointed toward the washroom, and I shook my head.

"Bed," I grunted, stepping toward the object of my infatuation.

"Bath first," he responded, and he crowded me, forcing me to take a step closer to the washroom.

I growled at him and pushed him away. "I just want to sleep."

"I didn't bring you here to sleep. This is my room. Wash, and I'll take you to yours."

"Your room?" I said in horror, peering around with new eyes. "Why would you do that?"

Irrik's eyes flashed black.

"Jotun was lurking outside your quarters." Scales erupted down his

159

forearms, and he thrust me back in one powerful movement. The air whooshed from my lungs as my bare feet slid over the smooth stone floor before I lost my balance and rolled the rest of the way, almost to the washroom doors.

I dragged myself into a crouch and looked back.

Irrik was gone.

I blinked, my mind trying to assemble what I was seeing in his place.

Lord Irrik had shifted.

His dragon head was at least four hands wide, his horned crest extending higher than I stood. His scaly hide was as dark as the sky on a moonless night, and he took up the majority of the huge room. He exhaled warm air through his nostrils, so hot it shimmered and steamed, billowing around me. His dark eyes were level with mine, and my heart pounded with acknowledgement they were Irrik's eyes.

I should've been terrified, but the air, much like his persuasion-breath, only warmed me, making me relaxed and a little sleepy. He pushed me toward the doors with his snout, and I batted him with my open hand.

You need a bath, he spoke in my mind.

Talking animals were too much for me right now. "I'm tired," I slurred. "Why can't I just sleep?"

He snorted and turned his head away. I knew what the Drae was saying without him voicing the words. I stank. I'd sweated in the dirt all day. *Of course* I stank. My stink just didn't bother me. In fact, I felt reasonably clean compared to the dungeons, like I was an aired-out rug. Clearly, there was no reasoning with an eighteen-foot Drae. "Fine, but then I'm going to sleep."

He snorted again.

I pushed through the doors then slammed them shut and looked straight at the large copper tub full of water. *Holy pancakes.* I shed my clothing, tripping and stumbling in my haste to reach the liquid bliss. I slipped into the tub with a sigh. The water was lukewarm, but there was no way I was complaining. The water circled and swirled with the intrusion of my body, and I dunked my head under the surface, holding my breath. I let the water pull away my tension along with the dirt and grime. Perhaps there was a little reluctant gratitude to the Drae for making me bathe.

I came back up, gulping at the air, and my eyes inadvertently went to the door. The open door!

Where Lord Irrik stood in his black aketon and breeches.

"Stop looking, creeper." I'd meant to yell, but the words came out in a whisper. "What are you doing in here? Go away."

"You don't want hot water then?" he asked, his lip curling. "I can't very well have you drown yourself, Phaetyn. When you're done bathing, you need to eat."

Nuh-uh. "You said I could sleep."

The Drae raised his brows and replied, "No, you said you wanted to sleep. But you're far too scrawny, and I'll not have you collapse out in the fields because you wanted a few extra minutes of sleep and didn't eat anything."

I glared, wishing I knew a way to hurt him.

"Cover up," he said, drawing closer.

"How am I meant to do that?" I screeched. "I'm naked."

His face paled, and his eyes flashed black once more. Recovering, he averted his eyes with a look of annoyance and approached the bath. I froze as he dipped one of his fingers into the water by my hip. The water nearest to the tip of his forefinger rippled, and the temperature rose to steaming within ten seconds.

I groaned, resting back. "I finally see a point for Drae."

He choked, and I cracked open an eye to check if the sound was somehow laughter. It wasn't. The scales were reappearing rapidly, and he was already back at the doors.

"Thank you. But next time, please do it before I get in," I mumbled.

"Next time don't rush in here and strip off your clothes while I'm shifting back."

"*Next time*, don't throw me in that general direction and then turn into a Drae." I listened and celebrated with a smile when he didn't reply.

"If you want sleep," he said, leaning in the doorway, though he rotated so his back was to me, "hurry up. You're exhausted, and I'm not leaving. If you die, the next decade will be hell for me."

I grabbed a bar of soap and scrubbed, all the pleasure of a steaming hot bath now gone. He didn't *need* to be here, what with his stupid Drae powers. But the living nightmare in front of me probably got off on intimidating me. "I hate you."

Irrik glared over his shoulder. "You've made that abundantly clear. If you don't pick up the pace, I could send for Tyr. Perhaps having him here will help you speed up the process?"

My heart stopped as did my scrubbing. How much did the Drae know? I knew he'd sent Tyr to clean up my Phaetyn blood, but Irrik's tone implied he knew *more*. Did he know things between Tyr and me were changing? Were things changing? Had Tyr said something to him about our meeting the other day? I wouldn't have thought so.

But clearly, Lord Irrik knew enough to threaten me . . . I swallowed and shook my head. The last thing I wanted was to bring the Drae's wrath on someone who had only ever showed me kindness. Whatever Tyr might feel for me, I definitely cared for him. "That won't be necessary. I apologize, my lord. I'll hurry."

Irrik growled another curse in his Drae language and threw a towel on the floor by the tub. "Your continued attention will eventually cause him harm, Phaetyn." He threw a new set of clothes by the towel. "The king will seek to control you through him. Tyr and everyone else you think you care about."

His words strangled me, more so because I could see the truth in them. I was the most important thing to the king. Anyone I tried to contact, anyone I was close to was a way to manipulate me. They would be the ones to pay for anything I did wrong or failed to do right.

"Why bother with the warning? You've made it clear how you feel about me, so why expend the energy and do something nice? You give me a warm bath, make sure I don't fall asleep in it, and then threaten me. Why?"

"I'm fairly certain I didn't threaten you."

"Right. You just said you'd hurt someone that matters to me if I didn't hurry up with my bath. That's not a threat," I said sarcastically.

"You *think* he matters to you, but do you even know him?"

"I know he takes care of me," I snapped. Tyr was kind, gentle, and risked his life to care for me. Unlike Irrik. But the doubt he'd planted nagged at me. I lathered my hands and scrubbed at my scalp and skin. Something inside me burst, and I continued vehemently, "You showed up in *my* room, acted like you wanted to help, but for what? Maybe that was just for Mum, not her stupid Phaetyn daughter, who couldn't really be her daughter if Mum was killed by a blade dipped in Phaetyn blood. Which means my whole life has been a lie, and no one knows the real me, not even me. Then I get beat all the time. *Now*, something good happens to me and you're going to destroy that, too. Of course you are. Drae means death." I'd been half joking when I'd said the words before, but this time they dripped with honesty. "I hate you."

The tub was filled with suds from my vigorous scrubbing, and I'd done all I could to be clean. I wanted to be out, to be done. To have this terrible interlude with the Drae be over and *finally* get some sleep. Finished with my tirade, I huffed my frustration as I reached for my towel.

In a blur of movement, he was at the tub, standing over me. I shrank down, under the suds, cowering from the anger he radiated.

"You think you understand the game that's being played?" he asked in a low voice. "You know *nothing* of betrayal, pain, or real suffering.

You can't fathom what's going on. You say you hate me, but you don't know me. Every single thing I do has a reason. Everything. You? You're a cyclone recklessly acting on emotion and impulse. You're only alive now because of the generosity of others and your Phaetyn powers, but if you continue down this path, you and everyone you care about will be—" He froze and pursed his lips. Then, raising his voice, he said, "You're the worst kind of fool. *Tako mi je žao.*"

"I get it, al'right," I screamed. More and more, every minute, every second, my hate grew. I hated that he was right, and I hated myself for my stupid, selfish actions. I wanted to cry for the hurt I'd caused Mum, Ty, and most likely Tyr, Arnik, and Dyter. I'd been a fool, but I was done. I steeled my heart and swallowed my emotions. They would do me no good here. "Please leave so I can get dressed."

I would do everything the king told me, everything. I would make him think I was the most compliant prisoner ever. I wouldn't ask for anything more than what they gave, and I wouldn't put anyone I loved at risk. I would be patient until the moment was perfect. Then, I'd make sure they all paid.

When I stepped out of the washroom in my fresh clothes, Irrik was barking orders at two guards in the room.

"I said to put it on the table there," he snapped, pointing at the short table by the couch. "Then you can leave." The other guard stood, waiting. Irrik held a scroll of paper in his hands, reading. The first man set a large silver tray down and went to the door where he waited for the other guard.

Irrik snorted, a sound I now recognized as his favorite expression of disgust, and crumpled the paper into a ball. "You may tell King Irdelron I have received his message. I'll only dispose of those I perceive as *immediate* threats to her life. You're dismissed."

The guards eyed the Drae warily, but as they turned to the door, I caught one sneering at me. Gritting my teeth, I tilted my chin up and walked toward the couch where dinner waited. My legs were weak from not eating, and my heart pounded from the exertion of the day. I was determined to eat everything on that tray. Even if I threw it all up later. But my mind wasn't as strong as my body, and four bites into the rich meal, my head swam and my vision blurred.

"I think they poisoned me," I slurred, sliding sideways on the couch. "In the food. I'm dying."

I closed my eyes as my stomach roiled.

I laid my head on the soft cushions and decided this was the perfect place to die. Irrik couldn't be mad at me because I'd been poisoned.

Darkness swallowed me in its arms, and as it claimed me, I heard Irrik say, "You can't be poisoned, *Khosana*."

21

The sunlight woke me, and I stretched with a luxurious slowness as I took inventory. I was whole, my soreness gone thanks to my Phaetyn blood, and I was ravenously hungry. I sat up and looked down at the table for the silver tray with food. But it was on the other side of the room, by the couch.

The couch where I'd fallen asleep . . . and was no longer lying.

I gasped, sure I must still be in a nightmare because there was no way I'd willingly be in Lord Irrik's bed. But I was. Fully dressed, thank the stars, but in his bed nonetheless.

The Drae was gone, and the panels were wide open, exposing a large expanse of sky from a short balcony. I strained my ears to listen, but couldn't hear him in the washroom. My curiosity swelled, and I jumped from the bed and crossed to the terrace.

I could see all of Verald, the main roads snaking through the pale dust of the Harvest Zones. There were small patches of green here and there, dozens of them throughout the kingdom. As I stared, I thought of my mother and her green thumb, and I wondered if those were the places she visited to help. Had I moved dirt at each of these places? Had I sprinkled Mum's special water mix over them? A mix I was fairly certain contained my bodily fluids?

A dark bird pulled into the air from one of the zones, but as the bird neared, it grew, and I realized Lord Irrik was on his way back to his tower. The Drae screamed and beat his wings, and I stood staring in awe. As much as I hated him, I had to grudgingly admit he was beautiful.

He flew closer until he was just beyond the ledge of the parapet, hovering. His breath flowed over me, and I reached out to touch him, caught in some kind of thrall. My fingertips grazed his armored cheek before he pulled away.

The massive Drae dove to my right into the room. The air shifted and the scent of leather, steel, and smoke blew by me. His powerful wings wrapped around his body. The air around his Drae form shimmered. He tucked, rolled, and stood in a fluid motion that spoke volumes of how many times he'd done it.

"You need to eat, Phaetyn." He turned and indicated I follow him with a wave of his hand.

He stood to one side, and as I passed, I risked a glance to assess his mood. His eyes were hooded and dark, his face an impassive mask. A smirk pulled on one side of his lips. "Did you know you sleepwalk? You're lucky it's comfortable to sleep on the ground in my dragon form."

I closed my eyes and grimaced. I'd sleepwalked to his bed? *Mortifying*. At least he'd left and slept on the floor, so he *said*.

"Did you know you shape-shift?" I asked with a quirk of my lips. "But don't worry, you're black, inside and out."

I edged past him to the couch, where I ate the rest of a loaf of bread and a large wedge of cheese for breakfast. And grapes. An entire bunch. And a small bowl of figs.

Irrik disappeared into the washroom then reappeared as I finished my meal.

Wiping my sticky fingers and smiling, I stood and asked as sweetly as I could, "Are you ready for today, Lord Irrik?"

His only response was a narrowing of his eyes that sent my heart racing now that I'd seen his true form up close. His eyes shifted, and his advance became predatory. I scanned the room, but Irrik was positioned between me and the doorway leading to the stairs. The only escape open to me was off the balcony. So not going to happen. Why was he stalking me? I'd pissed him off plenty in the last day. This was nothing in comparison.

He ran toward me, but I was distracted by a pounding on the door. Before I could move, he'd hooked an arm around my waist, and in a heartbeat, Lord Irrik pulled me off the terrace and into the air. I tried to scream as we plunged to the ground, but the fear was trapped in my chest, and I couldn't voice it against the rushing wind. Then Lord Irrik was gone and a black dragon held me wrapped in his powerful claws. My mind caught up enough a few seconds later to tell me nothing about being clutched in the digits of a beast was normal.

Don't be afraid, the Drae said in my mind. *We're landing now.*

I wasn't afraid. Irrik was bound by oath to keep me safe, Drae and human Irrik. The fear that had been trapped in my chest morphed to shock and then . . . joy. Because there was something about the freedom of flight that made my heart light. I wasn't afraid because all I could feel was elation.

We dipped toward the ground, and I closed my eyes, wishing we could stay airborne. But there was no way I was asking, so I bit my lips closed and enjoyed the last moments of flight into the fields.

I opened my eyes. "Why are we here?" This was where I'd worked yesterday.

My jaw dropped.

The uprooted plants were taller than I was, but most shocking were the potatoes attached to them. Piles of *huge* potatoes. The size of pumpkins.

The Drae opened his mouth and let out a low rumbling sound. He reared his head back, stretching toward the sky, and bellowed. Vibrant-blue fire shot out from between his fangs at the massive plants and vegetables to the left of me.

I flinched away from the heat, closing my eyes as the acrid smell singed my nostrils.

When I opened my eyes, Lord Irrik stepped away from the field of ash, past me, to the shade of the beautiful willow tree from yesterday, now double the size and a healthy green from when I'd rested my hand on it. He stooped down to the ground by the trunk and picked up a small bag of potatoes there, a look of grim determination on his face.

"Here," he said, holding them out to me. "You've got about an hour to grow these before the king arrives. I suggest you keep them potato size."

"Why?" Wouldn't bigger potatoes mean more food for the people? Would Irdelron really care if I could grow big potatoes?

A growl rumbled through Irrik's chest. "How much power do you want to give him?"

Only enough to stay alive until I could get away. "Not much?"

He rolled his black eyes. "The more powerful you are, the tighter Irdelron will attempt to tether you."

"You don't trust him." I didn't see how anyone could, but I wanted to hear Irrik's answer.

"I only trust myself. Everyone else will betray you if they have enough motivation."

I furrowed my brow. "And Tyr. You trust Tyr, right?" Irrik sent him down to care for me.

He frowned, and his gaze darted to my lips, making me blush. Finally, he said, "Only to a point."

I'D BEEN JOGGING FOR AN HOUR BY THE TIME THE KING'S CARRIAGE appeared, bouldering down the mountain path and smashing my peace to bits. I glanced toward the rows where Irrik finished burying the potatoes an hour ago. He'd made me roll each of them in my hands and count to ten. How did he know that would help? If he'd known that all along, why was he only sharing it with me now?

My sweat and spit had caused patches of the potato plants to erupt into massive potatoes—that were now ash. I doubted the king would be happy with the large bald patches between them. I'm sure there was a way to make a whole field uniformly luscious and plentiful and *normal*, though I had no idea how to make that happen. It wasn't like I grew up with any instruction. Aside from rolling the tubers in my hands and lying in the freshly overturned dirt—courtesy of Irrik's powerful wings and claws—doing dirt angels, I had no idea how to go about any of this.

—*Phaetyn or Faking?*—

—*Ryn, Last and Worst of Her Kind*—

—*Patchy Phaetyn, Can't Bring Home the Bacon*—

—*Skill-less Ryn, Still Skill-less, Even Though Her Spit is Magic*—

The king's carriage dipped and disappeared in a valley, and I hurried to the revitalized willow tree where Irrik hadn't risen. Silent guards had arrived steadily in the last half hour in preparation of the monarch's visit. Having them watch had been disconcerting, but Irrik barked at me, and I cared more about not having him yell than having them stare.

"Do you think it worked?" I asked, leaning against the willow tree. I rubbed my hand over the bark, staring at how different it was now compared to last night. The pale leaves had darkened to a vibrant green, and the trunk itself seemed thicker. Could I grow it large enough to take over a whole Harvest Zone? That would be cool.

He shrugged, finally deigning to stand, but didn't meet my gaze. "Guess you're about to find out."

I surveyed the Drae, who still had me completely thrown. He'd planted smaller potatoes in the ground to fool the king into believing I was less powerful? But why help me? The only conclusion I came up with was that he either helped or hindered, depending on which suited his agenda. As to what his agenda was, I had no idea. Like no freaking clue.

"Thanks," I chirped sarcastically. "That's super helpful."

Turning toward me, he met my gaze, but his expression remained completely flat. "I wasn't trying to be helpful."

Hinder it was.

We made our way to the king across the overturned dirt, Irrik several steps in front of me as I pushed my feet into the sunbaked dirt. As we neared the king, I stole a peek at his face. *Drak.* My feet tripped over each other. He was pissed. A definite step below his usual mild façade, which meant he was in viper mode. And the worst thing? Jotun was behind him, a cruel smile on his lips as he stared at me.

"The progress seems . . ." the king started as he turned to survey the area, his grimace hardening into a glare. His cold gaze flitted over me to Irrik. "Quite thin."

He held a handkerchief over his mouth and nose as if I smelled bad. I thought back to the last hour. I probably did stink. Served the stupid king right.

"I agree," Irrik replied without glancing my way. "She's lazy."

My mouth dropped open, and I turned to him. I'd been busting my butt! How *dare* he?

The king shifted his attention to me. "Is that so?" He pointed at Jotun and asked, "Do we need to add more incentive?"

I snapped my mouth shut and wiped the glare from my face, bowing to hide my frustration. Mumbling, I said, "I'm still figuring out how it works."

Made more difficult by the Drae who'd burned everything to the ground in the last couple hours to allegedly help me. Only now he was throwing me under a moving cart. Having Jotun here wouldn't help me grow anything, except more hate and bruises.

The king gave me a kind smile, which made my skin crawl instead of offering assurance. "Of course, you are, dear Phaetyn. Of course." He chuckled like I was a niece he held a soft spot for. "Just don't take too long, or I'll have to see if Jotun's brand of motivation is more convincing."

His threat hung heavily in the air between us. As if I didn't have enough pressure on me. *Grow the entire kingdom food, Ryn. Be quick about it, Ryn. I'll torture you if you don't, Ryn.*

Irrik snapped his fingers at a guard in a green aketon. "Dig."

The guard frowned and looked around. The Drae growled and picked up a nearby garden hoe, chucking it at the man. "Dig."

"Where, my lord?" the guard stammered.

"In the ground, you idiot. Anywhere." Irrik pointed at a mound of freshly turned dirt. "There."

The guard hurried over and dug the hoe into the soft soil. He pulled the tool back, and two large potatoes tumbled from within the bunched dirt.

Those spuds were larger than the ones Irrik had put in the ground. Much larger.

"But what's this?" the king neared. "Potatoes." His gaze narrowed, and he pointed. "Dig there." He pointed to a spot where Irrik hadn't buried potatoes.

The guard dug, but nothing came up.

"It only works in patches," I offered lamely. "I'll try to smooth it out."

The king smiled back at the potatoes. "Yes, dear Phaetyn. Do that." His expression smoothed, and he stared at Irrik for several moments before giving a curt nod. "Make sure it works."

Oh, great. I wondered if I was the *it* he referred to. Probably.

I'll get right to work, A-hole.

22

The king clambered back into his carriage with all his silky layers and jewels, but I didn't breathe properly until Jotun and the guards dispersed and the blood-red vehicle was out of sight.

"Next time, keep your mouth shut," Irrik snarled.

Thinking to dig holes by each plant and put a drop of sweat in each, I stooped to pick up the forgotten hoe. I froze before slowly standing, my anger flaring. "Excuse me?"

"You heard me. Don't make me repeat myself."

Glancing back, I opened my lips to retort, but the hoe slipped from my grip, and the edge sliced through my forefinger. Blood welled as I bellowed, "Ouch!"

"*Sto je dovraga*," Irrik snarled in his freaky language and turned to face me. Glaring, he asked, "Are you completely incompetent?"

After a month and a half of abuse, fear, starvation, and grief, I saw red. I swiped my bloody finger over the sharp edge and swung the hoe in a wide, vicious circle, then released it straight at the Drae.

His eyes widened, and my jaw dropped as the tool careened

toward him. Irrik raised his arm to protect his head and the blade sliced into his forearm.

"*Mistress Moons.*" I covered my mouth with my hands, and the hoe dropped to the dirt with a thud.

Irrik ran his fingertips over the deep gash. Black blood dripped down his arm. "Did you . . . just attack me with a garden hoe?"

I was a fool. Irrik was bad, but Jotun was worse. If Irrik died . . . I rushed to him, crying out, "It had my blood on it!" My hands fluttered over the grotesque wound. "Tell me what to do. I don't want it to kill you."

He moved to look at me, a curious expression falling over his face. "You regret hurting me?"

"What? No. Well, killing you, yes." My stomach rolled at the thought of murdering something, some*one*, anyone. "How long will it take to set in?" I asked him, trying to remain calm. "Should we try cutting off your arm?"

Lord Irrik's brows rose. "Cutting off . . . ?" He broke off and threw his head back in laughter. The gruff waves of it rolled across the potato field.

Did Phaetyn blood make Drae go mad first? Would he lose his sanity and go berserk? Would he turn on me?

Irrik continued to laugh, wiping his eyes when his laughter brought tears. He wasn't going mad.

"Well, die then," I snapped, picking up my Drae-killing weapon.

The laughter faded. "Your blood won't kill me, Ryn."

He said my name. Then his words registered, and I gaped in surprise. "What? Yes it does. I'm a Phaetyn. You're a Drae." I lowered my voice. "I'm your weakness."

Lord Irrik glanced away, a shadow falling across the top of his face. "No. It just can't."

"Why?" I pressed. "Does *he* know that?" The king had seemed adamant my blood was the bees-knees of Drae poison.

"No," the Drae said. "If you value your life, you won't breathe a word of it. Not to anyone. To Irdelron, you are nothing more than a drop of water in the bucket, a foolish Phaetyn, and if the—" He glared in affront at my raised hand.

"A drop of water!" My eyes were like saucers. "That's it? I thought for sure I was worth two." Grinning, I dropped the Drae-killer and hustled over to the beautiful willow. The stream it hung over was more of a disheartening trickle, but there was enough for what I planned—what Mum had figured out long ago. A worker's station wasn't far away, and I jogged over and rifled through the spades and pitchforks until I located a wooden pail.

I hurried back to the stream and placed the pail in front of the strongest current—a lazy rivulet. My finger, upon closer inspection, had already sealed, but dried blood still coated the digit. Once the pail was full, I wobbled back to the willow tree and set the pail down.

"What are you doing?" Lord Irrik inquired, standing over me.

Huh, he really doesn't seem to be dying. Add another puzzle to the heap.

"Making magic fertilizer." I stuck my bloodied finger in the water and swished it around, watching as the blood flaked off and dissolved in the cool liquid. Then, picking up my pail of garden juice, I tottered to the nearest row and walked down, dribbling the water on the anemic dirt.

—The Last Phaetyn has the Last Laugh—

—Everyone Respects Ryn After She Does the Impossible—

Maybe I would wait to see if it worked before shouting my victory to every Harvest Zone.

"That was a decent idea," Irrik said from behind me.

I rolled my eyes. "Don't sound so surprised. Anyway, I thought I was incompetent."

"You are. But maybe you won't always be so inept."

Fire-breathing jerk.

For the next several hours, I did the same, substituting good ol' spit when my injured finger was clean. I'd covered around half the rows in the field by that time. I had no idea if this would work or what the best concentration was. I'd have to work on it so the vegetables didn't show up oversized, or we'd have to go through the whole "tricking the king about Ryn's powers" routine again. With that in mind, I began to put less spit in the buckets from the halfway point and less still a few rows later.

After another eternity, I groaned and straightened, holding my hands behind my back to stretch. A cursory glance at the Drae told me he was still alive but asleep, or perhaps he just wished to appear asleep so I'd leave him alone.

The sun showed the time to be around three or four in the afternoon, and I was achy and sore from lugging around a full pail. Not that it mattered how I felt. I picked up the pail for another trip, and my heart panged with memories of helping Mum in gardens not that long ago. I turned to gaze in the direction of Harvest Zone Seven. Did our house still stand empty? Had someone seized the opportunity to move into the empty abode? Was Mum's garden dead? *My garden,* I realized. I knew better now. My mind ran back to all the times she'd poured the bath water in the gardens or soaked blood-soaked rags after I'd hurt myself. What happened to that water afterward? Had it gone into our neighbors' gardens and the other gardens mother had regularly traveled to around the kingdom?

I'd always assumed the ointment she rubbed on my skin when I was hurt was to help me heal. After witnessing how quickly I healed, I knew this couldn't be true. Tyr had used it on me, too, and I made a mental note to ask him when I next saw him . . . *if* I saw him again.

Mum had kept so many secrets from me. Was anything about my childhood true?

The faint clamor of voices broke over the hill a few fields away. I raised a hand to shield my eyes as people appeared—farmers come to work the Quota Fields, by the look of them. They turned my way.

I peered to where Lord Irrik still slept and then back, heart in my mouth. Did I know these people? There were around ten of them. They were coming closer.

After Irrik hadn't killed a single guard today, I had no doubt the king had tightened the rules of protecting me. But I was also sure the new rules wouldn't protect these men and women.

They were getting too close.

I held up my hands in a stop position and thanked the Moons when they halted. One of the men in the middle raised his hand in the air and made a fist.

My body trembled.

"*Arnik*," I choked. Hope burst forth inside me, and I took three steps closer before remembering the fearsome Drae at my back, and what he could do.

If I ran away, he'd kill all of them.

Had Tyr managed to get a message to Dyter or Arnik? Was that what had led them here? Or had word spread about the king, his guard, and the Drae at the potato fields. Had they come to see what was happening for themselves?

I raised my fist in the air, and tears slipped down my dirty cheeks as a grin spread over Arnik's face.

Hope bubbled in my chest, and my desire to escape became a desperate need. I wanted to race to Arnik, to my friend, to the safety and the ignorance of my former life. What if Tyr hadn't spoken to them? I didn't want to rely on anyone else, which meant I had to at least try. I stepped forward, but Arnik and his friends were pointing at the slumbering Drae by the vibrant willow tree. One by one, they disappeared back over the mound until only one remained. Arnik looked at me for another few seconds.

Then he disappeared, too.

"You'll be taken somewhere else tomorrow," Irrik said on the walk back. "And somewhere else the day after. The king wants you working throughout the kingdom."

"What?" Fatigue fled as panic hit me. I'd hoped Arnik would come back. How would he find me again if I was constantly changing locations? How would I get my message to him? "What about the rest of the potatoes? I mean, there are still lots more rows—" I stumbled and fell forward, scraping my palms on the path. I hit it in frustration. Why was nothing working for me? All of it. Everything against me.

Irrik grabbed my arm and pulled me up, but my legs refused to support my weight, and I slumped back to the ground. I'd used up all my energy on the fields. "I need to sit for a minute."

"You're not eating enough," he snarled. "I told you I wouldn't tolerate weakness."

"I had breakfast," I retorted. "I didn't know I was supposed to pack a picnic."

His mouth snapped shut, and he narrowed his eyes as I sat on a mound, but he made no further comment.

Ryn: One. Lord Irrik: One million

I was equal parts dejected and elated after seeing Arnik. Until today, I wasn't sure if he was alive. How had he found me? Had the rebels been trying this whole time? I desperately wanted to be back with him, in safety. Away from this nightmare.

I stared with unseeing eyes at the yellowed grass under my hands, then I dug my hands through the crunchy grass to place my palms against the ground. I wanted to heal the land so it was as beautiful as my mother told me it once had been in her lifetime. I wanted to heal it so people weren't scrounging for food each day and dying of starvation in their beds overnight.

The fountain garden in Harvest Zone Seven rose in my mind,

abandoned and falling apart. That place could be bustling and full of life again if the land would just grow.

If the people weren't so afraid.

Healing the land while evilness sat in the Verald throne wasn't enough. The evilness had to be ripped out by the roots. The king had to die.

And the rebels had to do it.

I pushed my fingertips into the pale, anemic dust we called soil and begged the ground to hear my plans and help me. I begged the land to listen to me, to feel my need and heed it. It was time to feed the people again.

Time to take down the man who crippled them.

I stifled a yawn as I trudged after Lord Broody-pants and snickered at my own joke. *Broody-pants. Classic.* He was extra broody today. I knew his moods well after three weeks in his company, going to field after field, hoping each day that Arnik would reappear. All that time had also left me reasonably confident of which of the Drae's buttons I could push, and when.

He pivoted before I'd finished laughing. "I'm pleased you still find ample amusement in your enslavement. I'm certain Jotun's guards will report your frivolity to him. He, more than anyone, will want to share in the enjoyment with you."

All the humor was sucked out of the air with the mention of Jotun, and I couldn't help a nervous glance around the stone hallway—if the incarnation of evil were present, he remained in the shadows.

I glared at Irrik, hating him for making me feel weak. If he were one centimeter closer, I'd punch him. Maybe. "I was laughing at you," I snapped. "Dimwit."

The Drae clutched my elbow. "I don't see the humor in the joke, *Khosana.*" He wore his usual black aketon, but an equally dark expression was in position on his face today, too. Despite his obvious brooding, the Drae remained alert, his muscles coiled, anticipating attack.

I batted my eyes at him. "Oh, do go on. I *love* when you talk Drae to me."

Reckless. But calculated. Irrik stayed by my side often, and while his words often stung, he'd never hit me. I was pretty sure he acted this way because of how the king controlled him. Everything the Drae did seemed geared to work around the king's orders in some way. Even if what Irrik did made very little sense to me, I could respect his need to thwart the person controlling him.

His eyes shifted, and a low humming rumbled in his chest. He inhaled and shoved me into the wall. I smacked into the stone, my head bouncing off the rough rock. The Drae stood in front of me, his hand circling my throat. "You would do well to remember you are a prisoner here, not a—"

"Lord Irrik." Irdelron's mild voice reached us from around the stairwell corner. "Do not harm my Phaetyn."

Irrik's gaze roved my face, the pad of his thumb stroking the side of my neck. His gaze held me captive as he said, "Yes, my king."

He dropped his hand to my elbow, where he cupped it gently and then tugged me to his side. Without looking at me, he said flatly, "My apologies, Phaetyn." With more sincerity, he added, "And to you, my lord."

Right. Crackbrained Drae. He wasn't fooling anyone with his apologies.

The king nodded.

He was dressed in a white aketon with a golden filigree wrapped up and over his right shoulder, but my gaze zeroed in on the splattered drops of crimson marring the pristine fabric. My thoughts went to Ty and Tyr, my stomach twisting in knots.

I felt immeasurable guilt that Ty was still in the dungeons while I was in daylight. There was no way to know if he still lived without taking a risk and asking Irrik.

Tyr hadn't been in touch since the dungeon, and I'd been left wondering if he was okay and whether he'd reached Dyter with a message. I missed him—a lot—and a growing part of me hoped he missed me, too. I'd never felt anything for a man before, not even Arnik, but there was something with my hooded protector, the tendrils of beginning.

Until I was free of this toxic place though, I shouldn't contemplate anything like that. Not while King Irdelron could use the relationship against me. Because there was no doubt he would.

Irrik tightened his grip and brought my attention back to their conversation.

"Where are you taking her today?" the king asked, looking at me as if I were something to eat instead of being the source of his food.

"Wherever you'd like, my liege."

My skin crawled with Irdelron's attention and I inched closer to the Drae, but his grip kept me rooted at his determined distance.

"My wine cellar is dreadfully bare. Let's have her visit the vine-yards." His gaze met mine with calculated intensity. "I believe that's your old Harvest Zone, my dear."

Irrik's expression was blank stone. The only indication of the emotion humming in his body was his gloved grip on my elbow.

"Take her by her mother's house. There's nothing quite like a trip down memory lane."

I flinched at the thought but kept my mouth shut.

The Drae inclined his head. Still holding my arm, he turned to leave.

"Irrik," the king called, halting our retreat. "Those commands are not up for interpretation. I expect you to respect your oath."

I glanced at the Drae and saw he was battling to keep his form.

Black scales appeared on his skin, and his nails dug into the soft skin on the inside of my elbow. I grimaced, clenching my teeth.

His black talons pierced my skin, and blood seeped from the wounds.

As soon as we stepped out of the hall and into the morning light, I whispered, "Please let go. You're hurting me."

One talon tore through my flesh as he released my arm, and I sucked in a breath as I clenched my inner elbow.

"I'm sorry," he growled in a barely audible voice.

He trembled beside me, trying to hold his human form, and I released my arm grabbing his, instead. I hissed, "Don't you dare shift."

I had no idea what was going on, but I knew if Irdelron detected anything odd between Irrik and me, he'd exploit it or send Jotun to guard me instead. My words were only meant as a warning, but as soon as our skin touched, electricity pulsed between us, and Lord Irrik's thoughts were in my head.

I will fail.

He brushed my hand away and snapped, "Don't touch me. I don't answer to you."

Had I really been considering a reversal of my hate for this turd-twat?

I followed him around the Market Circuit road. We walked through Zone Nine, and then Zone Eight. When we neared Zone Seven, my inner monologue of hate toward the Drae was ripped to a screeching stop.

Words failed me.

Harvest Zone Seven was gone.

Standing in the middle of the surviving road facing outward from the castle, I could see where the rows of buildings of the Money Coil *should* have begun, but the normally clear definition between the Money Coil, the start and end of the Inbetween, and the narrow housing rows in the Wheel where I'd lived were gone. There was nothing. For as far as I could see, there was nothing except the charred land.

Behind me, the Quota Fields remained untouched.

The air was clean and crisp, and the blackened soil damp from last night's rain. I leaned over, pulled off my shoes and socks, and stepped across the invisible line onto the blackened ground.

Shock rendered me speechless, so I said nothing as I traced the now nonexistent paths of my childhood. I went through the Money Coil, trying to remember where the House of Tal had been and wondered if they'd known what was coming. They'd ruled this Harvest Zone on behalf of the king. He hadn't spared *anyone*.

Was anyone alive? Arnik? Dyter?

Was everyone I knew dead now?

I kicked at the piles of ash and wondered if it was better to be burned alive because it was faster than Jotun's torture. I had no idea when I crossed from the Money Coil to the Inbetween and into the area where I'd lived with Mum and the other peasants. My landmarks were gone. Everything was gone.

Eventually, the shock waned enough for me to feel the ache of loss. This zone had been my home. These people had been my family. I wandered through the streets, not even sure if I was standing on what used to be a street or a house.

There was only one creature capable of destroying an entire Harvest Zone with fire. How long had Irrik breathed his fire on my zone? How long had it taken to destroy everything? I closed my eyes and pinched the bridge of my nose.

"When?" I choked on the word and had to ask again.

Irrik stared over the horizon at something only his Drae eyes could see. He didn't answer.

I bent down, grabbed a handful of ash, and threw it at him, screaming, "When? When did you do this?" I shoved him, pushing his rock-solid body uselessly as I continued my tirade. "Why would you do this?" I pounded his chest. "These were good people. You . . ."

My voice broke, and I covered my eyes with my hands. I fought to keep my emotions in check, knowing the king had forced Irrik to bring me here, but my emotions only registered the pain I felt. The pain I'd caused my friends and family by being so careless and stupid.

Lord Irrik put his hand on my shoulder. "The king likes to remind his subjects of his supremacy, Phaetyn, *all* of his subjects. Never forget it, and don't waste your tears here. Save your powers for the vineyards."

I snapped my head up, glaring daggers at the insensitive Drae, but his wide eyes stopped my retort. He rolled his eyes to the side and cocked his head the same way. My gaze followed to where Jotun and several guards stood, silently watching. The chief torturer met my gaze, and his lips curled in a wicked grin that chilled the blood in my veins.

"What are they doing here?" I whispered, my heart pounding in terror of the visible, immediate threat. They were watching us? Would they report this back to the king? Tell him all about how I broke down in response to his power play?

He had Irrik burn down an entire Harvest Zone to show me I was nothing.

I couldn't understand the depravity that required.

Irrik shook his head. "You still have work to do, Phaetyn. I'm done watching you sob all over the place." He grabbed my arm, much higher than where his talons punctured my skin minutes, or was it hours, ago. Even as his fingers circled my bicep, his grip remained as light as a feather. "Let's go."

He led me and our silent entourage back toward the Quota Fields. Because, of course, *they* still existed. Why would the king destroy his food source? He wouldn't. Just the people who worked the fields. Just his subjects. All because he had a shiny new Phaetyn who could do their jobs better. A few less mouths to feed was probably his twisted idea of a solution.

"Here we are," Irrik announced as we crossed from blackened ground to the anemic brown soil of Verald. "Work your magic."

I stared at the skinny vines weaving their way up the wires and old posts. I wondered if there was a way to poison the king through the grapes. Or perhaps make the vines grow fast enough to choke the guards. I stood staring at them, long enough that the rest of the world disappeared.

Icy-cold water hit my face, and I brought my hand up just in time for it to absorb the impact of the wooden bucket.

"Stop," Irrik growled. "You're wasting water, you fool." He picked up the bucket and threw it back at a sneering Jotun. "Go fill it again." Pointing at another guard, he said, "Bring yours here."

The man in the blue aketon was as silent as Jotun, but this man's hair was flaxen and shorn close to his head. His eyes were muddy brown, and he limped as he carried his pail of water.

"Your watering idea is working so well the king has sent you some extra hands." Irrik nudged me and pointed at the cut on my arm that he'd caused when he partially shifted. "Start with that."

The silence as I began was oppressive. It wasn't like Lord Irrik was a Chatty Cathy, but over the last few weeks we'd developed a mutual tolerance for being around each other. Today was different. He was uneasy about something, and that had me nervous.

The silent guards who carried the pails of water made my skin crawl, and as the day wore on, the collisions of their pails or knees with my body became more frequent, making it obvious that the strikes were no accident. No doubt Jotun was behind it. Was it wrong that I felt betrayed by Irrik? I shouldn't have. He was the king's Drae, after all, not mine. But the king had yelled at Irrik for hurting me, so why wasn't Irrik or the king yelling at Jotun's men?

The sun rose in the sky, the heat pounding the moisture from my body. I washed my bloodied arm in pail after pail, until my skin was clean of all traces of the wound. Then I scrubbed my hands, my arms, and my face. I washed my feet in the pails and spit in them. The men kept coming, one after another, giving me no time to rest.

The heat shimmered off the dirt. The day was uncommonly hot, which I rationalized as the cause of my blurry vision. Wavering, I sat down heavily in the dirt, too dizzy to stand. The guards didn't stop their progression, and as they tossed the buckets, I took the additional beating now that I was closer to the ground. My hands and lips were chapped, my thin shift soaked with sweat, and instead of feeling hot, I shivered with chill, which I knew was a bad sign in the heat.

I needed water.

I glanced up in time to see a bucket swinging at my head, but I wasn't fast enough to lift my hands. The metal ring at the bottom of the pail smashed into my forehead, and a burst of stars traveled behind my closed eyelids. I sucked in a breath, and the warmth of my blood trickling down my face was both a curse and a blessing. At least I'd have something for the next bajillion pails of water.

I wiped at the blood, dropping my hand so I could rinse it in a pail.

"You bloody fool," Irrik growled over my head.

I kept my eyes closed and waited for his verbal lashing. At least he was accurate in his assessment today. I *was* bloody. "Next pail."

A roar split the air, followed by a series of crunching sounds, and a shadow blocked the sun's rays. Not nearly as good as a drink, but the shadow offered some reprieve from the heat.

"Next pail," I murmured again, slumping to the ground.

24

*I*rrik crouched beside me, tracing my forehead with his fingers, and he swore in Drae. A cool cloth covered my forehead, and I sighed in relief.

The Drae lifted me, and the space around us blurred as he moved. I mean, *really* moved. Air circulated around my body for a full minute before he stopped abruptly. A moment later, he submerged us in deliciously cool water. It was up to my chin, held as I was in his arms. One of his arms disappeared from beneath my thighs, and a cup was brought to my lips soon after. I greedily slurped the luke-warm fluid, smiling when I recognized the nectar. It reminded me of Ty and Tyr.

Awareness seeped slowly into my consciousness, as I truly realized I was being held by Lord Irrik. In the water. In only my undergarments. How the hay did that happen?

My eyes flew open, but there was only black. "Where am I?" I croaked. "Why can't I see?"

"This is my lair," Irrik said, his voice resonating through my back. "You had heat stroke. It was getting severe."

He had a lair? Why didn't that surprise me? I swallowed back my panic. "Where?"

"I'm going to lift you out of the water. There is an aketon to the right you can wear."

"Wait!" I buried my face in the water, washing the grime away. I opened my mouth to rinse and choked when the taste of nectar hit my tongue instead of the water I'd expected. I swallowed and sputtered as I came up for air. Irrik grumbled in Drae, but I didn't care what he was saying. My mind stuttered on the thought of a pond, lake, or maybe even a river of nectar. "Is this the source of the nectar we drink in the dungeons?"

Silence met my question, and I wondered if he was trying to keep the nectar's source hidden. Given the healing properties, I could understand why. But how come Ty had it, too? "I won't tell. I promise. I just can't believe there's this much of it. I thought it came from a fruit or something. Is it a river?" Then a thought made my mind skid to a halt. "Can it heal the land? It makes *me* feel better."

Lord Irrik coughed. "No."

My shoulders slumped. "Bummer. That could've saved me a lot of spit."

I rolled my shoulders back, relishing in the relief seeping in through my skin. Irrik withdrew his arm from around my waist and pulled away, leaving a hand resting lightly on my arm.

I wiggled and squirmed, splashing a little in the nectar, not even caring that I'd basically drunk my bath water. I took a deep breath and submerged myself, running my fingers through my thick hair still cropped unevenly in clumps but longer than I remembered. I opened my eyes, wishing I could see in the darkness, and jerked when my pale skin began to glow.

Irrik yanked me higher. His eyes were wide, his dark features frozen in shock. In my periphery, I saw a massive cave of jagged black stone, the expanse of it melting into the depths. An inkiness that seemed to go on forever. But my attention was drawn to the Drae standing in the pool of clear liquid.

"Turn it off," he ordered, mottling and shifting into scales the same color as the rock. But pulsing underneath the black plates of skin was a vibrant, electric blue. His muscles tightened, and his chest swelled. The water rippled with his unrest. In a hoarse tone, he said, "If you value your life, stop glowing."

There was nothing threatening in his tone. In fact, the air sizzled with his panic. Just like that, as if my power understood his fear, the pale silvery light was gone and we were lost in the darkness. My mind reeled with confusion. "What was that?"

He sighed. "A Phaetyn is light and life as surely as a Drae is darkness and death."

His grip on my arm tightened, and he drew me closer, before lifting me out of the water. Honestly, I used a similar technique to wash my clothes in Zone Seven. Dunk the tunic, give it a swish, and then pull the drenched tunic out. I felt like a tunic. But as he lifted me out of the water, my thigh brushed his chest. He said nothing as he set me on the stone ledge, but I closed my eyes at the searing sensation caused by the simple touch.

Holy-freaking-Drae.

The water swished and droplets poured from Irrik as he climbed out. I patted the ground, feeling for the aketon he'd mentioned, my skin prickling with energy.

"Here," he said, his gravelly voice a whisper on my neck.

Blushing, I straightened, and he pulled the garment over my head.

Drak. What was wrong with me? Yes, he was hotness with wings, but he was *the* Drae. I delivered a major reality check to myself as I wrapped the ties of the aketon as tightly as possible. The stupid thing was so big I practically swam in it. "What about my clothes?"

He snorted. "They're ruined."

Of course they were. I patted the thin fabric to my body, letting the cloth wick the moisture from my skin, then pulled the bottom hem up to my head.

"What are you doing?" he asked, clearing his throat.

"Drying my hair," I said, words muffled between the folds of fabric. "It's cool in here, and my wet hair is making it worse."

I did the best I could, but my hair was still damp. With a sigh, I let the aketon fall to my knees and turned to the left. "What's next? Did I get my work done? Are we staying here for a while?"

"I'm over here," he said from my right with a low chuckle. "We're going back to Seven. It's only afternoon, and you have several hours of work to finish before we return to the castle at sundown."

I took a deep breath, wishing there was some way to not have to go back. I never wanted to see the damage, *the ruination*, of Harvest Zone Seven ever again. With Seven gone, there was no hope of ever getting a message to Cal, because I had no idea where Dyter would now be or if he was even alive. Which meant Ty's plan was no longer an option. All my hopes for escape had gone up in smoke with those I loved and their homes. I dropped my chin to my chest, sucking in air as I fully grasped the king's blow. He'd swiped away my home and unknowingly destroyed my hope, just like that. I glared into the darkness as determination pulsed through me. I was not going to let him destroy my land, my home, and my family and not pay for it.

"Irrik?" I asked. "Did . . . anyone live?"

He paused. "Most got out." His tone was foreboding, and I knew not to press him further. I didn't need to. *Most got out.* My heart tripped with hope at his words. Maybe Arnik and Dyter had escaped. Perhaps they were still okay.

The time in the pool of nectar had healed my body and rejuvenated me. The news from Irrik regarding the inhabitants of Seven still being alive made me giddy. The darkness offered enough anonymity that I braved a question I'd long wondered. "Is it true about your oath to the king?"

If I could understand this, maybe I could understand Irrik. Here in his lair, I dared to ask him, and in my mind I dared him to answer.

He stood in front of me now. I felt him, his strong presence, the warmth radiating from his chest, reeling me closer. He rested his hands on my shoulders, and I looked up. But I was blind in the darkness. He could've stuck his tongue out at me and I wouldn't know. I chuckled with the ridiculousness of the thought. Warm tingles of energy spread from where his hands were, and my thoughts went to another time when his mouth had been on mine. My heart quickened, and yearned to close the distance, even as warning bells chimed in my head.

"Whatever ideas you have for escape, forget them," he said, his voice husky. He stepped closer, pushing his body to mine as one arm encircled my waist, holding me flush. "Whatever traitorous aspirations you're hoping for, let them go. More than anything, don't trust anyone."

We were playing a game of chicken with our words, and he was pushing me with his body. I swallowed my nervousness and pressed back. My hands slid up his chest, and I smirked when he sucked in a breath. "What about you?" I whispered, playing with the tendrils of hair at the nape of his neck. "Should I trust you?"

Despite the playfulness of my question, it was in earnest. I wasn't ignorant that Lord Irrik had helped me more than once. But his motivation eluded me. Certainly, his game with the king wasn't that twisted. Was it?

The Drae's chest rose and fell against mine. He circled the back of my neck with his hands, setting every nerve ending in my body on fire. He lowered his head, his breath caressing my skin with the sweet smell of the nectar, and I licked my lips and inhaled. Irrik kneaded my neck with his fingertips and spread his hands over my back. With a gentle touch, he massaged my shoulders, working out knots I didn't even know I had. I moaned, and he kneaded harder, down my back, and when his hands fell to my waist, he pulled me to him.

"Especially not me," he said with an exhale.

A stupor blanketed the warning voice in my mind, and I pushed closer, threading my fingers into his damp hair.

Black scales appeared at the top of his chest, the centers pulsing blue. His nose skimmed the soft skin of my neck, tracing under my jaw to my ear. He pushed his lips to my neck in soft kisses. He nipped, and I threw my head back to give him better access.

My mind clouded with desire and want, and the voice of warning faded. I forgot everything else except my need for him. Gripping his shoulders, I begged, "Please."

He growled, a low sound of lustful hunger that called for me to feed him.

"Please," I whispered, standing up on my tiptoes, pushing my body to his as I pulled him to me.

He crushed his mouth to mine.

Energy pulsed between us, a mixture of longing, need, desperation, and something so strong I couldn't even put a name to it. I clung to him as he kissed me, and when my lips were free, I murmured his name, which brought his lips back to me.

"Sleep," he said.

My knees grew weak, and a blissful torpor settled over my consciousness. I reached up in the darkness to touch his face, to caress his cheek, and to touch his lips again.

"*Tako mi je žao,*" he whispered.

I AWOKE WITH A START, LYING IN THE DIRT OUT IN THE VINEYARDS, clutching my arm to my chest. *What the hay happened?*

"Ah, she's awake," Irdelron said.

My arm burned, and I stared at it through bleary eyes. It was slashed. Four deep cuts, evenly spaced, were spread from my shoulder to my wrist on my left arm. The blood oozed in rivulets of maroon, soaking into my borrowed aketon. Irrik cut me? On purpose?

"I see you were right. The vineyard is already much improved in the areas you have used the watering experiment," said King Irdelron.

"Much more could have been accomplished today if Jotun could keep his hands to himself," Irrik said, his face smooth.

Irdelron turned and addressed another. "Do you see? Brutality for its own sake is wasted. This is why he will always be my first and you my second, Jotun."

I risked a glance up. The sun blinded me, and I couldn't see their faces. But I could feel Jotun's hatred as much as I could feel the sun on my face and the dirt on my hands.

"Take him back," Irrik said. "It's difficult enough to get results out of her without having to watch over him and his Druman."

Irdelron's cruel laugh made my stomach lurch. "You mean *your* Druman, Irrik."

My vision returned, but I kept my gaze low, away from the sun's punishing light. I saw Irrik's hands clenched in fists, but he said nothing in response to Irdelron's comment.

"Very well," Irdelron said. "Jotun, it appears you and the Druman aren't needed at this time, after all."

The king moved away and barked, "Back to the castle."

I closed my eyes, remaining silent. What did it say about me that I would happily live with scars on my arm if it meant Jotun and his men would be gone. When I heard the bugs chirp and the birds trill again, I knew the king and his entourage were gone. The pain in my arm was waning, my Phaetyn powers helping to speed the healing process.

"Here," Irrik said, tossing a water skin at me. "Here's some . . . nectar."

I flipped the lid off and took a sip. The velvety liquid quenched my thirst. Its sweetness coated my tongue and slid down my throat. "It seems thicker," I said, "more concentrated."

He snorted. An answer that was no answer. We were back to that again.

"Pour it on your wounds," he said. "Then get back to work."

But I want to know what a Druman is. I watched his dark figure retreat several paces away to a thick wall of green vines dotted with clusters of deep-purple grapes. The vines were thick and at least a head taller than the Drae.

The Drae grabbed a basket and extracted a thin sheet of material from within, spreading it over the ground. Then he sat with his legs extended in front of him, hands propping him up.

Scowling, he stared up at the blue sky.

I wanted to say something, but I wasn't sure *what* to say. Should I be grateful or angry? He'd hurt me, yes, but he'd also healed me. This was all kinds of messed up. I kept my thoughts to myself and dribbled the viscous solution on my arm, rubbing the thick fluid into my wounds. My skin responded, knitting together from the inside out until only a thin pink line remained. I took another draught of the nectar, this time a long one, and let it work its magic from within.

The buckets had been discarded all over the vineyard, and I picked up several empty ones and went looking for a stream.

I shouted my intentions to the Drae, but when he didn't even glance my way, I figured that was consent enough. As I rounded the corner and he didn't stop me, a weight lifted from my heart.

There was no one watching me . . . for the first time in months.

Irrik was around the corner, but still, I was out of direct sight. I burst into a sprint, row upon row blurring in my vision, until I stopped at the end of the vineyard and dropped the pails. I dug my toes into the soil and let the energy of the ground seep through my skin. I lifted my arms to the sky and, closing my eyes, turned around, feeling free for the first time in as long as I could remember.

Faux freedom? Undoubtedly. But freedom from Jotun and the king for one glorious moment was freedom, nonetheless.

"Ryn?"

The voice hit me like a slug to my stomach, and I stopped spinning with a gasp. My gaze locked with his, and I blinked, willing him to not be an apparition of my desperate mind.

Arnik didn't disappear.

He and several other people I recognized were scattered amongst the rows. My eyes widened, and I shook my head and held my finger to my lips. If Irrik heard them, he'd come.

Arnik nodded and tilted his head to the side, toward the rows of still anemic vines.

My heart filled with joy so strong I thought I would lift off the ground. I ran down the row, ducking between the scraggly vines until several rows separated me from the Drae.

When Arnik rounded the corner, I crashed into him and wrapped my arms around his waist. I clung to him, smelling the sunshine of my childhood, the steadiness of his friendship, and the hope of my dreams. He was really here. "You're alive. I didn't know. Zone Seven was burned to the ground, and I didn't know." Tears ran over my cheeks.

"Ryn," he whispered, cupping my face in his hands. "*Drak*. I can't believe it's you." He fingered my hair and looked into my eyes. "You're really here."

He brushed his thumbs over my cheeks, and I smiled at him, ready to burst.

"I have to hurry. We don't have much time," I said. I pulled him down so we were nestled between vines, a poor attempt at stealth considering the sparseness of the crop here.

"What do you mean? You need to come with me, now. I can get you out of here. We'll hide you—"

"It won't work. I-I'm . . ." The word got stuck in my throat.

"You're the Phaetyn," he whispered. "We know. We've been watching you for weeks, waiting for a shot. We've seen what happens to a field after you've been there."

I stared at him. "You know?"

He nodded, smiling. "You're the last Phaetyn, Rynnie. I could hardly believe it. But then I began to remember some stuff your mum used to do, being so meticulous about the water in your house . . ."

"I'm pretty sure she used to make me rub an ointment on that stopped me from healing. I heal really fast."

Arnik swallowed. "You do?"

I could practically hear the questions about to burst from his lips.

"Arnik, listen. You need to get a message to Cal. You need to make sure he knows the king has a Phaetyn in his power. And . . . I met a friend. He said to tell Cal that if the rebels kill the king, the Drae will be free from his oath. That he might join the rebels." I agreed with Ty now. I didn't think we needed to worry about Irrik if he wasn't under the king's control.

Arnik worked his mouth, open, closed, open, closed. Nothing came out.

I glanced behind, aware that sooner or later, Irrik would come after me. When I turned back to Arnik, he was shaking his head.

"What?" I asked.

"How could you know that? How could anyone know that?"

I replayed the last minute in my mind and realized he was talking about what Ty told me about the oath. I understood his doubt, but he didn't know Ty like I did. "His family was raised near the Drae, before Irrik was oath bound. His father told him. Plus, he's been a prisoner in the castle for a long time."

"Wait," he said, drawing back to look me in the eye, "Whose father? Who told you?"

"Ty. He's my dungeon buddy." When Arnik frowned, I amended, "He's in the cell next to mine."

Arnik pulled me close again and kissed my forehead. "*Drak.* I've been sick with worry. Are you al'right? You look like . . ."

He was asking if they'd mistreated me. What could I say to that? Should I tell him of the horror of my dungeon life? If I did, what purpose would it serve, except to make him worry more?

"I'm fine," I lied, dropping my gaze to the ground.

He sighed, his chest pushing against mine with his breath. "I miss you so much, Ryn."

My throat clogged as I thought of my mother, Dyter, and the life I'd had. All of it gone in a blink, along with the rest of Harvest Zone Seven.

"I have to go," I said.

Arnik held me fast.

"It's time to leave, Ryn," Irrik growled, a second before he yanked me out from under the vines. "Tell your lover goodbye."

The ringing note of finality in his voice made me twist to face the Drae. I saw his eyes, cold and reptilian, and I shook my head. "No, Irrik, please."

His jaw widened, and his face seemed to swell, and I knew he was shifting. I *wasn't* letting him kill the one friend I had left. I grasped his half-Drae, half-human face in my hands. Razor sharp fangs sliced through the soft pad of my thumb, and I hissed at the sting.

"No," I pleaded, pulling my hands away. "Don't—that's my only friend, Irrik. Please don't kill him."

His features snapped back to human, and he shoved me away, down into the dirt. "Go home, human. Don't contact her again."

I couldn't watch Arnik leave. I just listened as his running footsteps faded.

"There's work to do," Irrik said.

25

"*W*here are we going?" I asked Irrik. My head was fuzzy with fatigue, and it took me longer than it should've to notice we were taking a different direction through the castle than we had for weeks. He wasn't leading me to my new room. My eyes widened. He was—

"Where are you taking me?" I blurted.

"The dungeon," he said in a cool voice.

"What? Why?" I shrilled, desperately. I remembered the darkness and Jotun's thudding footsteps as he'd come to collect me for more torture. Nearing the edge of hysteria, I tried to reason with Irrik. "I haven't been there for weeks."

Irrik gripped my arm lightly, probably sensing I was about to bolt. "Because, Phaetyn, you must learn that what is given can be taken away just as easily. Today, you spoke to your friend. Do you know what Jotun or the king would've done to him for that? What I'm still contemplating doing? You would be punished, too."

I shut my mouth at his threat against Arnik.

As we wound down the stairs that haunted my dreams, my

thoughts went from Jotun to the other occupants of the prison. I'd be able to talk to Ty. My heart leaped at the thought that Tyr might come to see me as well. The Drae glanced at me with one eyebrow raised, and I wiped my smile away. His previous warnings about showing affection for Tyr rang in my ears.

He swung open my cell door.

Home, sweet home. "It seems bigger than I remember," I said cheerfully.

Lord Irrik rolled his eyes and jerked the door shut, twisting the key in the lock. "Sleep tight."

"Don't let the Drae bite," I finished in a singsong voice.

He paused. "What did you just say?"

I blanched. What *did* I just say? I did not quote a nursery rhyme at him. *Mistress Moons*, please tell me that didn't happen. "Nothing."

The dim light gleamed on his now bared white fangs. "You better hope I don't bite you, Phaetyn."

I held my breath, adrenaline raising my skin in small bumps. His teeth disappeared, and I strained my ears to hear the door down the hall slam a moment later. *Phew.*

"Is that you, Ryn?"

Hearing his raspy voice, I grinned. "Ty!"

"Long time, no talk. How've you been?"

I groaned and sank down against our wall. "Oh, just fabulous," I said, sarcastically. "They put me in a nicer room."

"You sound upset about it. It's worse than here?"

Wincing, I said, "Not really. I just missed you is all." *And Tyr.*

The familiar drip marked the moments before he responded, "I was teasing, Ryn. Maybe someday they'll take me to a better room. Although, nothing could beat this cell for acoustics or morbid ambience. In fact, I'm fairly certain no female could resist it," he rasped.

I laughed. "What about Jotun?"

"He was my first victim."

He trailed off, and I sat in my dungeon cell, unreasonably happy to be there talking to a friend. "I've missed you, Ty."

"Ditto. I can just see you out there singing to the plants and playing in the dirt. Mud lady."

I did not want that to catch on. "I'm not a mud lady."

"Do you wear shoes out in the fields?"

I scrunched my nose. "Well, no."

"Mud lady," he reaffirmed. "Admit it. You love the soil and the life it gives. You love helping the plants grow. You like squishing your toes in the dirt."

A hum left my lips. I supposed I was a mud lady. "Hey, Ty? What's a Druman?"

Ty coughed then asked, "Why?"

"The king mentioned them today. Said Jotun and his Druman didn't need to watch me in the fields anymore. I've never heard the term. You're the most knowledgeable person here with that stuff."

He snorted. "Thanks. As it happens, I do know," he said in his hoarse timbre. "A Druman is half Drae and half human. All are male, all are infertile, and all are ten times stronger than a human. Jotun is Druman—as are most of the king's personal guards. They're the ones dressed in the navy aketons, not the green."

I stared into the shadows of my cell, mouth ajar as I processed this. "Half Drae? But how? There's only one Drae."

Ty made no answer, and my face warmed.

"Oh," I said hastily. "Is that Lord Irrik's choice?" Not that I should care, but for some reason the idea of him intentionally doing that . . .

Ty sighed. "As much as I dislike the scaly bastard, it was the king's doing. At least that's what I was told. Irdelron uses that oath like a collar to control the Drae, slowly tightening it year after year."

I blinked several times as a well of sympathy for Irrik surged inside. Or maybe it should be empathy. He was the last Drae, and I was the last Phaetyn. Who could guess what my fate would be once the fields were healed. I shuddered at the thought. I'd die before swearing an oath to the king that he could use to control me in that way. "How many of them are there?"

"Here in Verald? Hundreds. But the Emperor of Draecon has hundreds, too, if rumor is to be believed."

I whistled low. "That's a lot of children."

"Irrik's been around for a long time, and Emperor Draedyn even longer. Druman are long-lived, too. I believe Lord Irrik hates the sight of them. I'm sure you've seen it. Because of the oath, the Druman answer to the king, not Irrik. The king trains the Druman to be beasts without compassion. They only speak violence. That's why the king has their throats burned with acid, as a reminder that brutality is their only language. *Most* turn out like Jotun."

My attention caught on Ty's slight stress on the word "most."

"Tell me, did you get a message to the outside? Or were you able to make contact with anyone that could pass along the message?"

"I'm not sure if my friend was able to, but I did," I said grimly. I filled him in on my encounter with Arnik that day.

Ty's gravelly voice was tight with excitement by the end. "Ryn, do you know what this means? We might finally get out of here."

Times like these made me realize I had nothing to complain about. Ty had been down here for *drak* knows how long.

"Someone's coming," Ty whispered.

I listened for several moments, but all I heard was the silence of our dungeon. "I don't hear anyone."

Ty didn't reply, but I trusted his judgment. My inclination was to sneak to my mattress and lie down. But I was done being a coward. I took a deep breath. Things were either going to be really good or really bad.

I so wanted it to be Tyr.

A hooded figure loomed at the door, and he rattled the key in the lock. My insides clenched in anticipation, and I cursed the dim light.

But when he stepped through the doorway, I recognized his broad shoulders, his sculpted lips, and his clean-shaven jawline. His lips parted, as if he would speak, and he reached a tentative hand toward me.

"Tyr," I mouthed. With a small sob, I threw myself into his arms, burying my face in the folds of his cloak on his chest.

He locked me in a tight embrace, pressing his lips to my forehead, and then loosened his grip enough to stroke my hair. After two months, it was nearly down to my chin. Silver strands now that Mum wasn't here to dye it.

His long fingers brushed my cheek. *I have missed you.*

My chest filled. "I've missed you, too. You couldn't get up to my room?"

A frown appeared, and he shook his head. Still touching my cheek, he spoke in my mind, *I would never be able to see you up there in the light.*

Initially, I'd thought Tyr was Jotun's cleaning lackey. Then I thought him a guard doing what he could against the king. I'd even wondered if he was part of the rebellion at one point. After that, I found out Irrik sent him to keep my Phaetyn powers secret. But I'd never really thought about how Tyr got in here with all the food and drink, or how he disappeared after with buckets of bloodied rags.

I tipped my head back to see into his hood. Black veiled his eyes like always. I inched my fingers up to the shadow, but though I could trace his face underneath, I could not see through the darkness. This had to be Drae magic. Ty had said that Druman *tended* to be violent beasts. Was Tyr the exception?

Was he Irrik's son?

Tyr picked up my hand and rubbed gentle circles on the inside of my wrist. I tried not to show my reaction to his touch though heat flooded my cheeks.

I was able to get a message to Cal through your old friend, Dyter.

The floor fell away. Dyter was alive. He'd gone to Cal. "Y-you did?"

I couldn't sit still, and I jumped up and strode to the door and back. Fevered hope filled me. I tasted freedom on my tongue. I reached for Tyr, holding his hand in both of mine. "Do you know what this means?"

The corner of his mouth pulled up in my favorite wry smile. He shrugged, and I eyed him in outrage before realizing he was teasing. He caught my hand before I could hit him on the shoulder. *It means the rebels plan to ambush you in the fields soon. Very soon. It is set in motion.*

I'd expected several more weeks spent in the fields, waiting for Arnik to get the message to Cal. But Tyr made it happen. "Like, days?"

Tyr nodded solemnly.

My breath caught. "I can't leave Ty here." Ty, who was probably listening to every word, was my friend. I stared up into the darkness, wishing I could see Tyr's face. "Can you promise to get him out when the king's army goes out to fight the rebels?"

Tyr didn't move.

I whispered, "You'll be coming too, right?" When he didn't answer right away, I squeezed my eyes shut, fearful of the answer I would see in the set of his jaw, or the frown on his lips.

He sighed. *I will do everything in my power to make it so.*

I rested my forehead against his chest. "Why is it that you're saying the right words but I don't believe you?"

Arnik— Tyr ripped his hand away, but not before I caught the word in his thoughts.

My eyes narrowed. "What about Arnik?"

He avoided my gaze, extracting food and nectar from his cloak. A curious thought occurred to me. "Tyr? Are you jealous of Arnik?" I'd never openly acknowledged the growing depth of feeling between us before, and I held my breath as the question slipped from my lips.

His shoulders stiffened, and humor lit within me alongside a tight bundle of nerves in my stomach because Tyr felt jealous over *me*. I held back my wide smile, saying, "Arnik is a childhood friend."

He set the flagon of nectar down and spun in a blur. He cupped my face with his strong hands, his thumbs stroking my cheeks.

My heart thumped in my chest as I stared up at Tyr. I traced my fingers over his lips, and he caught my finger between his teeth. Desire burned low in my belly.

I have wanted to kiss you . . . for so long.

Triumph at his words made me smile, and I stepped closer. "I want you to kiss me, too," I whispered, rising onto my tiptoes. "I've wanted it—"

There was a flash of his white teeth before he crushed his lips to mine. His fingers threaded into my hair, and his other hand dropped to my waist to pull me tight against him.

I gripped his arms, drowning in him. His kiss turned tender, small brushes of his lips against mine, and then across my jaw line and down my neck. I tilted my head back, and I worked my hands up toward his hood. I wanted to run my fingers through his hair, and pull his head down to me. I wanted to wrap myself around him, and feel his heart beat. I wanted to be as close to Tyr as possible for as long as I could, for as long as he'd let me.

I whispered his name, and he pressed his lips to mine. The tender kisses turned desperate, my heart pounding with increased fervor. He nipped my lower lip, and I moaned.

Ryn.

I wasn't a fool. He'd given me no promise he'd join me. If the rebels saved me, I may never see him again. A pounding pressure seized my heart, and I broke off the savage kiss, panting.

My passion fled as reality of what would happen when I left doused me. Looking down at where my hands dug into his forearms, I clung to hope.

"Tyr, I can't leave without you." I choked and stumbled over the words, and my body started shaking. "I'm not leaving without you," I said in a stronger voice. "I'll wait until you can get out."

He shook his head, and the silence stretched.

My hope waned, and then I saw a droplet appear beneath the shadow of his hood.

I lifted a finger to catch it and then leaned up on tiptoes to kiss where the tear had been. His skin was warm under my lips. I would not abandon him. "I'm not leaving without you."

Loud, running footsteps echoed down the hall. We'd missed them in our fear-filled embrace. Tyr lifted his head and then thrust me back, spinning on the spot . . .

. . . and disappeared into thin air.

I gaped at the spot he'd been. I'd already suspected he was Druman, but now I knew for sure. I should feel betrayed, but if Tyr was a Druman, I could understand why he hadn't told me.

The door was thrown open behind me, and I whirled as a panting Jotun stalked into the room. His eyes were bright and his face lit with eager anticipation. He smiled, a cruel jeer, showing yellow-white in the shadows.

I shoved aside the most recent groundbreaking revelation and told myself to focus on the man here to bring me pain.

Days, Tyr said the rebels would be here in days. I couldn't screw this up. I couldn't give anything away. In only a few days, they'd come get me in the fields. But . . . I did have something over Jotun. I straightened and said, "You can't harm me. The king has ordered it."

Jotun stopped in his tracks.

I celebrated my victory but didn't press him further. Oh, but I wanted to. *Jotun, remember that time the king hit you and you whimpered like an animal? Remember the other day when Lord Irrik, the guy you hate who also happens to be your dad, gave you the biggest butt-whipping of all time?* "Jotun, your face is like a masticated, spat out piece of grisly meat."

I smiled at my witty inner dialogue, shrieking in surprised fright a second later when Jotun roared and charged at me.

I glanced down, picked up the chamber pot, and swung with all my might.

No one was more surprised than I when it connected with his head. Jotun's eyes widened then rolled back in his head, and he hit the ground like a sack of rotten spuds. I stared at the chamber pot in shock and then at Jotun. His finger twitched, *I swear*, and I screeched a second time, bringing the pot down on his head again.

"Having fun?" Lord Irrik drawled, leaning against the bars.

I jumped and moved away from Jotun, but the Drae just snorted, eyeing the chamber pot in my hands.

Fire licked up my arms, followed by an intense prickly sensation. I dropped the pot and scratched at my suddenly itchy forearms. My fingertips encountered a row of smooth rolling bumps. *What the hay?*

"Clearly I can't trust Jotun to keep his hands to himself," Irrik mused. He waved me forward. "Come with me. I'll return you to our room."

"*Your* room, and what about the lesson you were teaching me?" *Shut up, Ryn!*

He arched a brow, face cooling. "Would you rather stay?"

"Lesson learned," I blurted. I hurried out of the cell, skin tingling as I brushed past the Drae.

Irrik strode into the cell and searched Jotun, detaching the keys from his belt. Then the Drae joined me in the hall, shut the cell door, leaving Jotun immobile on the floor, and chucked the keys down to the far end of the hall.

I had to say, I almost liked the Drae.

I tried to peer into Ty's cell as we passed, but Irrik placed me on his other side and hustled us down the hall. My arms itched again, and I traced the bumps in the darkness, wondering what they could be.

My heart rate began to slow, and I let out a short laugh. I had just beat up Jotun! I was going to be in a world of pain if he ever got a hold of me alone again, but *drak* had it been worth it to see his twin moons go out like a dampened fire. It made me see how far I had come since my first introduction to the dungeon. Perhaps the bargaining chip I now had gave me power, but I no longer felt like the shredded girl who would only do what was necessary. I didn't feel like I would crawl anymore. At least around Jotun. I couldn't speak for the cold terror the king still instilled in me.

We passed out of the prison, and I held up my forearms to the flickering flame of a torch set on the wall. Smooth, sun-bronzed skin met my eye. I stopped walking and frowned, running my hands over the previously bumpy skin, but my fingers confirmed what my eyes told me. *Odd, I could've sworn . . .*

"What are you doing, Phaetyn?" Lord Irrik growled.

The day was long over, and I gathered the Drae was not pleased at having to attend me this late. His fault for taking me into Jotun terri-tory. "I thought there were bumps on my arms earlier," I mumbled. "Never mind."

He reached me in two steps and turned over my hands.

My heart pounded, and his eyes widened as he ran his finger down my inner arm. I shivered as tingles erupted underneath his touch.

He looked me in the eye. "When is your birthday, Phaetyn?" he demanded.

Avoiding his inky gaze, I tried to free my arms. They were itchy again.

He repeated himself, and I sighed. "I don't know. I don't even know what month it is."

His eyes shifted reptilian again and black scales dusted across the bridge of his nose. "Lunar twelve, day nine."

That meant nearly three months had passed since my capture. "In a little over a week."

I brightened, I loved birthdays. Though as I glanced around, my insides twisted. This year *might* not live up to past years.

Irrik let go and grumbled under his breath in his freaky Drae language.

I brought my arms up. Smooth skin. I shook my head and started after the moody Drae. I guessed his broodiness was my fault. *Again.* This man had serious anger problems. Still, I only had to deal with him for another handful of days. My stomach churned at the thought, and I wasn't sure what to make of the tumult I felt. Over the months, I'd discovered Lord Irrik was not at all what he seemed. Though what he *was* I still had no idea.

It's why I couldn't like him. He was still playing a game with the king.

Putting one foot in front of the other, I steadied myself for the days ahead. I hoped Cal and Dyter had something great planned to outwit the king's Drae because it was going to take a lot more to win than sneaking up to talk to me in a vineyard.

Hope quivered within like an arrow waiting to be loosed from the bow. *But if the rebels' plan worked . . .*

Maybe I'd have a dungeon-free birthday after all.

As we marched up the stairs to his room, my mind whirled. By now, after nearly three months in the castle, I knew the routine: bath, dinner, bed. Irrik was a stickler for routine . . . and cleanliness. Just like Mum, except now I knew *why* they were sticklers for cleanliness.

Jotun and his Druman continued lurking outside my "official" room, and Irrik wouldn't leave me to their mercy there—thank the moons—so this was my "unofficial" room. A fact I'm sure the king was well aware of, seeing as the guards had delivered missives here on several occasions.

I followed Lord Irrik inside, dreaming of the steaming bath water I'd be soaking in soon. Two nice things about the Drae's rooms: I got to bathe and the food was yum. I slept on the couch. Or at least I *started* each night on the couch. Something in my body or brain would click off after falling asleep, and a thread of insanity made me climb into his bed. I liked to think my affinity for his bed was the softness of his blankets. After the same thing happened several nights in a row, he told me it would be easier if I just started there and he slept on the couch. That way he didn't have to move to avoid my *bumbling* sleep-walks. So I guess there were three good things. I'd bumped the king's Drae out of his own bed. I was a force to be reckoned with.

"Go bathe," he grumbled as we stepped in the door. He crossed to the tray and lifted the top to inspect our supper.

I shifted from foot to foot. Normally, he went to the washroom first to heat the bath the servants had already filled. His change in routine wasn't appreciated. Had he forgotten? Why couldn't he forget the routine of waking me at the butt crack of dawn, instead? "Will you please warm the water?"

Irrik remained where he was, back to me. He dropped his head into his hands, shoulders slumped with unseen weight. Several seconds passed as I watched him. He sucked in a deep breath, and with hands on either side of his head, he massaged his temples.

My head had been filled with thoughts of the all-consuming kiss I just shared with Tyr, but in that moment I felt something for the Drae: pity, or possibly compassion. He'd been cruel, but he'd also been kind, even if his reasons were self-serving. I took a deep breath and asked, "Can Phaetyn heal Drae?"

He stilled but remained silent.

Was I suggesting something preposterous? Was it somehow insensitive? The rules that the Drae played by were largely a mystery to me, so I had no idea if what I'd suggested was horribly offensive.

"Look, I'm not being a jerk." *Not this time.* "I want to know if I can help you. You've done some nice things and . . ." I wrung my hands then clasped them to prevent any more dirt falling to the floor. Maybe I *was* a mud lady. "Anyway, if I can do something to help, I feel like I owe you. And don't worry about the bath. I should be grateful . . . I *am* grateful that I get to take one."

Could I sound any stupider? I shook my head and hurried to the washroom. Stripping out of my clothes, I caught the gaze of the girl in the mirror and wondered how Arnik recognized me. I didn't even recognize *myself*. I pulled the tie out, and my silver hair tumbled past my shoulders. Wide violet eyes, framed with thick dark lashes blinked back at me. My skin was still pale, but more like the first blush of tan on toasted meringue. As if the thought of food had called it, my stomach growled.

I looked at the stacks of soaps lining the counter and selected one of my favorites, lavender and mint, and slid into the tub. The water was cooler than I was used to but not unpleasant. I made quick use of my time and had just wrapped a towel around me when Irrik tapped on the door.

"You need to eat," he said.

The reflection in the mirror said I had been eating—enough so my body didn't have that cachectic famine look anymore.

"I'll be right out," I hollered and pulled on my shift and hose. I ran my fingers through my damp hair and opened the door, but I pulled up short.

Irrik blocked my path.

I peered up at him. The confusion marring his features had my stomach twisting in knots.

"What's wrong?" I asked.

He schooled his expression and pointed at the table. "Your supper is ready."

Lord Irrik was officially weirding me out, which was saying a lot because I was pretty sure "weirding" wasn't a word. I was inventing words because my vocabulary had no words for him. "I thought supper was ready when we came in." I raised my brows and continued down the pathway of insanity I was quickly growing accustomed to. "Just like every night." I closed my eyes and bit my tongue to stop my sarcastic comments. "I'm sorry. I don't know what it is about you that makes me say those things."

He chuckled, and the sound stroked my frayed nerves. "At least I always know where I stand with you."

Really? Because he confused the everliving life out of me.

He stepped back from the doorway, and I inched past him, every nerve attuned to his proximity. When he stepped into the washroom and closed the door, I sighed with relief and crossed the large empty expanse to the couch and table. I stared at the high ceiling, trying to collect my thoughts. When that proved useless, I turned my attention to supper.

My silver platter was laden with food.

A large roast of meat, sliced thick and still pink in the center, sat in the middle, surrounded by roasted potatoes the size of my thumb. Yeah, I'm pretty sure those weren't grown by me and my Phaetyn powers. They were way too small.

A small dish of brussel sprouts fried with bacon and a small basket of yeast rolls competed for my attention.

My mouth watered as I looked for my plate. Only there wasn't one. There was one set of silverware and one mug for the flagon of nectar. Which meant he'd intended to leave me in the dungeon all night.

"Why aren't you eating?" he growled, coming out of the washroom not long after, his liquid black hair still glistening with water. He held a towel in his hands and was drying his muscular chest and torso.

Heat crept up my neck, and I averted my gaze. Did I want to? Maybe not. I'm sure Tyr would have something to say if I didn't, however.

—*Lord Irrik—Friend or Foe?* —

—*The Drae—Damned or Demented?* —

—*The King's First—by Intention or by Accident?* —

"Why do you keep saving me?" I asked, glancing back.

He crossed the room to the wardrobe, picked a black aketon from a row of black aketons, and pulled it over his head. It must be so hard for him to decide what to wear each morning.

After fastening the ties, he faced me. His dark gaze pinned me to the soft cushions. Several seconds of silence hung in the air around us, but I was determined to not add anything else to my question. I wanted his answer. I wanted to know *something* about the Drae.

"You continually need saving," he said flatly. Instead of coming to share the food, he went to the bed and perched on the edge. He threw me a dark scowl. "If you don't start eating, I'm going to come over there."

"That's rich," I laughed. "In one breath you tell me you continually have to save me, and in the next you threaten me." I picked up the fork, speared a glistening sprout, and popped it in my mouth. I would miss the food when I left. Waving the silver utensil in the direction of Lord Broody-Drae, I said, "I wish you would make sense. Just once."

I sliced into a piece of meat and dipped it in a creamy white concoction on the tray. I sniffed at the sauce, which had a pungent peppery smell, and took a tentative bite. The richness of the meat and the sauce married perfectly in my mouth. My entire world became the tray for a few minutes, but after several bites in silence, I looked up to see Irrik watching me. Still.

Creeper.

I poured the nectar and took a long drink but couldn't help peeking at him over the rim of the mug.

He raised his eyebrows.

I set the cup down and studied him. "I can't understand you at all. And believe me, I've tried. Nothing you do makes sense. You said you wanted me to learn a lesson in the dungeon, which I assumed would mean Jotun—"

My thoughts skidded to a halt, and I covered my mouth. Him suddenly collecting me from the dungeons. His break from routine. His slumped shoulders. My hunger disappeared, my stomach now filled with the unease of questions I wasn't sure I wanted answers for. In fact, I was *certain* I didn't want answers.

He hadn't warmed the bath water, and I could only guess that meant . . .

"You're not going to try to breed with me, right?" I asked, determined to know my fate. The idea of being intimate with the Drae was terrifying for more reasons than I wanted to consider.

Irrik's features hardened. "Are you asking me this because I didn't heat your bath water?"

"No." *Okay, maybe that was a leap.*

He clenched his jaw. "The king can't make me do that anymore, so no."

I blew out a loud breath. "Thank the Moons for that."

His eyes flashed to Drae slits before flashing back to human. "Just so we're clear, I've never forced myself on anyone. The women, the mothers of the Druman, were all willing." He clasped his hands in his lap and dropped his gaze to them.

I swallowed the rest of my questions, not sure if I believed him. The two women I'd seen him in company with had seemed happy for his attention, sure, but I'd also seen what his freaky breath could do to them. I knew what his kiss had done to me.

"I know what you're thinking," he said.

"Can you read minds?" I asked, rolling my eyes.

He snorted. His most common response to my questions. *Lovely.*

"No, Ryn. Your expression is a clear window to your emotions. I don't think I'd need to read your mind."

Drak. I flinched at his words. I'd have to work on a blank expression, like the one he did so well. And the thought that he could actually read minds was a little terrifying. *Stupid Drae powers.* He ignored my response and continued talking.

"I would never use my Drae powers to be intimate with someone. Never. And there's no way the king can twist the oath to that end again."

Really? "Why not?"

"Because he can't," he growled.

Obviously, I'd touched a nerve. But, knowing the king couldn't make him mate was a relief, for him and for me. I was glad the king didn't have total power over him. Something else was bothering me though after Tyr's disappearing act in the dungeon. I gathered my courage and looked Lord Irrik in the eye. "Is Tyr your son?"

Waves of emotions crossed his face—frustration, sadness, anger—before he slipped his features into the flat expression he wore most. "No. He is not."

I'd learned more this evening than all the weeks of working outside with him.

He ran his hand over the soft comforter on the bed, and his mask slipped. He closed his eyes and took slow deep breaths. His pain and weariness hung in a cloud around him, drifting all the way to the other side of the room, to me. Maybe I wasn't the cause of his current heartache. Maybe his anguish wasn't my fault. But I was certainly adding to it. I'd seen enough over the weeks to know that while Irrik was bound to the king, the Drae was not aligned with the brutality of Verald's monarch.

"I meant what I said. If I can heal you, if there is a way for me to help you, I will." I scratched my wrist, the itching from before returning with pruritic fire.

Irrik shook his head. "You don't know what you're offering."

His gaze dropped to my hands.

I stopped scratching and looked down at my wrist. My fair skin looked normal, but I ran my finger over the rough patch. "Do you know what's causing this? Did I get some funky disease down in the dungeon? If I did, I would've thought my Phaetyn powers would heal it." He said nothing, and I fixed him with a pointed look. "Do you know how to make it better?"

"I'm not certain what it means, but I can assure you it's not a disease. You might find that the . . . nectar helps." He sighed, a tired and melancholy sound. "But it might make it worse, too. I don't have a better answer for you."

"Why do you say it like that? If it's not nectar, what's it called?" It wasn't like I was all privy to the Drae's language.

Lord Irrik chuckled. "You can call it whatever you want, Ryn."

Okay. I poured another mug of nectar and sipped at it. The sweetness brought a diffusion of tranquility with it. I dipped my finger in the clear liquid and rubbed it on the rough patch of skin on my wrist. The itching melted away. "Hey," I said, smiling with the relief of my discomfort. "You were right."

He stood. "If you're done eating, we should get some sleep. Tomorrow will be another long day."

"Why don't you take the bed?" I asked, lying down on the long couch. "You look like you need it more than I do."

He quirked a brow. "Do you mind if I have some supper?"

I blushed, stood, and hefted the tray with both hands. "Sorry," I mumbled. "Here you go."

I carried the tray halfway across the room where he met me. Our hands brushed as we transferred possession of the heavy platter. He quickly adjusted it so he held it underneath by one hand. "You didn't eat very much. Are you sure you don't want anything else on the tray?" With the other hand, he grabbed the flagon of nectar and held it out to me. "You might want this close by, in case your skin disease comes back."

"Hey, you said it wasn't a disease," I shot back. I accepted the flagon, grabbed a roll to nibble on, and then went back to the couch, feeling his gaze on me.

When he was done eating, Irrik extinguished the lights and opened the panels to the night. He drew near, and I watched him in the dark, my heart pounding. He pulled a blanket out of a drawer of the wardrobe and dropped it on my feet.

Seconds later, the bed groaned and sank under his weight. I'd been

217

waiting for this. The obscurity of night bolstered my courage, and I asked my last question in a whisper. "How can I use my Phaetyn powers to heal a person?"

I knew from my mother's tales that the Phaetyns of old could do this—though they were probably much stronger than I was. She'd never told me how, and I wondered if she knew.

He blew out a slow breath before he answered, "How do you heal the land, Ryn?"

I spit, bled, and sweat on it. Was he saying I had to put that on a person? *Sick.* "Hey, but if a Phaetyn is supposed to heal stuff, why is their blood lethal to Drae?"

"Phaetyn are life, and Drae are death. We are able to kill each other. It ensures balance in the realm."

I thought about it. "But my blood doesn't work on you?"

He chuckled. "Apparently not. I thought you were offering to heal me?"

Drak. "Yes, sorry. So, I can heal you—even though you're Drae?"

"Perhaps. I have no idea. I doubt it would harm me, seeing as your blood didn't."

"Do I have to sweat on you?" The idea of running around and wiping my sweat on Irrik was immensely funny. Then another thought made me laugh out loud. "Or spit on you?" I pulled the blanket up over my mouth as I snickered with the thought. Pretty sure he wasn't going to let that happen. Ever.

"I would have to ingest it," he said, his voice as dark as our room.

Eww. "You would have to lick my sweaty body?"

That was disgusting. Like seriously . . . Then my mind actually went there, and I shivered. "But you kissed me before."

"You would have to be willing to heal me," he said, roughly. "I can't take it from you. If I stole another kiss, I wouldn't be healed unless you're willing it to happen at that moment. Otherwise Phaetyn would've always been enslaved by man, right?"

"But the plants in my cell grew, and I wasn't willing them to grow. I just cried or bled on the seeds."

"I don't know. I'm Drae," he said, his voice tight with frustration. "My education is limited. I've told you what I know."

I snuggled under my blanket with a yawn. I'd pushed him far enough. "Sorry," I murmured, then, more quietly to myself, I added, "No need to get your aketon in a twist."

The wind blew, and clouds skittered past the first of our twin moons. I sighed as the night brushed over me, absently scratching at my forearm. The night air up on the top of the king's mountain was much cooler than in the valley, and I wished Irrik's room had a fireplace.

"Are you warm enough?" he asked. "Do you need another blanket?"

I yawned again, but my muscles bunched with the cold. "Is there another? It's really cold with the panels open, but I don't want you to close them."

The bed creaked, but he moved silently across the room, nothing more than a silhouette of darkness. The wardrobe opened, and seconds later a warm blanket settled over me, followed by a third blanket, which effectively trapped the warmth.

I sighed and stretched out beneath the covers. "Thank you."

With the shadows reassuring me and the heaviness of the blankets warming me, I fell into a dreamless slumber.

Morning broke with golden light chasing the darkness from the sky. I sat up, and the covers puddled at my waist. I'd managed to stay on the couch all night instead of sleep-walking to the bed. *Go me.* My stomach rumbled a stern warning.

"I'm starving," I said, stretching to look at Irrik's bed.

The Drae was gone.

I tugged a blanket back over my shoulders as I rose to sitting and saw another silver tray on the table. Hopeful, I yanked the lid off. The smells wafted on the air, and I attacked the food with an intensity no one would be proud of.

After eating and going through my morning routine, I sat back on the couch to await the Drae. I didn't have to wait long.

Irrik roared from outside on his approach, and I ran to the corner of the parapet to watch him land. Only, he didn't. He beat his wings and hovered near the edge of his room.

"Am I in your way?" I asked, ready to duck back inside if he nodded. Could he nod as a Drae? Or did it make him all reptilian when he was in that form? He tilted his head at me, and I wondered what he was trying to say. But then I remembered I'd felt his thoughts before.

I reached and held my hand out, waiting to see if he would let me touch him.

Irrik inched to the side and brushed my hand against the smooth onyx scales.

Come. I want to show you something.

Come where?

He unfurled his right foreclaw.

"You want me to climb inside your razor-sharp talons?" He had to be kidding. I knew the stories. He could cut through trees with those things. And what if he dropped me?

I won't drop you. Come on. You'll like it. I promise.

Right. I climbed into the palm of his upturned claw anyway.

He tucked his wings when I was sitting cross-legged in his claw, and then we dropped. The air blew over me, warming as we descended into the valley. He spread his wings, and we soared. The last flight with the Drae had been short-lived but thrilling none-theless. This one was magnificent. We flew over Verald, and as we circled the king's Quota Fields, I saw patches of lush green there now.

That's you. You're doing that, Irrik spoke in my mind.

I couldn't help the grin spreading across my face. I clambered up and stretched, standing on my tiptoes to stare through his curved talons at the beauty I'd brought to Verald. We flew in a circle, from zone to zone.

Every one that I'd visited was flourishing.

We soared higher. There was still so much barren brown. Occa-sionally, I'd spot a garden or cluster of gardens that held the same verdant qualities of the Quota Fields. I rested my cheek on his scaly hand, and when Irrik dropped lower, I recognized the homes Mum had taken me to. *To help her move dirt.*

I swallowed back the fierce burning in my throat.

It's right that you miss her.

"She lied to me about everything." What did he know? My heart ached for her, and at the same time I felt the sting of betrayal. "She made you kill her."

Perhaps not for the reasons you think.

I wasn't an idiot. "I know it was to protect me, but she still lied. I don't even know if she was my real mother." I felt hurt and betrayed still, but mostly I felt sad. I wanted to talk to her about what was going on. I wanted to hear her laugh. I wanted her wisdom.

You know she loved you. That should be enough for now.

"For now?"

He didn't answer, and all too soon we turned back toward the castle. As we got closer, I saw horses lining up far below, the silent Druman in their navy aketons leading them. Between the horses, a single carriage sat awaiting its occupant, door open and ready. One of the horses nickered, drawing my attention, and a Druman sheathed a wicked blade in his scabbard next to the warhorse.

Pressing my hands to Irrik's Drae skin, I asked, "Where are they going?"

Irrik shielded me from his thoughts. Like closing the folding panels in his room so no one could see into his private quarters, only he was shutting *me* out.

Where are they going? I thought at him, feeling a little foolish.

We dove toward the courtyard, and my breath caught in my chest.

His muscles bunched and twitched, and I closed my eyes, tensing for the bone-crushing impact. Then I was falling. The bloody Drae had dropped me. I was pummeling toward my death. I opened my mouth to scream, but my voice was trapped. My heart pounded, and I berated myself for ever trusting him. Irrik was the enemy, and this was probably just some form of—

I opened my eyes in time to see Lord Irrik snap into his human form as he hit the ground in a roll. Before I could blink, he was up and running.

I crashed into him, and he absorbed my force as we fell to the stone path. I lay sprawled on top of him, panting to catch my breath. "You need to work on your passenger landings."

He pulled me up next to him. *Be brave today.*

I turned to him with a jerk of my head, but his chiseled features were cold, and my questions never left my mouth.

"Lord Irrik," Irdelron drawled. "Your timing is impeccable. I noticed you flying this morning. Is everything in motion?"

"Yes, my liege," the Drae said, inclining his head.

"Excellent. And my dear Phaetyn, your efforts are coming along nicely." King Irdelron smiled as though his compliment were sincere, but the gleam in his eye said otherwise. He waved his hand, beckoning someone. "I've asked Jotun to accompany you to the fields today. The two of you are already well acquainted, so I expect you'll be productive in his company."

Dread filled my soul, and my knees trembled. Jotun was going to *kill* me for knocking him out with my chamber pot. I looked around in panic as my torturer advanced, grinning and carrying a whip. Irrik was drinking from a water skin, ignoring me. The king turned away and barked orders at another guard.

Irrik stepped between Jotun and me, facing the Druman. "If you kill her, she'll be no use to the king or the land. Not that you care or are compelled to listen to me anymore, but Irdelron will be livid. Who do you think he values more out of the two of you?" He turned to me and shoved the water skin at me. "Don't forget to drink while you're out there. You need to be able to spit, Phaetyn."

I narrowed my eyes at him, unsure if there was a hidden meaning in his words. Maybe he was just giving me the water skin.

The Druman mounted their horses, and Irdelron yelled something to Irrik that made the Drae's earlier words clear and my mouth go dry.

"Let's go, my Drae," the king said. "It's time to hunt our enemies."

No! They were hunting the rebels? Why now? Blood drained from my face, leaving a buzzing sensation behind. Why did this happen when I was so close to freedom? Irrik turned to me and then away as he stood apart to shift into his Drae form.

Jotun ushered me in the opposite direction, but I kept twisting to look behind me until Irrik's black form was out of sight.

Jotun hadn't touched me while Irrik was still in view, but the crack of leather announced Jotun's confidence that the Drae was now far enough away. The sting of the leather strip ripped through my thin shift and into the skin on my back. Hate was not a strong enough word for what I felt.

Jotun grabbed my arm and yanked me forward on the road toward the next field. As soon as I recognized our path, I wrenched free from his grip. He rewarded me with another lashing, but the sting of the whip was worth it to have him not touching me.

As I walked across the blackened ground of Zone Seven, I wished Irrik would burn Jotun to a crisp. I'd love to see his face shriveled and scorched from the Drae's fire. I wanted Jotun dead.

My back would be a map of his ministrations within the next hour, and if he kept it up, my strength would drain, too. If the rebels came for me today, I had to be ready to run and have the energy to fight. Too many more lashes, and I wouldn't be able to do either.

The whip cracked against me again, and an almighty roar rocked Verald. Jotun raised the whip for another go, but he blanched and swung about, searching the skies.

Courage swelled with the sound of the Drae, and I couldn't help gloating. "You know Irrik will find out, Jotun," I said. "If not Irrik, I will be sure to tell the king about your mistreatment later. You can flay me now, but you'll be dead by sunrise if you keep at it."

His face twisted, and I crossed my arms over my face as he whipped me again.

The threat was worth a shot. He must be a bit sour over the chamber pot thing. Maybe I'd try the garden hoe trick on him and see if it worked. Ever since my being a Phaetyn was revealed, Jotun had taken extra precautions not to come in contact with my blood. It's probably why he was using the whip and not his gloved fists.

We turned right as we reached the vineyards and entered the infertile fields of Zone Eight for the day. I took off my boots and socks and squished my toes into the ground. *Carrots.* The answer came to me unbidden. Sure enough, a quick search confirmed there were a few green and yellow carrot tops scattered about the pale dirt. The fronds were limp and weak.

I set to work, going between the nearest water source—which was a well between the two zones—and the Quota Field I was working on today. Jotun stood halfway in the middle of the six fields I had to lug water between, monitoring my progress. When I had to pass him, I gave him a wide berth. The king had taken all my usual "helpers," and by the time the sun was high in the sky, I'd only watered a third of the fields with my Phaetyn juice super fertilizer because of the distance to the well. Whenever I bent down to fill another bucket with water, I cast my gaze over the surrounding rolling hills, searching for my friends, wishing for my escape.

How would Cal do it?

When would he do it?

As the sun began to sink in the sky and I reached the last row of the carrot field, I gave a weary sigh and dusted my hands. Clearly, today wasn't the day. I wondered if the sight of Irrik in the sky had scared them off. Waiting until the king had stopped his hunt would be wise, but how long would that take? Weeks? Months? Would there be a rebellion left by the time he was done?

I trudged back across the six fields, past Jotun with my empty pail, keeping more than a dozen feet between us so he didn't add to the wounds on my back. They'd healed hours ago, but the muscles still ached, and I had no doubt the back of my sleeping shift was a bloody, tattered mess. I set my bucket on the ground and lowered the pail down into the well, covertly checking that Jotun was still three fields away. I didn't trust him; he could easily sneak up on me when my guard was down. Pulling up the pail from the well with a muffled groan, I tipped the water into my bucket, taking the opportunity to lean against the well's rocky wall for a brief rest. Taking a few breaths, I blinked at the blurry surface. I'd need to get a drink of the nectar before my next pass. My fatigue was starting to affect my vision again. I rubbed a "clean" part of my hand over my eyes and knelt to sip from the bucket.

The surface of the water rippled.

I frowned and peered at the ground. Tiny granules of dirt were shuddering. As I watched, they began to jump around, and I could feel the reverberation in my feet.

I raised my head as a pounding noise sounded in the distance. Forgetting my pail, I straightened, stomach leaping into my mouth. I scanned the horizon in a circle. In my periphery, I noticed Jotun standing several fields over and doing the same.

Now the smaller stones were joining the surrounding dirt, shaking and bouncing off the ground.

Then I saw them.

I covered my mouth with both hands as I stared past Jotun at the waves of rebels pouring over the rolling hill just by the field I'd worked that day. At the front . . .

"Arnik!" I gasped. This was it. They'd come for me!

Between me and my freedom with the rebels stood six fields, and, more importantly, the Druman Jotun was in the middle. Anger flashed across his face, and he ran toward me.

The bucket tipped back into the well, and my pulse pounded in my ears as I searched the ground for a weapon.

Several rocks were in the dirt, and I scrambled to find one I could use. My palm scraped against the sharp edge of a stone, and I tugged it free of the dirt. The rough edge came to a wicked point, and I pressed the tip into my palm until my skin broke and my blood covered the edge of the black stone. The rebels had just reached the far side of the carrot field. Jotun was far ahead of them, and *fast*. He covered twice the ground they did in the same time. *Half Drae.* He'd be able to cart me away over his shoulder before the rebels even reached me.

His eyes were blazing with a wild edge, and I knew he'd read my intention to resist. I dug my toes into the ground and got ready to throw myself to the side. The roar of the rebels, at least two hundred of them, made my heart thunder, and their courage pulsed with each beat. They were here for me. I *would* do this.

This was my chance. Tyr's chance. Ty's chance.

Jotun's arms pumped by his sides as he drew closer. Twenty feet, ten feet . . .

His hand blurred, and my eyes widened as the leather of his whip sliced toward me. I'd forgotten about his *whip*. I raised a hand in front of my eyes and shouted as pain burned across my forearm a second later. I dove to the side, some part of me remembering to get out of his trajectory despite the pain.

Rolling in a cloud of dust, I gasped and opened my eyes even as I jumped to my feet. But Jotun had stopped, still ten feet away from me. I glanced down and saw the end of his whip wrapped about my forearm, the other end in the dirt.

He lunged for the loose end, and I yanked my arm back, drawing the end to me. Jotun straightened with a growl and *came for me*.

I wasn't fast enough to use the whip.

The air whooshed out of me as he dropped his shoulder and bouldered into my stomach. We crashed to the ground with a force that had me seeing stars. Still clutching the rock in one hand, I wiped at my face with the other. My blood dripped onto my shift, and as Jotun drew his gloved fist back to deal a blow that would certainly finish me, his gaze took in all the blood, and he hesitated.

"That's right, Jotun," I slurred. "My blood kills Drae."

The world blurred, and I remembered all the times this beast had hurt me. He'd nearly destroyed me. Every single one of my horrific memories could be linked to him. My hands shook with the need to rip his life from him. The roaring wave of pounding blood crashed in my ears, and in its wake, the steady beat calmed my heart.

Jotun's gaze met mine, and when I smiled at him, his eyebrows pulled down in confusion for a fraction of a second before his eyes widened in horror . . .

As I drove the sharp edge of the rock deep into his side.

The effect was immediate. Jotun threw his head back and an inhuman roar escaped his lips, echoing his pain as my Phaetyn blood attacked his Drae nature. The sound was a gurgling mess, unable to be more without a voice. He writhed on the spot, caving in on himself, limbs contorted in agony.

I staggered to my feet, still clasping the rock, and ran toward the rebels. Tears coursed down my cheeks as I saw their faces—focused, hopeful, determined.

"Ryn!" Arnik yelled.

I aimed for him, my hope giving me strength to pump my legs harder than I thought possible.

"Arnik!" I was going to make it. A powerful elation burst within me like a dam had been released, and I sobbed with abandon at the sight of my salvation.

Just as a shattering roar split the air.

Cold horror ripped through me with the force of a hurricane.

Terror blanketed the valley, and every living thing held its breath in a brief moment of silent dread of what was coming. From behind the rebels, the harrowing black form of the Drae rose in the distance. Some of the rebels turned to look, and their screams broke the silence. Beating his wings, Irrik covered the distance at a furious speed.

No one could outrun such power, and all the power of the Drae was sworn to the king.

"Run!" I screamed at the rebels, waving my hands, imploring them to heed my words. "Run!" I sprinted for Arnik. "Run, Arnik. He'll kill you all!"

Whether it was my horrified screams or their own survival instincts, the rebels began to scatter in all directions as Irrik roared high above.

All except Arnik.

My chest burned for air as I sped toward him, panic propelling me faster than I'd ever moved before.

Irrik circled once, and dozens of rebels changed directions as he herded them back into the open fields. Then he lined up with the field full of rebels, a molten glow building in his exposed chest.

Dread filled me. His reptilian eyes found mine in that moment, and I screamed, "No, Irrik. Please, don't!"

But the Drae answered only to the king.

He reared back and then threw his head forward, jaws gaping as flames shot from between his fangs. The inferno raced across the sky, blazing toward the rebels. The conflagration would swallow them all.

Arnik was in the firing line. The world blurred as I crossed the distance to him.

The heat was blistering, and a second after I'd wrapped myself around Arnik's frame, fire licked my back. I screamed at the scorching heat, yelling words to Arnik in an indistinguishable torrent as the fire seared my open mouth. *Hold on, Ryn,* I begged myself.

I had to hold on.

As consciousness slipped from my grasp, I rested my head against the back of Arnik's neck. He'd always been my friend. Would I ever see him again? Then darkness filled my vision, and I crumpled into his arms.

Hold on, a familiar voice whispered.

I groaned, rolling onto my back. My head was pounding. *What happened?*

Screams and the roar of fire echoed in my head, and flashes of the inferno burst across my eyelids. The field! My throat tightened. The *rebels.*

The stench of char singed my nostrils, and my throat felt raw. I rubbed the blurriness from my eyes and stared up at dark stones and pale phosphorescent light I knew all too well.

I was back in the dungeon.

"No," I wailed, rolling from my bed. I fell to my knees. "No!"

The tears caught in my throat, and my chest heaved as I knelt in the middle of my dungeon cell. It didn't work. My head bowed, pictures flashing behind my eyes of the consequences of my failure: burning bodies, the acrid smell of molten flesh, moaning screams of *hundreds.*

A sob escaped, and I pushed trembling fingers to my mouth, my body convulsing with the weight of my guilt.

The king's force had left in the opposite direction of Jotun and me. How . . . ?

I closed my eyes as realization dawned on me.

A ploy. The king played us. They'd gone in the opposite direction to lure the rebels out. The king threw out bait, and they'd bitten, coming out in droves.

Tears trailed over my cheeks, and I choked out the worst part, "I was the bait."

I sucked in breath after breath as the horror settled on my shoulders. I couldn't breathe. *Arnik,* I thought. Had he survived? Had Dyter been there? Cal? Had I desolated the entire rebellion because I couldn't bear my enslavement?

I screamed wordlessly, scratching at my head as I saw how selfish I'd been. Hundreds of people died for *me.* I pounded the sharp stone floor with my fists, feeling no relief even when my skin split and blood covered the floor. I would never, ever forgive myself if Arnik had died.

Time passed, and when I'd exhausted myself, I toppled onto my side and wept. How was I even alive? I'd felt the heat on my back. I'd seen what Irrik's inferno could do with my own eyes. It laid an entire Harvest Zone to wreck. He'd torched a field full of potato crops without lifting a finger.

I'd healed myself. How much time had passed?

I remembered Irrik's words: *Be brave today.* I sat up, a new awareness hitting me with fresh revulsion. He hadn't reassured me against Jotun. Irrik's desolate behavior from the night before the attack now made perfect sense. He'd known what would happen. He'd been forbidden from telling. Someone had betrayed our plans to the king.

Mistress Moons. Irrik had known those people were going to die?

But how? There were only three people here: me, Ty, and Tyr. My heart couldn't allow either of them to be the traitor. But I knew what happened to people in the torture room. I knew the strongest resolutions could be shattered under the right duress. I hadn't shared. Which only left them.

Had Tyr betrayed what lay between us to be free of whatever tethered him here?

Or had Ty betrayed our friendship to secure his release from the dungeons at last?

Or was it possible one of Cal's force was a traitor? Maybe. That would be equally despairing but less heartbreaking for me.

"Ty?" I called out.

He wasn't here. He wouldn't have listened from afar as I screamed and pounded the ground until I bled. Why wasn't he here?

I sank to the mattress and remembered all the times Ty had been gone in the past, disappearing and reappearing to no routine. "Jotun comes for me fortnightly," he'd said, but was that true? I had no idea, but my head told me it couldn't be. My mind scrambled for more details. He'd had such in-depth knowledge about the castle, the Druman, Irrik's oath.

Another possibility came to me, one I hadn't contemplated since the first time Ty spoke to me.

Was Ty planted here to get information from me?

I dug my palms into my eyes. I'd fallen for it. He'd mentioned Cal, and I'd tripped over my feet in my haste to tell him everything. I'd ruined my own chances of escape. Tyr was probably being tortured as I sat here in this decaying prison. Fresh tears leaked from my eyes. *Tyr, I'm so sorry.* I hoped he'd gotten away. How could I have been so stupid?

I killed those people.

Whether through my selfishness or through my idiocy.

I killed them.

The door creaked open down the hall, but I didn't budge. I stared at the far wall as shocked numbness settled over me. Madeline had told me to find my corner of strength. But the corner I found early on, the corner full of my people who gave me strength to fight . . .

That corner was gone. I couldn't feel it anymore.

"You've been summoned before the king," Irrik said. His voice was devoid of emotion, but his dark eyes were haunted.

I stood mechanically and moved to the front of the cell. Lord Irrik pushed open the door and let me through. I blinked to break our shared gaze and began walking down the hall.

He'd been beaten. The king's Drae. His face was still mottled with bruises, and he was limping. It had to have taken a force of epic proportions to inflict so much damage on him. I knew the rebels didn't have a chance to get to him, so the king was the culprit. Why? What had Irrik done afterward?

"How long was I out?" I asked in a strange, faraway voice. I told myself it didn't matter. Nothing mattered. I could see the broken girl, and I wanted her to have relief at last.

His reply was hoarse, "Three days."

As I shuffled after him, I said nothing more, and neither did he. We walked all the way to the throne room in silence, up the stairs, past the two lines of guards which I now knew were Druman, through the foyer, and to the double doors.

I couldn't look at Irrik. I couldn't look at anyone. But most especially, I could not look at myself.

Out of the corner of my eye, I saw Irrik open his mouth several times, and I wondered what he was struggling to say. Was it an apology for what he'd been made to do? Or was it a warning of what was ahead?

I reminded myself I didn't care. I didn't want his help, and I didn't deserve any mercy. I placed both hands on the gilded doors but paused when the Drae wrapped his long fingers around my wrist.

Khosana, his voice echoed in my mind, heavy with pain, *I am so sorry. Please, forgive me.*

I peered into his inky eyes, glimpsing the dead look in my eyes in their reflection. He should feel guilty for killing all those people, just as I did. Not replying, I pushed the throne room doors open and walked in.

I passed the table laden with food, and its smell didn't stir my hunger. The rows of guards in the room registered but didn't raise any fear. My hands and face were numb, and my ears buzzed. This game of lies and pain had finally destroyed me.

"Phaetyn," the king greeted in a cheerful voice. "Thank you for coming."

Thank you for serving up the rebels on a platter? I didn't bow when I reached him, just stared at the wall behind the throne without emotion, waiting for him to lead me into the next horror.

"It has been a week of revelations for my kingdom. But I am happy with the result thus far." He tapped a ringed finger on the arm of his gaudy throne. "*Thus* far," he repeated. "All that remains is to find the rebel leader and end his pathetic uprising once and for all."

His words startled me. *They haven't found Cal?*

"Of course, now that we know where to find Dyter, that shouldn't be a problem."

My stomach roiled.

"You look quite defeated," the king crowed, clapping his hands. "After hearing of the little escape plan you'd arranged, I was ready to have Jotun drain you of blood. Then I came to see how I could use your plan to my advantage. Of course, Jotun still hasn't awoken after the injury you inflicted upon him. If not for his human-half, he would be dead, did you know? Your phaeytn blood killed his Drae side." He surveyed me anew. "You have proven to be more resourceful than I ever anticipated, and you have concealed far more than I could have believed." His eyes softened into a mocking expression. "But not everyone is as *resourceful* as you, dear girl. Not everyone feels the same loyalty to their peasant kin." He lifted two fingers. "Bring in the boy."

So he would tell me, would he? He'd reveal the person who had betrayed us all by revealing Dyter's location. He'd destroy the last traces of me by parading Ty or Tyr in front of me. He'd crush my last sliver of love.

I couldn't handle it. I wanted to go on believing Ty had been there for me, and Tyr had gotten free and was working to save me still, not willing to stop until I was safe. I didn't want to know.

But it had to be one of them.

The doors were pushed open behind me, and I heard twin sets of marching footsteps, accompanied by grunts of pain. The person was thrown onto his knees in front of the king and the black hood ripped off of his head.

My chest tightened, and I swayed on my feet. My heart thudded painfully.

"Ryn," he said, spotting me. He wobbled, trembling and shaking as blood oozed from his torn lip, his face a mottled mess of bruises and battered skin. What had they done to him?

What had they done to Arnik?

I lifted my eyes to the king's.

A cruel smile danced across his lips. He held a ringed finger just underneath it on one side. "Not who you were expecting, dear Phaetyn?"

Arnik groaned, and one of the Druman guards kicked him savagely to the ground.

The king stood and sauntered from the dais, radiating triumph. He glanced toward Arnik then faced me. "Your friend has been most accommodating," he said. "We have a number of locations and names that we didn't before. But he doesn't seem to know where the mysterious Cal is."

"I don't know where he is," Arnik mumbled, mindlessly, as blood dripped from his chin to the ground.

The king bent over and patted his cheek. "No, I don't believe you do." He straightened. "You're quite useless to me now." He stepped away from Arnik with a gleam in his eye. "Irrik. At your hand."

My knees shook. "No," I whispered as Irrik moved toward Arnik. "No, Irrik! Please!"

The king laughed. "Why are you pleading with him, Phaetyn? He answers to me and only me."

"I'll do anything," I screamed at the king.

He laughed harder. "You already will, dear girl. You already will."

I sobbed, crying in fear for what I knew would come. Through my tears, I could see Arnik crying, too. I tried to reach him, but two Druman forced me to kneeling. Arnik lifted his head, turning his face toward me, his swollen eyes barely open. Could he even see me?

"Did you ever wonder about us, Rynnie?" he asked, choking on my name. "Did you ever think of us married with children?" He shook as if he knew Lord Irrik was nearing him.

I brushed away my tears, nodding. A long time ago, but I had thought it many times back then.

"Yes," I said, knowing I was misleading him.

"I thought about it all the time, Rynnie," he whispered, voice breaking.

The king's Drae shifted one hand into a massive claw, black talons shining like a scythe.

Arnik's lip quivered. "I love—"

29

$\mathcal{I}$ screamed and closed my eyes as Arnik's head slid from his body and hit the throne room floor with a wet thud.

I heard his body slump to the stone, and I screamed again and again, the image of his head leaving his body seared behind my eyes.

"Shut her up," the king boomed.

Lord Irrik was back with me, his now human hand over my mouth. The same hand that had killed Arnik. I kicked and twisted to free myself. *Get that hand off me,* I pleaded with him silently.

He choked on a breath and removed his hand.

I didn't scream again, but I cried, my shoulders shaking as I grieved, unable to look back toward Arnik. Dead. Another person I loved was gone. I didn't blame him for the information he'd divulged. I didn't judge him for it. He'd been broken, and I'd come close enough more than once to know what that felt like.

Nausea rose in my throat as the coppery smell of his blood permeated the air.

I gagged, and Irrik pulled me farther away from Arnik.

King Irdelron returned to his throne, white aketon splattered with

Arnik's blood. Reclining in the seat, he stretched his legs out and offered me a contemptuous smile. "Do you see?" he asked. "No one can deny me. No one will thwart me. If you don't change your loyalties, Phaetyn, you will meet that same fate."

His threat broke through my mourning like he'd fired an arrow at my heart. I whirled on him, charging forward until Irrik grabbed me around the waist. He held me fast. Unable to break his hold, I leaned forward, screaming, "Why should I care? You've already taken away everything—"

"Everything?" He snapped his question, rising in his throne to glower at me. "How wrong you are, girl. I'm just getting started! This Dyter person will be next. I'm told you once worked for him. Then the peasants' precious Cal. I will find every single person you've ever thought you *might* have cared about, and I will slaughter them. I will not stop until your will is mine."

I stared at Irdelron until the horror inside me spread throughout. Before I'd been numb, but now, with my future laid before me, I broke. Racking sobs tore through my chest, and I made no attempt to stop them. The king already knew how much he'd hurt me. The only punishment I could return now was to make him hear. I sank to the floor and bowed to the power of my grief.

"Take her away," Irdelron barked. "I'm weary of her incessant cries." He wrinkled his nose in disgust as he peered down at Arnik's corpse. "And have someone clean up that mess."

My heart bled for my childhood friend. The deep recesses of my very soul had been torn and crushed. These were shattered wounds that my Phaetyn powers couldn't heal, and I was sick with the depravity of this person. The pathetic excuse of a man who called himself king.

Irrik tugged at my arm gently, but I couldn't look at him. When he lifted me, I buried my face in his aketon and continued sobbing. The silence in the foyer did nothing to halt my harrowing pain.

But when Irrik turned to go to his tower, something penetrated my cloud of despair. I sucked in a breath and shouted, "No."

Irrik's tower was a gilded façade, shielding me from the malevolence of Irdelron's power. It would be wrong to be in a soft bed or couch, to have food, warmth, or comfort. It would be wrong to delude myself that any of those things meant safety or approval. The dungeon offered no such mask. I saw through the faux freedom Irdelron had given me.

"I want to go to my cell," I murmured to the man who had killed hundreds of my people. To the man who'd ended Arnik's life with the flick of one great talon.

I wanted to loathe him, to hate the Drae with everything in me. I wanted to beat him and kill him for the death he'd caused and the blood he'd spilled. But the pain he radiated was mirrored by the haunted look in his dark eyes. I'd seen through the Drae's fearsome mask. Underneath it was the wretchedness of his life in chains. A life that was now mine, too.

We were both of us slaves.

"Why do you look at me like that?" he whispered.

I continued to study him, not sure how to answer.

He pivoted, carrying me as though he held air, and led us down the stairwell toward the dungeon cells, his gaze shifting to me and then away.

"Have you ever tried to resist?" I asked. He wouldn't need me to clarify that I meant the king.

He winced as if my question brought him fresh pain. Ducking his head, he said, "Every time I do, it is worse. Worse for me and for the victim of his brutality."

I furrowed my brow. How could that be? Dead was dead.

"I know the limits of my oath," he said after catching my frown. "The king can't make me kill anyone but those threatening his life or his rule."

Arnik and the rebels had been after both.

"For traitors," he continued. "There is a difference between a quick death and one that is drawn out and painful. When I have attempted to refuse him, the compulsion to act builds and builds until it seizes me and I cannot resist. I have nailed my feet to the floor to try to deny him." He swallowed hard, his jaw tightening. "So, when he gives me a command, and I can choose to make it fast . . ." He turned his face so I couldn't see, but his pulse feathered in his neck.

I couldn't do this. I couldn't imagine living that way for decades, and still . . . *existing*. There would be no part of me left. None. I tightened my hold and closed my eyes, terrified to see his reaction. But I did not want to continue living this way, this sick tortured life. I would live for hundreds of years, just like Irrik. "Will you kill me, if I ask one day?"

He was silent as we continued our descent.

"No." His chest rose and fell, and he said, "I'm sorry. I could never do that."

I nodded. I'd heard Irdelron command him to keep me alive. Even invoking the oath between them.

We arrived at my cell, and tears pricked my eyes as I contemplated the vile eternity before me. A small spark of compassion welled inside, and still in his arms, I glanced at the Drae. "Let me heal you."

Surprise and then confusion flitted across his face before he scowled. "Why?"

I rested my head on his chest, weary beyond measure, and let the steadiness of his heartbeat ground me. I was almost sure his recent injuries were because of me. Much of his behavior had always been a mystery, but I did know, looking back through our interactions, that he'd always decided on the lesser of two evils when he had a choice. Keeping my eyes closed, I told him the truth, "Because even though you are the one to inflict the pain, you are not the creator of it." We were both captives to the king, and for the first time, I felt a connection, an understanding, with the feared Drae. "And because if I heal you, I'll be defying him, just a little, in my own way."

Lord Irrik rested his cheek on top of my head and, to my surprise, he sighed. How very un-Irrik-y.

"Do you know what you're offering?" he asked.

I tilted my head and met his gaze. "Yes."

He set me down and reached around to unlock my cell door. I didn't want to go in. Not just yet.

I raised my hand, resting it on his stubbled cheek, the roughness of his whiskers tickling my palm.

He looked down, and the ghost of a smile crossed his lips. "You're not going to make me lick your body, are you?"

Two tears escaped my eyes, and two more tears chased after them. "I'm sorry I hated you so much. You aren't responsible for his maliciousness."

I stretched onto my tiptoes and pulled his face to mine. I closed my eyes as our lips touched, and I willed him to not only feel better, but to *be* better. The salt from my tears was on our lips, and I urged my Phaetyn energy to go to him, so his bruises would fade and the pain of his wounds would lessen. He sighed again and wrapped his arms around me, and I longed for his heart to be whole and his mind to be clear. He ran his fingers over my cheeks, and I wished for the scars in his heart to be gone and the ache in his soul to find peace.

Except when his lips parted in front of mine, I forgot to will anything and a wave of emotion rushed over me. I lowered with a gasp.

"Ryn," he murmured, touching his forehead to mine, warm breath caressing my face. "What was that? I've . . . I've never felt anything like that before."

I stared at him, having no idea myself, but understanding on some deep level that we'd just shared something beautiful.

His dark eyes were vibrant and pulsing with energy. He was

focused on me in a gaze of what could only be called reverence. His skin was smooth and almost glowing with health. His arms held me close, protectively.

"Do you feel better?" I asked breathlessly.

He nodded, blinking as he clenched his fists and moved his head. "Yes, *Khosana*."

An ache in my chest lightened. "Good."

Lord Irrik took a deep breath, and grim determination took over. "Do you trust me?"

His question caught me off guard, and I hesitated. Did I trust him? Not like I trusted Tyr. How could you fully trust someone who was controlled by another?

"Never mind," he said. "Just . . . If you get out of here, someday, make sure you go to the Zivost Forest. Go out through Zone Two into the mountains. Don't stop until you reach the woods. Perhaps there are still Phaetyn there. They are powerful enough to withstand me if the king finds a way to send me after you through the oath. I . . . I won't be able to hunt you there, and the Phaetyn will train you."

I smiled at him, a sad acknowledgment of my grim reality. "Thank you. That is kind of you, but we both know I won't be leaving."

I walked into my cell and sat cross-legged on the bed. The words escaped before I could stop them. "Is Tyr still alive?"

The Drae pursed his lips and gave a curt nod. "*Toliko vam volim kraljicu.*"

This time I snorted. "I have no idea what that means," I said with a yawn.

But there was one good thing to happen in this never-ending nightmare, at least.

Tyr was alive.

30

The click of a key in a lock awoke me. I sat, disoriented, my sluggish mind dredging up awful images of Arnik's death and a lingering nightmare of Irrik burning me with his terrible fire. But there were other images, too—like me kissing Irrik—that brought confusion. What was I thinking?

My thoughts dissipated when a hooded figure entered my cell.

"Tyr?" I whispered, certain I was still dreaming.

Instead of rushing to me, he waved me to the door, staying outside.

I crossed my cell, and he reached for me, pulling me to him, the bars between us. As soon as our skin touched, I heard his thoughts.

I've been so worried. He brushed his lips to my forehead. *I have no time to explain. Please listen.* When I said nothing, he continued. *My love, you must escape.*

My heart stuttered and I blinked several times. "You love me?"

I have loved you from the first moment I laid eyes on you.

"In the torture room?"

He pressed a whisper of a kiss to my lips. *Before that.*

Tyr loved me. A fierce joy bubbled inside me, and a grin spread across my face despite my attempts to control it. I peeked up at him and lifted a hand to stroke his jaw.

"I love you, too, Tyr." We shared an intense, desperate love born of the constant threat to our lives. My heart was full of this man, and my soul knew him. I sighed. "I'm not leaving without you."

How was it possible that Irrik told me to leave and then maybe a dozen hours later Tyr showed up to let me out? Even in my exhausted stupor I knew they must be working together. "What about you and Irrik?"

Tyr stilled. *What?*

"You heard me. When are you and Irrik going to escape? And what about Ty? Or was he the one who betrayed me?"

Tension rolled off Tyr in waves. When he pulled me to him, I went willingly, though seeing the walls of his secrets more clearly than ever before. Putting my hand to his cheek, I pushed my thoughts at him. *Do you know who betrayed the rebels?*

He nodded, slowly. A clank down the hall made us both jump. Tyr let go of me, set the key on the floor, and kicked it to me.

I stared at the glinting object.

Holy-freaking-Drae. I had a key.

When I looked up, Tyr was gone.

I SAT IN THE DARK AND COUNTED TO ONE HUNDRED AT LEAST A DOZEN times. By then, I felt ready to crawl out of my skin.

I fumbled with the key in the lock for a minute before I heard it click open, and I let out a shaking breath when I stepped through the doorway. I passed Ty's cell, a rumpled blanket on a mattress was the only evidence he'd been there. Curiosity seized me, and I stopped to see if the key would work on his cell.

It did. The door creaked as I swung it open, and I moved into my prison buddy's abandoned space. There was no way to know how long he'd been gone.

I lifted the blanket and discovered a heap of rumpled fabric underneath. I reached down, pulled up the loose fabric, and stared at it in stunned silence. It was a navy aketon.

A Druman aketon.

Ty told me Jotun had poured acid down his throat, and that was why he rasped. But that wasn't why at all. How much of his Druman throat was damaged? Which of the king's Druman had played me the fool? Had he gone back to his Druman buddies and laughed over me pouring my heart out to him about my mother?

I dropped the aketon and nudged it over with my foot. Beneath it was a dagger, the small blade was still in its leather sheath, almost begging me to take it. I scooped it up and swung the belt around my waist.

I glanced down at my pale shift.

"Crap," I muttered. There weren't any female Druman, but the uniform would help me blend in more than what I had on. Disgusted by the thought of wearing anything that had belonged to him, I pulled Fake Ty's navy aketon over my head. The aketon was long and provided plenty of concealment for the dagger belted around my waist underneath.

Perfect.

I crept out of dungeon-buddy-traitor's cell and headed to the stairwell. There, I stood at the bottom, heart pounding, listening for sounds of people descending. No hint of disturbance reached my ears. Swallowing back fear, I gave myself a stellar pep talk: *Run, Ryn. Run.*

With adrenaline coursing through my veins, I took the stairs two at a time. I ran for my life, forcing all the horrendous things that had happened to me—Mum's death, Arnik's death, Ty's betrayal—to the side.

Until I reached the torture landing.

A scream echoed down the hall, one filled with pain and anguish. A scream of bloodcurdling loss, one that petrified me.

For one second too many.

A door opened, and Jotun stalked out of one of the torture rooms, a gleam of malice on his twisted face. Our gazes locked—his momentarily startled to see me—and abhorrence rose so strong I could taste bitterness in the back of my throat.

I smiled back at him. I'd killed his Drae side in the fields. Jotun was *human* now, and still recovering.

I yelled as I charged, dropping my shoulder to deliver as much impact as I could. I thought of Irrik's strength and wished for it. I collided with Jotun, and the air rushed from my lungs as we skidded several feet over the rough stone. I landed on him, and my lip curled as Jotun absorbed the brunt of our fall.

He grunted beneath me, but I didn't give him time to recover. I struck at him with my fists, and when that didn't prove enough, I clawed at his face. Spittle flew from my mouth as I screamed a wordless tirade on him, the sound of someone who had suffered greatly and was bent on revenge. I cried as the nightmares he'd induced crawled and writhed to the surface. He whimpered beneath me. The only sound of pain he could manage—his equivalent of an agonized scream—but I had no pity for the monster who'd inflicted horrific torture on so many—inflicted it and found sadistic joy in it. He deserved to feel the same awful pain. I wanted to deliver it to him.

The dying light caught my tears on Jotun's face and broke through my relentless attack.

I *did* want to deliver Jotun pain. I wanted to draw it out for days. Jotun didn't deserve a quick end.

But I wanted my freedom more than I wanted vindication.

I shifted to pull the dagger from my belt. My eyes widened as I saw Jotun going for a blade at his side. I lunged for the hilt of his weapon, and we wrestled, falling back to the ground. His knee twisted beneath him, and his face contorted. His grip weakened, and I wrenched the dagger from his hands.

Placing my knee in the center of his chest, I drove the blade between his ribs.

Jotun bucked and threw me off. He was only human now and weakened, but he was still larger than me. Rolling away, I clambered to my feet and turned to run toward the stairs, picking up the sound of pounding footsteps.

I took two steps before slowing.

I was too late. Druman filled the passageway as I watched.

I should have run instead of wasting time in Ty's room. *Foolish girl.* I'd lost my chance.

I glanced at Jotun's writhing body, watching blood pour from his mouth as he flailed, until he stopped moving forever. *My sacrifice hasn't been for nothing.* I tilted my chin, strength burning within. A monster was gone from the world, and I was the one to banish him to death.

I stood and marched to meet the Druman rushing toward me.

I expected to be taken to a torture room or my cell. But my blood chilled as the Druman corralled me the rest of the way up the stairs, herding me back to the throne room.

As we exited the stairwell, the ring of Druman surrounding me parted and I came face-to-face with Lord Irrik. The air sizzled between us as he stopped directly in front of me. His eyes flashed with a molten fire I couldn't decipher.

He pushed past me and slammed his fist into the wall. He roared as he punched the wall repeatedly, and with his final blow, he simply asked, "How?"

The ground shook with the force, but his question wasn't for me, or the Druman, apparently. He stomped off, snarling in his guttural Drae language.

A bruising shove had me dutifully following the mass of Druman into the throne room. As soon as I crossed the threshold, I knew something was different. It took me a moment to spot it.

The massive quantities of food were gone. The tables laid bare and pushed to one side of the room, stacked one on top of another, much like Dyter had stacked the stools at The Crane's Nest. But the difference wasn't just the lack of false gaiety in the ambiance or lack of food on the tables. The air in the throne room was heavy with a thick expectancy, a dark anticipation, a shivering *tension*.

I thought I was marching to my death, and I'd been at peace. But that was shattered as I saw who stood amidst another group of armed Druman.

I'd forgotten the king's threats until my eyes locked on the only person I had left from my former life. I stared at my friend and mentor, lips numbing.

31

*U*nlike Arnik, Dyter was unmarred of any signs of recent torture, though he bore plenty of scars from serving in Emperor Draedyn's war, scars I knew from memory. Dyter's eyes widened as he saw me between two of the Druman surrounding him. Even with my silver hair and violet eyes, and in the enemy's navy aketon, he recognized me.

My gaze shifted from him to his companion, and my mouth dropped. It was the twenty-something blond man from The Crane's Nest. The young man who'd paid for his soup in coin.

"Ah, you're feeling better," the king said with a smile.

I turned to face him but blinked as I did so. I peered at the young man and then back at the king.

Even from across the room I could see the tightness in the king's features. "You see the family resemblance, I gather," he said, voice cold. "It seems my son, Irtevyn, hasn't been fighting at the frontlines of the emperor's war like I thought but rather plotting to overthrow his father, instead."

His son was plotting to overthrow him? But . . . that would make the young man, Cal. I gasped, and something huge clicked into place. Cal was this man's child?

I'd come here to face the music for trying to escape and for killing Jotun, but the king hadn't yelled at me, and I wondered if he knew.

Dyter leaned forward. "Ryn?"

His tentative question and familiar voice were a crushing weight to my chest. *Be quiet, Dyter*, I begged him silently. I hung my head, squeezing my eyes shut, but when Dyter said my name again, I couldn't ignore him. Everyone had heard by now.

"I'm sorry," I whispered to him. Sorry for Mum's death, sorry I'd been captured, sorry Arnik was dead, sorry the rebellion had failed, and sorry Dyter was about to die now, too, because he had uttered my name and confirmed to the king that we knew each other.

"I see you're acquainted, so introductions won't be necessary. I'm sure everyone in my entire kingdom is aware of the penalties of treason." He scowled at his son. "There are no exceptions."

Cal raised his chin. "I wouldn't expect anything else of you, Father. But know that it doesn't end with me. The people are tired of your oppressive rule. You can kill me and my first today, but another will rise up tomorrow. Your time is nearing its end, and whether I watch it here in Verald or from the stars, I will watch you fall, and I will cheer."

As the crown prince spoke, Irdelron's face reddened, darker and darker. "You speak of fantasy and dreams, boy, and you always have. This is reality: There is no one with the power to stop me."

The crown prince smirked. "You're wrong, old man. There are Drae, besides the one you've poisoned and corrupted, as well as Phaetyn in hiding. They'll join together, and they'll destroy you."

The king laughed, a harsh bray. "You know nothing. I have the only Phaetyn, right here," he said, pointing at me. "And we all know Drae cannot harm their own, if indeed you have more, which I doubt. Your pitiful rebellion will be gone within the week. Lord Irrik will obliterate the rest of the peasants, and that's all you'll be seeing in the sky. You and your pathetic, decrepit first," he mocked.

The insult to Dyter was enough to spark my anger.

"You believe your own propaganda. You're—"

"Enough!" King Irdelron yelled.

The king was going to kill Cal. He was going to kill Dyter. It would happen in the coming minutes. When that happened, he'd send Irrik out and obliterate Cal's rebellion. I wasn't under the same delusions Cal seemed to be. If he died today, there was no tomorrow for the rebellion. He was the myth, the uniting factor, and if it was not him, it wouldn't be anyone. If Dyter died today, I would cease to exist. I saw this clearly as calm acceptance settled over me. If Cal died, the kingdom of Verald died with him—what was left of it. My breathing became shallow, and the knife strapped underneath my borrowed aketon burned.

The doors to the throne room crashed open, and Lord Irrik strode in.

"My Drae?" Irdelron snarled, but his face paled as Irrik drew closer and what he was dragging became visible.

Dressed in his black aketon, the muscles of Irrik's bare arms were taught as he hauled Jotun's body behind him. The dead Druman's face was still covered in dried rivulets of blood. The red moisture was splattered on his skin. In Irrik's other hand, he carried a round object wrapped in black fabric. As he stepped up to the foot of the king's dais, next to me, something dripped from the bottom of the makeshift bag and puddled on the floor.

"What is this?" the king demanded.

For the first time since I'd been in the castle, the king's voice quivered.

Irrik threw Jotun's body, and it came to land sprawled across the bottom two steps of the raised platform. "His body was in the passageway of the interrogation deck."

Irdelron narrowed his eyes and pursed his lips as he studied Lord Irrik. He glanced at his son and Dyter and then the Druman around me. They melted back several steps.

The silence in the cavernous room added to the weight surrounding us, and the very walls seemed to be holding their breath.

The king turned to me after several moments. This time there was no superficial smile of friendship. The intensity of his fury radiated across the space, and the glower he wore twisted his face beyond the realm of anything I'd ever seen.

I knew he knew, and the calm that had settled over me didn't waver in the face of his wrath. His rage was almost as sweet as nectar.

He continued to glare at me, but his question was directed at Lord Irrik. "A good try, my Drae. You cannot kill your own blood. My Druman are compelled not to hurt each other, so tell me . . . how did she get loose?"

My heart stopped, and I prayed the consequences of my escape would fall to me.

Irrik dropped the parcel in his other hand next to Jotun's body. "It appears someone was helping her."

Lord Irrik pinned me with a dark, veiled look. But my eyes fell to the dripping black bag in his hands. I couldn't think. I couldn't even breathe because . . . because . . .

Only one person had helped me.

"Tyr," I choked on my strangled whisper, dropping to my knees.

The king's growing smile froze. "What did you say, Phaetyn?"

His question rolled right past me. I brought my bloody hands to my lips, eyes fixed on the blood dripping from the saturated material Lord Irrik held. The bag hung with a round weight inside, and I groaned low from my stomach as it occurred to me what and who was inside. My heart would know it. I began to shake. My *soul* would know it!

By now, my head knew better. Souls only existed so men like the king could destroy them.

"What did you say?" the king screamed, standing up from his throne. His voice rang to me as though from far away, but my eyes lifted to him as he stomped down the first step toward me.

Tyr was gone.

His head was in that bag. His blood was on this ground. And it was this man's fault.

Something deep within me snapped. I was done being a victim of this man's brutality. I was finished having him steal everyone I loved.

Five steps stood between us.

My hand grasped the dagger, pulling it from the leather sheath underneath my stolen aketon. Irdelron was still moving toward me.

Four steps away.

Three steps.

He stood over Jotun's body, screaming profanities.

Two steps.

I stood and lunged at him, shrieking at the top of my lungs, half in anticipation of killing and half in soul-deep pain.

I thrust.

The blade slid into the king's abdomen like it was butter, and he stiffened, gasping in shock. His hand wrapped around mine, his grip crushing my fingers to the hilt of the blade, but I barely felt it. My wild gaze was fixed on him, lapping up the pain in his eyes with desperate hunger.

Grasping my hand in an iron vice, he forced the dagger out, with me still attached.

He dug his thumb into the groove of my wrist, and a stabbing pain shot up my arm, causing my fingers to reflexively relax. I would not let go of this weapon until he or I died, or both of us. I owed it to Tyr. For what could have been.

Irdelron torqued my wrist, the pressure driving me to my knees. "How dare you?"

His blood oozed from the wound I'd created, saturating his white aketon. This time it was his own blood. And I had drawn it. Panting, he struck me with his other hand. My stomach churned, and bursts of white exploded behind my eyelids.

"Irrik!" Irdelron growled. "I require your talons, my Drae."

I stared at the seeping red spot on the king's side, willing it to grow faster, to drain him of his strength and energy, to end his life. But if will alone was enough to make things happen, I would have been gone from this place long ago.

"I will not," Irrik said in a quiet voice.

The king chuckled, relaxing his grip enough that I was able to blink the room back into focus.

Dyter was struggling against three Druman. He stared at me with wide eyes, scarred face blanched in horror. The prince, also surrounded by the king's guard, studied me as if I were a puzzle, which I assumed meant he was ignorant of my Phaetyn nature.

Tyr was gone.

I longed to see his hooded face, his wry smile. My heart yearned to feel his lips on mine one last time. We'd shared one kiss. . . I'd hoped to share many more with him.

Irrik tossed the black bag, and my throat squeezed in horror as it hit the ground with a sickening squelch and the head inside rolled out. I didn't want to see further evidence of his death or Irrik's forced cruelty, but never once had I seen Tyr's full face, and I wanted this one last thing before I died. I swallowed the lump of emotion at the back of my throat and let my gaze go to the decapitated head.

I blinked, my mind refusing to accept that the face of the Druman before me was Tyr. He was nothing like I'd pictured him. I tilted my head to the side, examining the young man's face. His dusky skin was smooth, but his lips seemed thinner than I remembered, and his chin . . .

The king released my hand and grabbed a fistful of my hair, yanking my head back to expose my throat.

"Kill her!" he screamed. "I command you. I invoke the power of your oath to me. Slay this traitor."

My gaze collided with Lord Irrik's dark eyes. The Drae stepped toward me, lips pursed, his eyes filled with haunted sadness. He was the bringer of death, and he would deliver me from the torment of King Irdelron. "Don't be sad," I said, choking on the words. I would be in the stars with Mum and Arnik in the blink of an eye. "I'll be free."

"*Už ti nikdy neublížujem,*" Irrik said, shaking his head. He held out his hand, and as he stretched his fingers, his skin darkened, his hand shifted, and black talons appeared on the end of his scaly digits. Razor sharp.

"Make it fast," I wheezed.

Lord Irrik broke eye contact with me, and then he lunged forward.

I closed my eyes, feeling the whooshing air of his movement brush my cheeks. The hair on the top of my head rippled. I felt the warmth of Irrik's body, and his terrible snarl echoed in my ears. The last sound I would ever hear.

I wasn't afraid.

32

*T*here was no pain.

There was no darkness.

There was no end.

The warmth receded. The air settled around me.

The king released my hair, and my eyes flew open.

Lord Irrik stood before me, boxing me between his legs and the king's. I twisted to look up.

Shock drove me out from between them, and I scrambled back, unable to tear my gaze from where the Drae's black talon was punctured clear through the king's neck, several inches of the tip visible on the other side.

Irdelron opened his mouth and gurgled. His eyes wide and disbelieving.

"You can't compel me to do that. Your blood oath isn't strong enough, Irdelron." Lord Irrik's eyes gleamed as he retracted his deadly talon, slowly. He lowered his arm to his side, the king's blood dropping from the sharp tip to the stone ground.

The king slumped to the floor as blood pooled from the gaping wound. He gurgled again, attempting to speak.

I began to hyperventilate, feeling my face and body, over and over again, certain my mind was playing tricks on me.

Irdelron continued his attempt to communicate, hands gripping the floor uselessly as his lips opened and closed. Head spinning, I stared at the dying monarch, unmoving as his movements became weaker and weaker.

I knew what happened next. I'd seen it happen to my mother.

His movements stopped.

Irrik crouched next to the king, staring into his fading eyes. "You sealed your fate," he said, jaw clenched. "With the command to kill her."

The king's expression slackened, and he looked past Irrik to where I was curled. Irdelron clearly understood what Irrik meant.

The life disappeared from the king's eyes as he suffocated on his own blood, but my mind said it should be me. *Why wasn't it me?* How had Irrik broken the oath?

I shifted my gaze to Lord Irrik. He shuddered, and black scales danced up his arms. He snarled a reverberating roar at the Druman, flashing his fangs. They dropped their weapons to the floor as though the swords were scalding hot.

Irrik continued to roar until every one of them was on their knees.

Dyter rushed to me and supported me with an arm behind my shoulders. "Ryn," he said hoarsely. "*Mistress Moons*, Rynnie. What have they done to you?"

I heard him, but Dyter's question didn't seem to want an answer as he clutched me to him, stroking my silver hair with shaking hands.

I couldn't tear my eyes from Irrik, and finally, *finally* he met my gaze.

"How did you do that?" I managed, glancing toward the king's blood nearly touching my extended foot.

"Not here," he replied tersely. His hand had shifted back to human, and the king's blood coated Irrik's fingers.

"No!" I shouted. I extricated myself from Dyter's arms and sprang to my feet, ignoring my shaking legs. "I want to know right now. Right now!"

Cal and Dyter gasped to my right at the way I was speaking to the king's Drae.

Not the king's anymore.

Irrik's fangs appeared again, and he forced them back, the struggle evident on his face. "There are too many ears here."

"Then get rid of them," I ordered. "But I'm not leaving here until I get answers."

"Ryn?" Dyter asked.

Irrik snarled an order in Drae to the Druman, who marched out of the throne room in ordered lines. He turned to Cal and Dyter, but I held up a hand. "They stay."

We warred silently, Irrik before me. He showed all the signs of being about to lose control and shift: scales, talons, fangs, inky eyes.

"As far as I was aware," Cal spoke for the first time, calmly—as if his father hadn't just suffocated on his own blood. It made me like him more. "Your blood oath was absolute. If there was a threat to Irdelron's life, you had to protect him. Him above everyone else."

Irrik sucked in a breath between his fangs, and the black glossy scales appeared up the sides of his neck. He shook his head. "There's always been a way to break it."

What? Without thinking, I closed the gap between us and gripped his forearms. "Tell me. Irrik, talk to me. Whatever it is, I can handle it. You know I can."

He turned his head, closing his black eyes and breathing thinly. "One hundred years ago, the emperor gave King Irdelron a choice. He needed to get the Drae to fight for the emperor or eliminate the risk they posed to his war plans. With the emperor's help, Irdelron slaughtered my kind. When all the male Drae were murdered—my brothers, father, uncles, grandfathers—he took me, the youngest, to where the females were corralled, unconscious from their mates' deaths. He then gave *me* a choice: I could swear an oath to him, or he would kill my female kin. I was nine and hadn't come into my power. There was no way I would've said no. And so I swore to protect him. But a blood oath is not infallible. There is one thing that is more powerful to a Drae, something which supersedes a blood oath, something that is unbreakable."

Shivers exploded down my arms.

"Irdelron had been well informed. He sent the emperor the females, and I was the only Drae left with him, so there was never any danger of the oath being broken, before now. I've always been the only Drae in Verald."

"What are you saying?" I whispered.

Irrik opened his eyes, human once more, and faced me. He slid back the sleeves of my shift.

"Drae cannot kill each other. I cannot physically kill one of my own. It is not magically possible. To tell me to do so would shatter the blood oath and allow me the freedom to protect my fellow Drae." He glanced down and, frowning in confusion, I did the same.

I gasped at the sight of the lapis lazuli gems stuck to my skin. Except . . . I stepped away from Irrik. They weren't gems. I swallowed. I thought I was Phaetyn? I sucked in a breath. "What . . . am I?"

His answer didn't come quickly enough.

"What am I?" I screamed at him.

He tried to get closer, but I shifted away to keep distance between us. His eyes went inky again, and when he spoke, his menacing Drae voice rumbled through the throne room. "You are Drae."

My legs folded underneath me, and I sank to the ground, staring at my arms. My blue-scaled arms. "I can't be," I said. "I'm Phaetyn."

"You are Drae, too," Irrik said.

Dyter's voice was incredulous. "How is that possible?"

"The emperor's experiments," Irrik answered tersely.

Cal and Dyter looked at each other in confusion. I'm glad I wasn't the only one.

"A female Drae can only breed with her mate," Irrik snapped. "What he was trying to do is unnatural." Scales rippled over his skin, and he trembled to maintain his human form.

"Do *not* shift on me right now," I yelled at him, climbing to my feet. I was pushed far beyond my coping level and unable to feel fear. I grabbed his arms and shook him, though he didn't even budge.

Irrik closed his eyes, and his black scales smoothed to skin. He rested his hands on my shoulders and took slow, deep breaths.

My breath was ragged. "So what? I'm Phaetyn and Drae?" I swallowed, and my voice shook when I said, "Apart from the scales, I don't seem very Drae. I don't shift. I don't . . ."

I didn't even know what other powers Drae had, but I didn't have anything else besides my Phaetyn powers. And those twinkling bumps.

"When is your eighteenth birthday?" Cal asked.

Irrik asked me that same question not long ago. I had no idea how much time I'd lost recovering from my injuries, so I took a guess. "A few days. Maybe?"

"A Drae does not come into their powers until adolescence," Irrik said. "Males come into them earlier, at age twelve." He fidgeted then met my quelling gaze and said in a strained voice, "Females later, usually around eighteen, when they are of mating age."

He did not just say mating. Drak, no. I backed away from him, suddenly needing distance. It hit me. "You knew I was Drae? This whole time? Was it my itchy arms?"

Irrik exhaled. "No, that's when I knew your transformation was close. I knew you were Drae the first time I touched you. I recognized you as my kind. But I first knew you were both Phaetyn and Drae when your mother told me, before . . ."

She killed herself. "My mother was Drae," I said in a daze. I'd suspected it once before, long ago, believing if she was that would mean I wasn't actually her daughter. But my mother had been Drae, and I was her daughter. That was something, it was outweighed by everything else at the moment, but it was something.

"The Phaetyn blade that killed her . . ." I had to know but couldn't actually ask.

Irrik's eyes flashed black, and his fangs lengthened. He trembled for a long moment before answering. "Yours."

I closed my eyes as a dead weight landed in my stomach. It shouldn't mean anything. I hadn't been the one to put the blood on there or shove it into my mother . . . but my blood had killed her.

"Why didn't you tell me?" I asked, hugging myself.

My question fell flat. I knew the answer before he parted his lips. Shaking my head, I answered my own question. "Because you couldn't trust me."

"Ryn, I—"

"No." I held up my hand to stop his excuse. I didn't want to hear him say it. My heart couldn't take anymore. "It's fine. You couldn't risk it in case Jotun got it out of me, or I screwed up in front of the king. I get it. Truly." I'd made that mistake with Ty. Arnik had been broken. Everyone cracked under the right pressure. My mind understood that.

Dyter's arms closed around me, tugging me to him. "My girl," he whispered in my hair. "What have you been through?"

So much. Too much. I couldn't even feel anything anymore and didn't know when I would. I turned to my friend, my mentor, and buried my face in his chest. A low grieving sound came from deep in my chest, but my eyes remained dry as my mind spun to take in all that had happened and all I had learned.

"You're al'right now," Dyter shushed, rocking me.

My eyes were drawn to where Tyr's head still lay facing me on the ground. I wasn't okay. I wouldn't be. I was a Phaetyn and a Drae. I wasn't stupid. I knew that would make me highly valuable, or highly threatening.

I returned Dyter's hug, my heart swelling. "Dyter, I'm so glad you're okay."

He choked. "I'm so sorry about your mother."

"No, please," I stopped him in an emotionless tone. "It's not your fault. It's not anyone's fault, except that man's." I pulled away and studied the king's body.

He was dead. But I didn't believe it yet.

Cal crossed to his father's body and pried the crown from Irdelron's head. The prince studied it, tipping the golden circlet side to side, and I wondered what he was thinking. Sighing, he held it out to Irrik and said, "This belongs to you. You slayed him, so his possessions shift to you, including control of the Druman. You are their alpha once more."

Irrik's nostrils flared, and he clenched his teeth. "If you held a Phaetyn blade to my throat, I would not take anything from the house of Ir."

I glanced over at him. *That's right*. Phaetyn blood *didn't* work on him, or at least mine hadn't. Yet it had killed my mother. I'd thought that I could only kill the Drae side in drumans, but if my blood killed my mum this wasn't true. So, why was Irrik immune to Phaetyn blood? Clearly, he wanted to keep this hidden from Cal and Dyter. I'd be getting to the bottom of that as soon as they were out of earshot. I was done with secrets.

"You will take the Druman, too. I concede my control over them to you. I hate the very sight of them. Plus, not all were mine. You'll need their protection once the emperor's Druman report back to him. He'll send others to attack if he knows you're vulnerable," Irrik said. "You must be the king the people of Verald need. You will need to become a king the entire *realm* needs."

Cal's face sobered as he accepted the weight of rule. "I intend to see this battle through to the end. The very end."

Irrik's eyes flooded black. "I would expect no less from the infamous Cal. And I intend to hold you to your word." His lip curled, and he snarled, "If you ever take your position for granted, I'll be back, and I will make you pay."

The prince tilted his chin. "I am not my father. In fact, I'll gladly renounce his name. The house of Ir no longer exists. I'll be Caltevyn of House Cal, my mother's house."

With a gleam in his eyes, Lord Irrik leaned over the fair young man and said, "A pretty speech, but I look forward to you proving the truth of it by uniting the three kingdoms against the emperor."

Whoa. My heart skipped a beat as I contemplated the meaning of the Drae's plan. Now he was free from Irdelron, he was pushing for the empire to be purged of its abusive Drae ruler.

Caltevyn pursed his lips and stared at the crown as if contemplating Irrik's challenge. After several moments, the prince squared his shoulders and looked up to the Drae. "I will need your help."

Irrik dipped his head. "You shall have it, King Caltevyn. As long as I agree with your decisions."

I was sure our king understood the underlying threat. But I agreed with Irrik. Someone needed to help maintain the balance of power. Mum's stories weren't just stories after all.

Cal frowned at the crown for a long moment before he placed it on his head. This was the man who had ordered potato stew from me at The Crane's Nest. I'd known there was something strange about him, something different, back then. But that he was a prince, never. Now he was king. The crown suited him, but I silently added to Irrik's threat. If Caltevyn or Irtevyn, or whatever his name was, abused his power, I would come back to end him myself. A deep sense of protectiveness bubbled up from within, and I felt compelled to remind him, "The people need you. Don't let them down."

King Caltevyn nodded, a grim look of determination on his face. "I will not fail them."

Dyter chuckled behind me. Placing his hand on my shoulder, he did his best to reassure me. "I've known Cal for more than ten years, Ryn. I believe in him."

Once, that might have been enough for me to believe in him, too.

Cal crossed the stone floor and knelt before me. Taking my hand in his, he bowed and brushed his lips over the back of my hand. He looked up into my eyes and said, "My lady, I hope you will come to believe in me, too, over time. These are trying times, and I must put the needs of my people before all else. I would implore you to consider their plight. Please, will you help us, too?"

My help? "With growing more food?"

I'm sure there would be more healing of the land that would need to take place, but I could teach them how to do it, and I had a few ideas so I wouldn't have to always be around for spitting in the pail.

The new king grinned. "Ryn, you're more powerful than you know." He sobered and looked me in the eye, all traces of humor gone. "When you turn eighteen, you will be unstoppable."

The thought made me uncomfortable. Despite Irrik's theory, I wasn't really sure he was right. I didn't feel like a Drae or someone who would soon become a Drae. Though . . . I hadn't believed I was Phaetyn at first either.

Cal released my hand and stood, casting a look at Irrik.

The Drae had been watching our exchange with sharp eyes, and he shifted his gaze from me to the king.

King Caltevyn smiled. "Lord Irrik, you are no longer tied to my father's house. I release you from your blood oath to the house of Ir. You are no longer to be called Irrik . . ."

Irrik's eyes widened, and he flinched as he turned back to me. The color drained from his face as the king finished speaking.

"You revert to your own house now, Lord Tyrrik."

Lord . . . Tyrrik.

The stunned silence gave me ample time to put it together. I turned toward Tyr's decapitated head again, taking two steps toward it before clutching the sides of my head and whirling back.

"Tyrrik," I shrieked. "No." I chanted my denial over and over again, pressing my knuckles into my mouth with bruising force. "*No,*" I gasped again.

Black agony filled my chest, and I looked up to Irrik, willing him to assure me that I'd misunderstood. Certainly, he wouldn't have deceived me, betrayed me, like that.

His face was a smooth canvas, blank of all emotion. Void of everything.

"You," I choked, unable to articulate the storming thoughts in my head through the ripping hurt inside.

Something torn flashed in his dark eyes, and then I watched as the darkness came to him, wrapping around him, shrouding him. My throat constricted as he became a hooded figure, slightly shorter, with light stubble lining his jaw. His eyes and most of his nose were beneath a shadowed mask. I looked down at his hands, but he had no reason to change them. His fingers were long, and my eyes burned with tears as I remembered their gentle touch.

His lips on mine.

His tender treatment and whispers of love.

"Tyr," I said, choking on my sob. Through my tears, I glared at the Drae, my heart freshly shredded by his betrayal. "You were pretending. You were Tyr this whole time."

A loud whining noise filled my head, and a blinding-white light exploded across my vision. I clutched my chest, feeling as if, at any moment, my ribs would shatter from the hurt.

"Yes," the Drae spoke.

Except it wasn't in his voice.

It was *Ty's* voice. My dungeon buddy's. Not raspy because acid had been poured down his throat or because he was a Druman spy. Raspy because it came from the partially shifted throat of Lord Irrik. "You were Ty, too?" I choked.

Ty. Tyr. Tyrrik. He'd lied to me this entire time.

He stepped closer. "The king ordered me to get information out of you by posing as a prisoner."

"*You* told him the rebels were coming? You betrayed us?"

"I didn't have a choice. I did what I could to get around the blood oath. I did what I could to be there for you and help you without endangering you. But as soon as the king's life was placed in danger, my oath compelled me to tell him."

"Then why ask me to contact Cal in the first place?" I shouted at the unmoving Drae.

His body vibrated. "Because I needed to get you out, but not while I was still under Irdelron's control. He would've sent me to retrieve you. I had to find a way to break the oath so you could be truly free, and *you* were the only way to do that. Drae cannot kill Drae. I thought I could play both sides and manipulate the oath without too many people getting hurt."

I snorted. He'd killed hundreds because of his game.

"You were wasting away before my eyes," he said hoarsely. "I couldn't bear it."

"That whole time I thought Jotun was hurting Ty, and you're telling me that was all one huge lie? Do you know how much time I spent worrying he would never come back?"

He dropped his gaze to the floor.

"Do you?" I choked. Irrik had been Ty. Ty hadn't been a Druman at all. He wasn't *real*. The thought pierced through the cloud of disbelief inside me.

And if Ty wasn't real . . . My eyes landed on the head I'd assumed was Tyr's. I let out a hollow sound.

Tyr isn't real, either.

I fell to my knees. "Why would you do this?" When he didn't answer, I screamed, "Why did you do it?"

I sobbed, digging my nails into my skin as though clawing to reach my heart.

"*Ticho teraz, moja láska. Ste v bezpečí,*" the Drae said in his language. Then he placed his hand on my arm, and in my mind Tyr spoke, *I will always keep you safe, my love.*

Safe? His words were a slap, and anger surged within me hot and swift.

"Keep me safe?" I asked shrilly, pushing him away from me.

Cal and Dyter stood back, watching the exchange with matching expressions of bafflement, but I had no time or inclination to explain anything right then.

I turned on the Drae and continued my verbal assault. "You manipulated me," I shouted, my body burning with rage. A heart-broken cry escaped my lips, and I pressed my trembling fingers against them. "You used me. Y-y—"

I stared up at Irrik and marveled that his expression was still smooth. *Uncaring.* How was I so affected and he felt nothing?

I crossed to him, lifting my hand, and slapped him before I knew what I was doing. But I *did* know he could have moved if he'd wished. He kept his face averted after the slap, but I wasn't done. My chest heaved, and I hurled my whispered accusation at him, my voice breaking, "You made me fall in love with him. How could you?"

He stayed turned away. Unflinching. Unmoving. Unfeeling. How could he have played Tyr? How could he be Ty, too? They were figments of his imagination. There would be no saving my dungeon buddy. Whoever that head belonged to, it wasn't my Tyr. But he was still dead.

Worse than dead.

He'd never existed.

Tears poured down my cheeks. Salty, disbelieving, excruciating, tears. There was no word for this kind of pain.

"He wasn't real," I said, staring at the Drae. My heart was shredded and the coward wouldn't even face me. Snarling with disgust, I snapped, "None of it was real."

Only then did a tear escape his soulless, empty eyes and trickle down over his sculpted cheekbones and clenched jaw. But still, Lord *Tyrrik* said nothing.

I turned away and told myself I felt nothing inside, either.

I left then. I walked out of the castle through the front door, once I found it, with nothing but the clothes on my back and Ty's dagger. After I remembered the blade and aketon were *his*, I scrambled out of the blue uniform and threw it and the dagger away with as much strength as I could muster.

No one tried to stop me. Not Cal, not Dyter, not . . . *him*.

As I walked into the night, I vowed I'd never step foot inside that castle again. Even though the monster who had ruled it was dead and gone, it would always be the place where I was broken and put back together again and again for the sadistic pleasure of others. Those men had once been more powerful than I was. I didn't care that I was stronger for it. I didn't care that I would be powerful. I didn't care that I was powerful *now*. I didn't care.

"I don't care," I screamed at the pitch sky, at the stars of those I loved. Then I bowed my head and walked. My throat was raw from crying. My feet took me on familiar paths, until I stared at the black-ened ground that had once been my home. Zone Seven. Where I'd had a mother, a best friend, and an uncertain but hopeful future.

Yet even my memories of that were now tainted by the truth I hadn't known at the time.

Lies. Ty, Tyr, Tyrrik . . . my own mother.

Everywhere I turned. My entire life. Lies.

I wanted something to be real. I *needed* something . . .

Tears fell from my eyes to the charred ground. My blue scales erupted, climbing up my arms as my heart began to race. I sank to my knees as racking sobs tore through me, again. Only this time, I cried for me. For my losses. For the girl who once was and never could be the same.

I closed my eyes from the starlight twinkling off my vibrant-blue scales as if reminding me of the truth. I hated them. I hated what they represented.

A truth that everyone knew but me.

I was already barefoot and filthy from my night spent mourning in the middle of the blackened and desolate Harvest Zone. I bowed low and sank my hands into the ground, digging my toes into the ash, too. My tears poured freely, dripping onto the char, and I shared my pain with the soil underneath. I shared with it my losses. I unfolded my heartbreak. I divulged my fears. I told the warm ground underneath my hands *everything*.

For hours I stayed this way, pouring my heart out to something that could never betray me, never report to another, something that could never spin my words to mean something that would break my heart anew. The soil would never judge me for how I'd changed, or shy away from the hardness in my heart now. I told Harvest Zone Seven all of who I was and could never be again. And when I'd shared everything, when I was empty and my tears had dried up, I collapsed to the ground and let the dirt embrace me.

It felt like an eternity when footsteps crunched toward me. I remained still, lost in memories of Tyr's wry smile and sure hands.

"Rynnie," Dyter whispered, tears choking his voice.

I felt his presence crouched by my head. My eyes were swollen, and I could hardly move in my exhaustion.

"I'm so sorry, Rynnie," he cried. "I'm so sorry I wasn't there."

Nothing else could have roused me except the tears of the man I considered my father. I moved my head to look at him.

"I went down to the dungeons." He gasped, his scarred face twisted in agony. "I saw—" He broke, his body shaking as he cried silently.

"Help me up?" I asked.

He hurried to do so. Pulling me to him as he sat, he propped me up next to him. He wiped his face, and together we surveyed what was left of our home.

"I can't believe it's all gone. It doesn't seem real, does it?" he asked.

I didn't reply.

He hesitated. "I'm sorry about the man you loved . . . Tyr."

I closed my eyes, trying to block out the memories that rushed at me. "Please, don't speak his name. He wasn't real."

Dyter sighed.

When I opened my eyes, he was still staring at the endless black.

He turned and looked me in the eye as he said, "But what you felt was real, and I'm sorry your heart was broken."

Not just my heart. It seemed deeper. I blinked away burning tears.

He spoke again. "Your mother . . ." He paused. "You know she only kept those things from you to protect you, don't you, my girl?"

I remained mute.

He nodded after a time. "You'll see it in time. But I hope you know she loved you with all her heart and soul. You were her reason for waking each day."

A tear slipped over my cheek. "I know," I managed. "I miss her, Dyter. So much."

A sob escaped the older man beside me. "I do, too, Rynnie. She was a good friend to me. Helped me when no one else would. I'll tell you just how one day."

I smiled at him. "I'd like that."

After a long moment, Dyter said, "He followed you when you left, did you know? He's been there, all night, watching over you." My mentor tilted his head to the rolling hills behind us. "If I could kill him, I would." He cleared his throat and added, "But being a Drae and all . . ."

His comment startled a laugh out of me. A strong reminder I hadn't lost everything. "Thank you, Dyter."

"What for?" he asked. In his haunted eyes, I could see he blamed himself for everything.

For being alive. "For being here," I said.

Dyter smiled, but it faded a moment later. "Ryn, I know this isn't what you want to hear right now, but Tyrrik"—he arched a brow at my dark scowl—"said you will make the transformation to Drae in just a few days' time. He said when that happens, the emperor will become aware of your existence."

A few days. Not long enough. My life had changed so much. I wasn't ready for it to change again. What would happen to me? Would I still be me when I transformed? Unfortunately, I refused to speak to the only person in Verald with those answers. "Why is that a problem? He can't kill me, right?"

"You know there are worse things than dying by now, Rynnie."

I did know.

He rocked me in his arms as we sat quietly in the burned remains.

"It's all gone," I said. How would we ever get back to what we had been? It wasn't possible, I knew. But we'd also defeated the king. "But maybe tomorrow . . ."

Maybe I could find the hope I needed tomorrow.

"Well, now look at this, my girl."

My Phaetyn power was healing me, my energy returned with a slow swelling, and I shifted to look at his scarred face. His gaze had softened and was fixed on my hand.

I wiped my eyes and gazed down.

Soft blue petals, a pale version of my scales, were blossoming between my thumb and forefinger. The flower was small, but as the breeze moved the solitary bloom, the petals glowed in the starlight. My heart skipped a beat as I stared at the only bit of life for as far as the eye could see.

"I've never seen a flower like this before," Dyter remarked.

I had.

Every day since I was two, Mum had held me up to stroke the petals of the welded flower in the Market Circuit. When I'd grown old enough, I reached to touch it myself whenever I passed it.

This was that flower brought to life.

My flower.

A flower that belonged to Mum and me—and to everyone who had perished in the last few months.

"It's a new flower," I answered him in a firm voice. A reminder of who I was today, and who I'd loved at this moment. In a few days, I would transform into a Drae, but I would always have this flower here as a sign of who I'd been once.

Dyter squeezed my other hand, and I returned the gentle pressure, whispering as I looked to the sky, "It's called a Tyr."

"A Tear," Dyter said, misunderstanding the name as I'd known he would. "That's a beautiful name, Ryn. I hope more grow."

My heart squeezed, but I took a breath, and air finally filled my lungs.

"As do I, Dyter." My gaze flickered to the rolling hills concealing Lord Tyrrik. In a handful of days, he wouldn't be the only Drae in Verald anymore. I'd be a monster, just like him. I took a shaking breath. "As do I."

Shadow Wings

The Darkest Drae: Book Two

Releasing February 8th

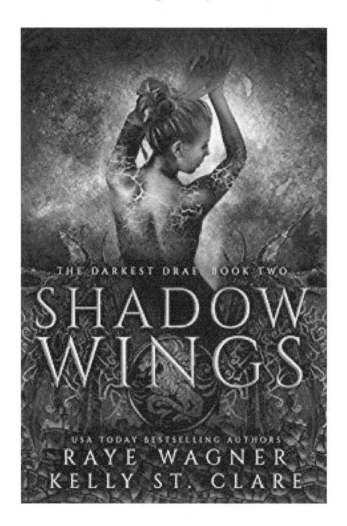

KELLY'S ACKNOWLEDGEMENTS

Holy pancakes! This book was a blast to write.

Thank you to the following people:

- Our betas, Michelle, Jennifer, and Kate, for providing amazing feedback.
- Our manuscript team for their hard work; Kelly Hashway, Krystal Wade, Dawn Yacovetta and Michelle Lynn.
- Our cover designer, Daqri at Covers by Combs for this badass cover.
- Our ARC team – you guys rock more than rockstars!

Thank you to my readers, who bring much joy to my life through social media shenanigans.

Thank you to the guy I stood behind in queue who read non-fiction books, but politely pretended to be interested when I told him I was co-authoring a book about dragon shifters. I could tell you thought I was crazy, but I appreciated your social efforts to remain non-judgemental for the five minutes we spent together in the post office.

As always, thank you to my incredible husband and best friend, Scott, and to my family and friends, who are wholly supportive.

Finally, thank you to someone who is legitimately crazy. Raye Wagner, Raye-Wagz, Wagneroo, you have been an absolute pleasure to work with. This book was 87% laughter, and 13% actual work. When I met you in Nashville, I knew we would be great friends. I can name the exact moment we *became* friends, too. It was when I asked you to search me for ticks because you freaked me out telling me they were everywhere in Nashville. Some might say that is a strange way to become friends, and they would be right, but it suits the dynamic we share. What I'm trying to say is. . . we're both really weird.

The same weird.

Lurv you!

P.S. If you grew potatoes, they would undoubtedly be the biggest and best in Verald.

Fun Facts About Raye Wagner:

1/ She could conquer the world while on her elliptical or washing her hair.

2/ She doesn't just 'join in' with the dancing. She *arrives* on the dancefloor, and dominates it. Respect.

3/ She didn't like the Marmite I took to the U.S. with me, and I wondered for a time if I could forgive her, but she liked the Tim Tams, so we remained friends and wrote this book together.

RAYE'S ACKNOWLEDGEMENTS

Books take time, and the older I get the more time becomes my most precious commodity. So thank you to Jason, Jacob, Seth, and Anna who allow me to take time away from laundry, dishes, and cooking so I can write. And thanks for listening, sometimes even with enthusiasm, to my ideas and stories, and MOSTLY thank you for sharing your time with me. My life is so much richer because you are in it.

Thanks to my parents who are not only two of my bestest friends, but who listened to me spout off the insane idea I had about a dragon-shifter while they were visiting. And for my brothers, sister, in-laws, nieces, nephews, cousins, aunts, uncles... Family buoys me up, mostly because I know we have each other's backs whenever we need it!

Our betas are awesome, as is our editing team. Michelle, Jennifer, and Kate you're the beta babes!! XOXO Kelly Hashway, I'll forever be grateful Ednah brought us together!! You're amazing! Krystal Wade, you have superpowers, don't you? It's okay, I won't tell. ;) And Dawn Yacovetta, I adore you and your sharp eyes!

Daqri at Covers by Combs- I'm pretty sure you were inspired. Your talents led to the most stunning cover!

To our ARC team- Muah!! There aren't enough hugs and kisses for how grateful I am to you!

Lela, Courtney, and Joy. You're truly angels! XOXO

Lela, you are the yin to my author yang!

Finally, I have to gush for my co-author, Kelly St. Clare. You make "work" so much fun! I can't even remember how we met online, but I'm so glad you were willing to organize a party with me and then hang out when you came to the U.S, and by hang out I mean come stay at my house! Hahaha! You've got mad writing skillz, sharp wit, and a hilarious sense of humor. I'm making plans for a bazillion more stories for us to write together. I'll forever consider it a gift that our paths crossed and merged. This journey has become exponentially more fun travelling with you!

BTW, if Kelly gives you a jar of stinky, black paste and tells you to lather it on toast... just say no. Tim Tams are totally worth it, though.

KELLY ST. CLARE

When Kelly is not reading or writing, she is lost in her latest reverie.
Books have always been magical and mysterious to her. One day she
decided to start unravelling this mystery and began writing.
The Tainted Accords was her debut series. The After Trilogy is her
latest work.
A New Zealander in origin and in heart, Kelly currently resides in

Australia with her ginger-haired husband, a great group of friends, and some huntsman spiders who love to come inside when it rains. Their love is not returned.

Visit her online and subscribe at:
www.kellystclare.com

RAYE WAGNER

Raye Wagner grew up in Seattle, the second of eight children, and learned to escape chaos through the pages of fiction. As a youth, she read the likes of David Eddings, Leon Uris, and Jane Austen. As an adult she fell in love with Rick Riordan's Percy Jackson series (shocker!) and Stephanie Meyer's Twilight (really!) and was inspired to pursue her dream of writing young adult fiction. Raye enjoys baking, puzzles, Tae Kwon Do, and the sound of waves lapping at the sand. She lives with her husband and three children in Middle Tennessee.

Visit her online and subscribe at:

www.rayewagner.com

Fantasy of Frost

(The Tainted Accords, #1)

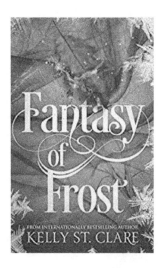

I know many things. What I am capable of, what I will change, what I will become. But there is one thing I will never know.

The veil I've worn from birth carries with it a terrible loneliness; a suppression I cannot imagine ever being free of.

Some things never change...

My mother will always hate me. Her court will always shun me.

...Until they do.

When the peace delegation arrives from the savage world of Glacium, my life is shoved wildly out of control by the handsome Prince Kedrick, who for unfathomable reasons shows me kindness.

And the harshest lessons are learned.

Sometimes it takes the world bringing you to your knees to find that spark you thought forever lost.

Sometimes it takes death to show you how to live.

COMPLETE SERIES NOW AVAILABLE

Cursed by the Gods
(The Sphinx, #1)

Hope has a deadly secret...

Hope has spent her entire life on the run, but no one is chasing her. In fact, no one even knows she exists. And she'll have to keep it that way. Even though mortals think the gods have disappeared, Olympus still rules. Demigods are elite hunters, who track and kill monsters. And shadow-demons from the Underworld prey on immortals, stealing their souls for Hades.

When tragedy destroys the only security she's ever known, Hope's life shatters. Forced to hide, alone this time, Hope pretends to be mortal.

She'll do whatever it takes to keep her secret safe— and her heart protected. But when Athan arrives, her world is turned upside down. With gods, demigods, and demons closing in, how long can a monster stay hidden in plain sight?

Join Hope on her unforgettable journey to discover what it means to live and her daring fight to break Apollo's curse.

COMPLETE SERIES NOW AVAILABLE